the WELL-PLACED *Lie*

A WISHVILLE  MYSTERY

kari lee townsend

NATIONAL BESTSELLING AUTHOR

OHB

For the crossroads that test us…and the choices we make that define who we become.

A special thank you to my parents, Chet and Marion Harmon, who have always been there for me, and have never made me doubt how very much I am loved. I am forever grateful to still get to love you back. 88 years and still going strong.

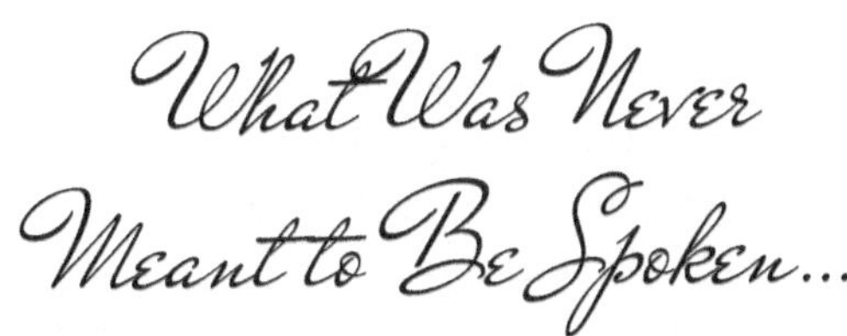

LONG BEFORE THE first WishFest lanterns were lit in winter, before snow softened the edges of Wishville into something harmless, there were words spoken beneath the mountain that were never meant to be heard again.

They were not wishes.

They were not spells.

They were not prayers.

They were promises.

When humans and Dwellers first ended their war, peace did not arrive gently. It was negotiated in shadows and stone, forged by those who believed survival mattered more than fairness. The agreement that followed was recorded carefully, sealed tightly, and placed beyond reach in a secret hall.

Not because it was fragile, but because it was powerful.

Too powerful to be remembered accurately.

Over time, the story of that agreement became simpler. Kinder. Easier to repeat at festivals and councils. What had once been argued clause by clause was reduced to tradition. What had been carved into stone was softened into legend.

And what had been deliberately removed was forgotten entirely.

The Elders believed this was wisdom. They believed that if no one spoke of the parts that frightened them, those parts would lose their power. They believed that silence could preserve peace longer than truth ever could.

So, they hid the record.

They buried it between Elarion and Wishville, in an area where no one dared to tread. They trusted that time would do what magic could not. That it would dull memory, blur intention, and make lies indistinguishable from history.

For generations, it worked.

Winter came and went. Snow fell and melted. A Guardian was chosen. New oaths were sworn. And the agreement—whatever its true shape had once been—remained intact enough to hold. Until winter came again.

Not with violence.

Not with war.

But with questions.

Because a revolution does not forget what once was. And a rebellion formed by the original Guardian demands justice for what the original Elder took away, and what the Entity continues to seek…

CHAPTER
One

IT HAD BEEN months since I'd last seen my mother, Serena, in the mountain caverns between Wishville, Vermont, and the realm of Elarion beneath it. I was still coming to terms with the fact that she hadn't just vanished a century ago. She had flipped to the other side as the leader of the Rebel Revolution against the Elders and the ancient treaty I was sworn to protect as Guardian of the Well. My mother had warned me the treaty wasn't what I thought, and the Elders had lied, then she'd escaped and was currently at large.

But that didn't mean I would stop looking for her.

In the meantime, I had a job to do. Winter WishFest didn't arrive quietly. It flared to life just before dusk, when the lights flicked on all at once and Main Street transformed into something that looked like a postcard come to life, with evergreen garlands wrapped around lampposts, lanterns glowing amber against the snow, and storefront windows lit so warmly they seemed to radiate heat.

I paused at the edge of the street with my clipboard tucked under my arm and my breath fogging the air. As Festival Chair, it was my job to make sure Winter WishFest ran smoothly, with vendors happy, walkways clear, and no rogue fire pits or screaming mechanical decorations.

Wishville loved its folklore. The wishing well. The stories. The festivals tied to the seasons. They just didn't know the realm of Elarion beneath the well was real, along with the magical creatures called Dwellers. With a human father and a Dweller mother, I was the only half-blood in existence, and three-hundred years old.

The town just knew me as thirty-year-old Lyra Wells, the Festival Chair.

Vex, my half-cat half-Whispen familiar, shifted on my shoulder, his claws carefully sheathed against my coat. His black fur caught the light with a faint silver sheen, like frost woven through midnight. Everyone thought he was my service animal, which wasn't exactly false. That meant no one objected when he followed me everywhere.

They've committed, he said in my mind, surveying the street. *Lights, music, sugar. The full ritual of pretending winter is charming.*

"It *is* charming," I said.

It's aggressive, he replied. *Winter should whisper. This is shouting.*

I smiled despite myself as I passed under the hand-painted arch at the base of the path that led up the hill to the festival clearing with vendor tents and the well.

It read, **WELCOME TO WINTER WISHFEST!**

Music drifted through the air as I made my way to the top. Fiddles and bells rang loud and clear near the gazebo, with laughter rising in bursts as people clustered around food stalls. Snow crunched under my boots. The scent of sugar and spice wrapped around me like a memory I hadn't asked for but didn't mind revisiting. Unlike the recent streak of crime we'd had, this was the version of Wishville people loved.

Cozy. Familiar. Safe.

I hope to keep it that way, I thought, as I moved into the flow of the crowd, already filling my mind with notes. Cocoa stand: line too long but cheerful. Candle booth: fine, but too close to the evergreen display. I made an actual note on my clipboard to separate them before someone accidentally summoned the fire department.

"Lyra!"

I turned just in time to brace myself as The Wellies descended. The Wellies—Tilda Nettlesblossom, Maribelle Crimp, and Dottie Quench—were three elderly women who were self-appointed assistants to all things regarding the well.

Tilly, a retired herbalist who now ran a spell jar booth called *Bibbidi, Bottles, & Boo*, led the charge wrapped in a scarf so long it could have doubled as emergency rope. Belle, a former opera singer who trained pigeons to carry secret notes instead of using a cell phone, followed. She was practical as always in a red knit hat pulled low. Dot, who sold wildly inaccurate fortunes in tea leaves at her *Quench and Snoop Tea House*, glided between them with her polka dot scarf arranged so precisely it looked like a sailor's knot.

"We need a ruling," Tilly announced.

"I am presenting facts," Dot said calmly.

Belle sighed. "She's lying. She's presenting opinions."

Vex lifted his head. *Oh good. A tribunal.*

I raised an eyebrow. "What's the issue this time?"

Dot gestured at Tilly's scarf. "That is not a scarf. That is an architectural feature."

"It has pockets," Tilly said proudly.

"For *what*?" Belle demanded.

"Emergency supplies." Tilly rolled her eyes.

I rubbed my forehead. "As Festival Chair, I'm ruling that scarves longer than their wearers must remain tucked in. For public safety."

Tilly gasped.

Dot smirked.

Belle looked vindicated.

"See?" Belle said. "Authority knows best."

"Authority has work to do," I warned, already backing away.

Fenrin, a full Whispen shapeshifting creature whose normal look was a ginger cat, chose that moment to appear, slipping out from behind a wreath display like she'd been there all along. One second the space was empty, the next, she stood perched on the display in all her colorful parrot glory at the moment, her amber eyes shining with mischief.

The Wellies blinked.

"Oh," Dot said faintly, pushing up her massive spectacles. "Well, aren't you a beautiful creature. What on earth are you doing in a Vermont mountain town during the winter?"

"LuLu's pet," Fenrin whistled. "Scarves inefficient. Feathers better."

Tilly's eyes lit up, and she clapped her hands. "Yes," she said in delight. "I like this bird."

Dot narrowed *her* eyes. "No."

Vex pretended not to look at Fenrin. She pretended not to notice him pretending.

I shook my head and started walking. "Gotta go make my rounds."

"Try the cider," Dot called after me. "Maisie has the good stuff out."

"I will," I promised.

The Wellies drifted off, still arguing, their voices blending into the general hum of the festival, and Fenrin vanished again. Wishville had a gift for noise that felt like comfort. I headed toward the first row of food stalls, with Vex leaning forward with interest.

This is the part where you get to eat everything, he said.

"This is the part where I *sample,*" I corrected. "For quality control."

Your teeth are not a committee, he said.

The lights flickered across the grounds, stopping me short. I frowned.

Maisie Flint spotted me immediately and waved me over from behind her *General Store* display. Jars of candy full of peppermints and taffy plus maple sweets poured over snow gleamed on tables, beckoning people to purchase.

"Festival Chair!" she called. "Come taste."

I glanced at my phone as I got a text at that moment from Mr. Finch. **Problem with the generator.** I groaned, hoping this wasn't the start of trouble. "I will taste all your samples later, Maisie. An issue just came up I have to check on. Any issues for you? Heat lamps? Power? If so, I can let Mr. Finch know, or his intern, Elliot Crane." Finch was a jack-of-all-trades and the best handyman Wishville had had in decades. His intern was following in his footsteps, eager to work.

"Just a few glitches with electricity, but nothing dramatic," she said. "Yet."

Fenrin reappeared at my side as a Great Dane, holding a small bag of samples in her mouth she definitely hadn't been officially offered, then sent Vex a gloating amber-eyed look. Vex rolled his bright blue eyes, and I just sighed at the two of them and their love-hate relationship.

"Maisie's candy will have to wait."

Vex pouted. *Duty before sweet treats is so last season.*

I stepped back into the glow of the festival, heading toward the back where the generator was located. People waved. Kids ran past with glowing wands. Somewhere down the hill toward the town square, Chief Holden Thorn's voice carried as he redirected foot traffic with calm authority. I didn't need to see him to feel steadier knowing he was there.

WishFest unfolded the way it always did, warm, loud, and full of small joys. And yet…as the snow began to fall in earnest and the lanterns swayed gently overhead, I felt it again. That faint prickle at the base of my neck. The sense that something was watching, waiting, and patient enough to hide behind lights and laughter.

I shook it off and kept walking. Winter WishFest had only just begun.

~

By the time the caroling began it was nearly six p.m. Winter WishFest had settled into its stride.

The lanterns glowed brighter as the sky darkened, their light reflected in the thin crust of snow that had begun to cling to the edges of the street. The music shifted from lively to reverent, with fiddles giving way to bells and soft harmonies drifting through the cold air. People gathered closer together, their cups cradled in mittened hands and breath rising in clouds that felt almost synchronized.

I stood near the edge of the stage, scanning the crowd with the practiced eye of someone who had learned that disasters rarely announced themselves. It had taken longer than expected to handle the generator problem, putting me behind schedule. I still hadn't sampled anything. That would have to wait until after the show. Kids darted between adults. Vendors leaned out to chat with familiar faces. The scent of cocoa and pine and sugar hung thick enough to taste.

This is the part they'll remember, Vex said from my shoulder. *The singing. Humans love collective noise.*

"They love tradition," I said. "It makes them feel anchored."

He flicked an ear. *Anchors can drag.*

I didn't respond. I was watching the choir assemble near the gazebo. They formed a loose semicircle of familiar faces bundled in matching scarves, holding sheet music with gloved hands. The Snowglow Sing was the symbolic heart of opening night for Winter WishFest. It was the moment when the festival officially shifted from marketplace to ritual. Not *that* kind of ritual, of course, just the human kind. Songs passed down, candles lit, and voices raised together because it felt good to do so.

Holden stood off to one side, his hands in his coat pockets and posture relaxed but alert. He ran a hand over his short, dark buzz-cut, then down over his beard. His stormy gray eyes caught mine briefly and he nodded as if to say, *Everything's calm, everything's under control. Relax and enjoy the show.*

LuLu hovered nearby, pretending to be deeply invested in a

tray of peppermint bark while actually watching the crowd with the sharp focus she never bothered to hide from me anymore. She was a sweet, petite, Hispanic journalist that fooled most, but her tough, feisty, determined personality usually got her whatever she wanted.

Something Chief Enforcer Calderis, a full Dweller from Elarion, loved most about her.

Calderis and I had grown up together and had always been drawn to each other. But after I met Holden and he met LuLu, we'd sort of formed an unspoken agreement that our time would come in the future since humans lived much shorter lives than me as a half-blood, and him as an immortal Dweller. It still wasn't easy watching each other date other people, but now was not the time to dwell on romance.

Pushing those thoughts aside, I focused on the scene before me.

The Wellies were front and center, naturally, standing by Alistair Hawthorne and swooning. He was a retired financial investment advisor who used to manage a hedge fund, and was about as charming as they came. He'd moved to Wishville for the quiet after selling his firm, and was already making a big splash, helping to sponsor the festival.

Tilly had produced battery-powered candles, and Alistair helped her distribute them with enthusiasm. Dot helped Alistair with his grip technique. Belle murmured something about tempo and diction, already invested in the performance like it was opening night at the opera. All three kept fighting for spots to stand by him.

Fenrin lingered just behind me in her normal ginger cat form. Vex sat taller on my shoulder, his sleek black tail swaying slowly as he watched the choir with an intensity that made my skin prickle.

"You're staring," I murmured.

I'm listening, he said. *Songs remember things.*

I frowned. "It's just caroling."

Nothing is just *anything,* he replied.

Before I could press him, the choir director raised his hands, and the crowd quieted. The first notes rose into the air, soft, clear, and familiar. A ripple of recognition passed through the people around me as voices layered together, weaving harmony out of breath and cold and memory. Someone behind me sniffed, already emotional.

The lead caroler, Violet Snowe, stepped half a pace forward. She was a local, one of those people you saw everywhere and never really thought about until you realized she was woven into the town like yarn. Middle-aged, warm-voiced, dependable. She smiled as she sang, her eyes half-closed, her breath fogging in steady rhythm with the melody.

I let myself relax…just a little.

The song swelled. Candles lifted higher. Snowflakes drifted down, catching the light as if the night itself were participating. Then Violet faltered. It was subtle at first, just a hitch in the note and a breath taken too sharply. She lowered her candle slightly, her brow furrowing as if she'd momentarily forgotten the words.

I straightened.

Vex went utterly still.

She tried to recover, drawing in another breath. The sound that came out wasn't wrong, exactly, but it was strained and thin, like air forced through something too narrow. She pressed a hand to her chest. The harmony wavered. Someone in the front row shifted uneasily. Violet's candle slipped from her fingers and hit the snow then blinked out. She took one step back, her mouth opening as if to speak…or gasp…or call for help. Then her knees buckled.

For a heartbeat, no one moved.

It was the kind of pause that comes from disbelief, from the brain scrambling to reconcile expectation with reality. This wasn't part of the program. This wasn't supposed to happen. Then chaos snapped into place.

"Hey—!"

"She fainted!"

"Someone call—"

Holden was already moving. He reached her side just as she collapsed fully, one arm flung out, and her sheet music scattering across the snow like startled birds. He knelt, his voice calm and commanding as he checked for responsiveness.

"Clear some space," he said. "Give her some air."

People stumbled back, their candles wavering.

The choir director, Thomas Whitaker, dropped to his knees with panic written across his face. "I—I don't understand," he kept saying. "Violet was fine. She said she felt fine."

I pushed forward, my heart pounding, and the cold was suddenly sharp against my skin. LuLu appeared at my elbow without a word, her hand firm on my arm.

"She's breathing," Holden said, then frowned. "But it's shallow."

Violet's skin looked wrong. It was too pale, with a faint sheen of sweat despite the cold. Her lips parted as if she were trying to pull in more air than her body would allow.

"Did she have a condition?" someone asked urgently.

"I don't know," Thomas said. "No...she never said..."

An EMT's voice crackled over a radio as someone finally managed to get through. The crowd pressed closer despite Holden's efforts, fear pulling them in like gravity.

I crouched a few feet away, my useless hands clenched in my gloves as I scanned the scene for something, anything, that made sense. This wasn't frostbite. This wasn't a simple faint.

Vex's claws dug into my coat. *This is wrong,* he murmured through my mind.

"I know," I whispered.

Violet shuddered once, her body tensing before going slack again. A sound escaped her throat, sounding thin and breathless.

Holden looked up at me, his expression carefully neutral, but his eyes were laced with concern. "Lyra," he said quietly. "I need you to keep people back."

I nodded, forcing myself to stand, slipping automatically into my Festival Chair voice that was calm, authoritative, and steady. "Everyone, please step back," I called. "Give them space. Help is on the way."

The crowd obeyed, reluctantly. Someone began to cry softly. The candles dipped and wavered, their warm glow suddenly fragile. By the time the EMTs arrived, the singing had stopped entirely, show over.

Winter WishFest held its breath.

They worked quickly and efficiently, lifting Violet onto a stretcher, checking her vitals, and murmuring terms I half-caught and half-missed. The choir director hovered with his hands twisting together.

"She just ate," Thomas said suddenly, as if the thought had only just occurred to him. "She had cider. Some pastries. A little pie. Hot cocoa. She said she wanted something sweet before we sang. She liked food. I think she sampled a little bit of everything today. Maybe she ate too much? I don't know."

I felt LuLu's grip tighten on my arm.

The stretcher was wheeled away, sirens cutting through the quiet like a blade. People stood frozen in its wake, unsure what to do now that the night had cracked open.

"We'll continue tomorrow," someone said weakly.

No one answered.

As the crowd slowly dispersed with their voices hushed and uncertain, I stood beneath the lanterns and stared at the patch of snow where Violet had fallen. The candle lay half-buried nearby, its light extinguished.

So much for no more drama this WishFest season.

I told myself it was a medical emergency. A tragic coincidence. A reminder that winter in the Vermont mountains was unforgiving and human bodies were delicate. But deep down, beneath the lights and music and carefully practiced calm, something cold and certain settled into my bones.

This wasn't an accident.

CHAPTER
Two

WISHVILLE WOKE UP CAREFULLY.

That was the only way I could describe it. The town didn't ease into the morning so much as tiptoe, like it wasn't sure what sounds might still be echoing from the night before. Snow lay fresh and unmarked on Main Street, smoothing over footprints and spilled cocoa, and up the hill to the place where a woman had collapsed on the stage beneath lantern light. By sunrise, it looked like nothing had happened.

Which felt like a lie we were all politely agreeing not to challenge.

I stood near the fountain in the town square, not ready to head up the hill to the crime scene and face reality. My hands were wrapped around a cup of coffee that had gone lukewarm without me noticing. Festival volunteers moved quietly around me, pretending this was just another Winter WishFest morning. Someone swept snow from the steps by the fountain, ready to start the second day of WishFest.

Vex sat on the rim of the fountain, his tail wrapped neatly around his paws. He hadn't said much since last night. That alone made me uneasy.

They're good at this, he said finally, watching the town come back to life. *Moving on.*

"They have to be," I replied. "Winter WishFest doesn't stop." It couldn't stop.

The town relied on the festivals to keep outsiders coming to visit since our mountain town was so remote. People came from all over each season to make one wish in the ancient well, hoping their wish might be the one to come true. When a wish came true, they chalked it up to wishful thinking and coincidence. They had no idea it was really magic. That the treaty between Dwellers and humans relied on one wish being granted during each season's festival to keep the peace between realms. If the treaty was broken, war could resume.

It was my job as Guardian of the Well to prevent that from happening.

Holden crossed the street toward me, his steps measured, his expression carefully neutral. It looked like that when he was carrying news he didn't like. He'd been at the hospital most of the night, checking in, making calls, and being the person who stayed when everyone else had gone home.

LuLu followed a few paces behind him, with her coat buttoned wrong, and her hair pulled back too tightly. She caught my eye and gave a small shake of her head before I could ask anything. I swallowed hard. That wasn't good.

Holden stopped in front of me. "They pronounced Violet Snowe dead early this morning."

The words landed with dull finality. I nodded, even though my chest tightened painfully. "What was the cause?"

"Cardiac event," he said. "Looks like she had an undiagnosed condition. They're leaning toward cold exposure and exertion as contributing factors."

Of course they were. It made sense. It was neat. It fit the story everyone wanted to tell, that winter was harsh, bodies were weak, and sometimes tragedy didn't need a villain.

"They're calling it natural causes," he added quietly.

I stared out at the street, at the lights still glowing softly despite the daylight, like they hadn't gotten the memo that someone's life had ended.

LuLu stepped closer, lowering her voice. "The town council's meeting in an hour, and then the mayor will give an update."

I looked at the vendors heading up the hill to set up again, and pictured Maisie Flint carefully lining up cider cups, Tasha Frimble arranging pies with hands that shook just a little, and Dot hovering at her tea stall like she was bracing for impact. I thought about the choir director's face when the stretcher rolled away.

"The festival must go on," I said. "But we'll scale it back. No singing tonight. We'll do a candlelight walk instead so we can honor Violet."

Holden nodded.

LuLu squeezed my arm. "That poor woman looked so healthy."

"She sure did," I replied.

And that was the problem.

～

The council meeting and mayor's update came and went in a blur of murmured condolences and careful phrasing. No one said *murder*. No one even said *suspicious*. They said *tragic* and *unfortunate* and *these things happen*.

Yet I couldn't shake the feeling that something was wrong.

By midmorning, the official story had settled into place. A woman with a hidden heart condition collapsed during exertion in cold weather. A terrible coincidence. A reminder to take care of ourselves.

Wishville accepted it with the practiced grace of a town that had learned how to carry grief without letting it spill everywhere. Too gracefully. I made my rounds with my clipboard in hand, checking in with vendors under the guise of logistics.

Betsy Plum snapped at me about oven temperatures and then hugged me hard enough to knock the breath out of my lungs.

Maisie pressed a peppermint stick into my palm like it was a talisman. "For later," she said softly. "You look pale."

Willa Hartman insisted I sit for a minute and drink something warm, watching me over the rim of her mug like she was cataloging every breath I took.

Dot didn't offer me tea. She just reached out and squeezed my hand, her eyes red-rimmed and fierce. "Violet was kind. She didn't deserve that."

No one did.

By noon, the story had spread beyond Wishville, stripped of context and softened by distance. *A sad accident at a small-town festival. Winter can be dangerous. Take care out there.*

I told myself to accept it. I told myself not to dig. But the words the choir director had blurted out last night wouldn't let go of me.

She just ate.

I stood at the edge of the clearing, watching people sip cider and bite into pastries, and tried to replay the night in my head. Not as Festival Chair or someone responsible for keeping things moving. As a witness. Violet hadn't stumbled before singing. She hadn't complained of the cold. She hadn't looked tired.

She'd smiled.

Vex sat beside me on the low stone wall by the well, his gaze tracking the crowd with unsettling focus. *You're thinking,* he said.

"I'm always thinking."

You're thinking past what they told you.

I lowered my voice. "You think they're wrong."

I think, he said slowly, *that when a story settles too quickly, it's because everyone wants it to.*

Wishville didn't know how to stop for grief. Not when there were schedules to keep and lanterns already strung. Instead, it moved more carefully, like a town stepping across thin ice. I crossed the festival clearing, heading toward the scene of the incident, my thoughts heavy and breath fogging the air as my boots crunched over snow that had been tamped down by yesterday's crowds.

Everyone's movements were slower than usual, with voices hushed as they lifted Styrofoam cups and samples. Someone was tuning a fiddle near the main stage, the notes soft and tentative, as if even the music was afraid of being too loud.

The gazebo stood at the center of it all, wrapped in white lights that glowed faintly even in daylight. Pine garlands trailed along its railings, dusted with snow. It looked exactly the same as it had the day before.

Except I couldn't stop seeing Violet there.

Right at the steps. One hand on the railing. The other pressed to her chest. Her breath coming out in short, startled bursts before she'd gone down hard enough that the sound had carried across the clearing.

Natural causes, they said.

A heart attack.

Exposure to the cold.

I told myself, again, that it wasn't my job to question that. But my feet slowed anyway as I passed the gazebo, my gaze snagging on the spot where someone had left a cluster of white roses tied with a silver ribbon. They hadn't been there last night.

Voices cut through the quiet.

Sharp and angry.

I turned.

Dana Snowe, Violet's sister, stood near the gazebo steps, her coat fastened neatly, every button on her expensive coat aligned with deliberate care. Her hair was pulled back in a smooth, controlled style that suggested habit rather than haste. At first glance, she looked composed—the kind of woman who prided herself on keeping herself together no matter the circumstances.

But up close, the control felt strained. Faint shadows bruised the skin beneath her eyes, and her smile—polite and practiced— never quite settled. Her jaw tightened and released in small, careful motions, as if she were constantly measuring what she allowed herself to show. She didn't look like someone falling apart.

She looked like someone determined not to.

The man facing her was a stranger. He stood too close, his posture aggressive in a way that felt deliberate. Tall, broad-shouldered, and wearing a dark wool coat that looked expensive enough to belong somewhere else. His voice carried, cutting through the muted festival sounds.

"This isn't how this works," he said. "You don't get to shut me out. Not anymore."

Dana crossed her arms. "I'm not discussing this here."

"You don't have a choice," he shot back. "Now that she's gone…tag, you're it." His hand gestured toward the gazebo.

My stomach tightened. "That's enough," I said, stepping closer before I fully realized I'd decided to.

Both of them turned.

Dana's expression filled with surprise…and relief.

The man's face hardened immediately. "This is a private matter," he said flatly.

"Not when you're yelling about it in the middle of Winter WishFest," I replied. "*Especially* not here."

His eyes narrowed. "You must be the Festival Chair. Lyra Wells."

"I am."

Something like disdain curled his mouth. "Figures."

Dana straightened. "You need to leave."

"I have every right to be here," he snapped. "I'm family."

"No," Dana said, her voice shaking despite her effort to steady it. "You stopped being family a long time ago."

A few people nearby had slowed, pretending not to watch while very obviously gawking. A vendor paused mid-unpacking. Someone's mittened hand hovered over a coffee cup.

The man leaned in closer to Dana, ignoring me. "Violet's gone. That changes things."

My skin prickled. "Back off," I said quietly. "Or I'll call the Chief of Police...my boyfriend."

He looked at me, really looked this time, as if weighing whether to push harder. For a tense second, the world narrowed to the three of us with the gazebo lights humming faintly above, and the festivalgoers holding their breaths. Two giant men in black suits and sunglasses stood off to the side.

His gaze locked onto them, then his jaw tightened as he turned back to Dana. "This isn't over. You'll hear from my lawyers." He turned and stalked away through the clearing, his boots cutting deep lines through the snow as he disappeared between the vendor tents.

The big men followed.

Dana's shoulders sagged the moment he was gone.

I stepped closer. "Dana, are you okay?"

She pressed a hand to her face, breathing out slowly. "I am now."

"I'm sorry," I said. "I didn't mean to interfere, but—"

"I'm glad you did," she said quietly. "He never knows when to stop."

I hesitated. "Who was that?"

"My cousin, Ozzy," she said without looking at me. "Estranged."

I blinked. "I didn't realize you and Violet had other family."

"We don't," Dana said. "Not really. Just on paper."

The festival sounds crept back in. Boots on snow, the low murmur of conversation, and the hiss of a coffee urn being opened.

"What does he want?" I asked.

Dana let out a short, bitter laugh. "Money." She leaned against the gazebo railing, the same one Violet had grabbed yesterday. "Our grandmother raised us after our parents died. She was... formidable. When she passed, she left everything to Violet and me."

"And your cousin?" I asked.

"He'd already burned every bridge he had," Dana said flatly. "Maxed out credit cards. Missed rent. Lawsuits. Violet helped him more times than I can count. Paid his way out of trouble, but it was never enough. He always came back wanting more."

"So, your grandmother put a stop to it," I said slowly.

Dana nodded. "She cut him out of her will. Legally. Completely."

"And now that your grandmother and Violet are gone…" I said.

"He thinks I won't fight him like they did," Dana said. "That death makes him entitled, and I'm somehow weaker than they were." She lifted her chin a notch. "He has no idea who I am."

"I'm so sorry," I said.

"Thank you." Dana nodded and then frowned. "I had no idea Violet's health was so fragile. It's so sad."

"She always seemed so healthy," I said. "She was in great shape. I saw her walking every day."

Dana shivered and rubbed her arms. "That's the scary part. You never know what underlying condition someone might have. Life is so fragile." Her lips quivered.

I nodded. "They said it was the cold."

"Maybe they're right. I'm no doctor." Her gaze drifted back to the gazebo steps. "Now I'm nervous that I might have some underlying condition I had no clue about." She shook her head.

I chose my next words carefully. "Did she say anything before…?"

"No," Dana said. "The night before, she joked that Wishville winters were finally going to kill her." Her voice cracked. "Our cook made her breakfast that morning, but she never ate it. Said she wanted to be good and hungry because festival food was the best."

I nodded. She wasn't wrong. We stood there while Winter WishFest continued around us. Music starting up again, vendors calling out greetings, and children dragging sleds across the snow like nothing in the world had shifted.

"I'm here if you need anything," I said quietly. "Meals. Help. Company."

Dana nodded. "Thank you, Lyra. I have a full staff who are like family to me. I just came to leave flowers. Now I have to plan a funeral." She took one last look at the gazebo before turning away and disappearing into the festival crowd.

I stayed where I was, the lights above humming softly, the cold seeping through my boots. Violet Snowe's death had already been labeled and explained. But standing where she'd fallen, listening to Dana, I couldn't shake the feeling that Winter WishFest was moving forward too quickly.

And that the cold might not be the only thing that had taken Violet Snowe down.

CHAPTER
Three

DR. OLIVER GREAVES'S clinic smelled like disinfectant and lavender. That clean, sharp bite that clung to winter air, rubber gloves, and the unspoken promise that whatever was wrong with you could be categorized into a chart and treated with something in a white bottle.

The **WISHVILLE FAMILY HEALTH** sign on the glass door had a snowcap of its own, and someone, almost certainly the Wellies, had stuck a tiny wreath to the handle with a red bow that felt aggressively cheerful under the circumstances.

I hesitated on the front step anyway, my gloved hand hovering at the door like I was about to walk into something contagious. Vex rode my shoulder, silent but watchful, his silver-sheened black fur stark against my coat.

You're stalling, he said.

"I'm choosing the correct emotional pace," I muttered.

Humans call that stalling.

Before I could argue, Holden opened the door from the inside, his broad frame filling the doorway like he'd decided my hesitation was now his problem. He'd trimmed his dark beard this morning, but the sharp line of it made him look more awake than I felt. His eyes slid over my face quickly, assessing.

"You coming in?" he asked quietly.

"I am in motion," I said, stepping past him.

His mouth twitched like he wanted to smile, but he didn't. We didn't have a lot of room for smiles right now. Not when the town was still insisting Violet Snowe had simply died. From what we had witnessed, Violet had been the picture of health. Her unexpected death seemed off. Hence, why we were here.

Inside, a small waiting room held three people bundled in coats, a toddler with a runny nose, and a teenage boy clutching a tissue like he was trying to strangle his own cold. A radio played quietly behind the counter. Some talk show discussing "winter wellness tips," with the breezy optimism of people who had never slipped on black ice and questioned every life choice that led them to that moment.

Fenrin was with us, in her ginger cat form, slinking close to my boots. To anyone else, she was just LuLu's cat. To me, she was one more secret wearing fur. Dr. Greaves allowed service animals, which everyone thought Vex was to me.

She flicked her tail once, slow and deliberate, then rubbed against my ankle.

"You can't come back here," the receptionist said automatically, glancing down at her.

Fenrin blinked up at her with innocent, enormous amber eyes.

The receptionist's resolve visibly weakened.

Holden cleared his throat. "She's LuLu's service animal, but I uh…borrowed her."

I turned to him.

His expression stayed perfectly straight.

I didn't dare laugh.

"It doesn't work like that." The receptionist frowned. "Just *borrow* the other one."

"He doesn't like me." Holden shrugged.

Fenrin chose that moment to leap up into a waiting chair like she'd always been scheduled for a 10:30 appointment and the clinic should be grateful she'd arrived on time.

The receptionist sighed. "Fine. But if she sheds on the upholstery, you're paying the cleaning fee."

Holden nodded gravely. "Understood."

Vex's ears flicked. *You're both ridiculous.*

I followed Holden down the hallway past exam rooms with paper-covered tables and posters that warned about flu symptoms and the dangers of untreated high blood pressure. The clinic was small. One of those places where the doctor knew your name, your aunt, your dog, and the fact that you only pretended to floss consistently.

Dr. Greaves was waiting near his office door with his white coat unbuttoned over a sweater that looked like it had been knitted by someone who loved him enough to bully him into wearing warm clothing. He was in his late fifties, with kind eyes and a face that had seen too much small-town grief to ever be surprised by it. Still, when he saw us, something tightened in his expression.

"Chief Thorn," he said, then looked at me. "Lyra."

"Dr. Greaves," I said.

There were condolences sitting between us like an extra empty chair none of us wanted to acknowledge. He opened his office door and gestured us in. Holden let me enter first. A small act that reminded me he'd been raised right. Neither of his parents were alive anymore. His mother dying when he was young, and his father murdered by a criminal Holden had put away back in Boston. That was the reason he'd moved to our small mountain town.

To get away from the violence.

The office was warm and cramped, lined with books and framed photos. A faded picture of the clinic staff at some long-ago holiday party. A certificate on the wall. A hand-drawn card taped near the lamp that said, *THANK YOU DR. G!*, in a child's looping handwriting. Wishville adored this man. If Violet Snowe had been truly sick, he would know.

Dr. Greaves sat behind his desk but didn't lean back like this was routine. He folded his hands instead and looked directly at Holden. "I heard," he said softly. "About Violet."

Holden's jaw tightened. "Yeah."

Dr. Greaves exhaled through his nose. "She was a good one."

I swallowed. I'd known Violet by repetition, shared spaces, and the consistent kindness of seeing her show up. She wasn't loud or dramatic. She was...steady. The kind of person who brought extra mittens for the kids' choir because she'd quietly noticed who always forgot theirs.

"I'm sorry to drop in like this," Holden said, his voice careful. "But we need to ask you some questions."

"I assumed you would," Dr. Greaves replied. His gaze slid to me. "You don't look like you've slept, Lyra."

"As Festival Chair, I consider sleep an optional myth," I said.

Vex flicked his tail against my collar. *Liar.*

Dr. Greaves's mouth softened briefly, like he appreciated my attempt at humor. Then the weight settled back. "What do you need?" he asked.

Holden glanced at me, giving me the opening.

I drew in a slow breath and forced myself to keep my voice calm. "The medical examiner's initial ruling indicates Violet Snowe may have had an underlying heart condition that led to her unexpected death. Did she have any known health issues? Heart condition? Medications? Anything in her history that could explain what happened?"

Dr. Greaves didn't answer immediately. He turned slightly, pulling a file from a stack on the corner of his desk, flipping it open with the ease of habit. His eyes scanned quickly. "No diagnosed cardiac issues," he said at last. "No hypertension. No arrhythmia. Nothing chronic."

My stomach tightened. "Family history?"

He shook his head. "Not that she ever reported. And she wasn't the type to hide things."

Holden leaned forward a fraction. "When was the last time you saw her?"

"Early fall," Dr. Greaves said. "Routine check. She came in for a stubborn cough, but her lungs were clear and vitals normal. She joked about how winter would be the death of her."

Her sister had said the same thing. A chill snaked through me. "She didn't come in recently?" I asked. "No dizziness? Shortness of breath? Chest pain?"

"No," he said, and his tone filled with certainty. "If Violet had felt something off, she would've told me. She wasn't reckless. She took care of herself. She walked every morning in the rain, snow, or whatever Vermont felt like throwing."

I'd seen Violet bundled in a coat on a snowy morning, walking Main Street while the rest of the town was still sleeping.

"Her sister said the same thing," I confirmed.

Holden's eyes stayed steady. "Could she have had a condition she didn't know about?"

Dr. Greaves hesitated. "It's possible. People *can* have silent issues, but..." He tapped the file gently. "She wasn't a stranger to checkups. Her baseline looked good."

The quiet "but" was the crack. Because it meant that the story everyone wanted, the neat one tied in a bow, wasn't as secure as it appeared.

I forced my hands to unclench. "What about supplements? Herbal blends? Anything she might have taken without thinking it mattered?"

Dr. Greaves looked almost offended on her behalf. "Violet was cautious. She wasn't swallowing mystery powders from the internet."

Holden asked, "Any chance she had an allergy? A reaction?"

Dr. Greaves shook his head. "No documented allergies. None she mentioned. And allergic reactions usually present differently." He paused, then his eyes met mine again, thoughtfully. "You're not asking this because you want reassurance. You're asking because something doesn't fit."

I nodded. "The medical examiner ruled her death as natural."

"I know," he said. "And I respect Dr. Bellamy. But initial impressions aren't always the full story."

Holden's voice stayed careful. "If we want more certainty, what do we do?"

Dr. Greaves leaned back slightly, as if choosing his words with professional caution. "If you have reason to believe there's uncertainty, then you request a full autopsy and expanded toxicology. Not just a basic screen."

Holden nodded. "I'm working on it."

"And you should," Dr. Greaves said, his tone firm now. "Because if Violet Snowe died from something other than an undiagnosed condition, the town deserves the truth."

The town, yes. And Dana. My gaze dropped briefly to the child's thank-you card on the wall. Gratitude preserved, like proof that people could be good. Then my mind flashed to Violet on the stage, her breath turning thin, her hand to her chest, and the way she'd looked startled as if her body had betrayed her without warning.

"Did she mention anything yesterday?" I asked. "Any stress? Any argument? Anything that could've pushed her?"

Dr. Greaves frowned, thinking. "Not to me. But I have heard through the grapevine that her estranged cousin, Ozzy Snowe, was back in town. Her sister also mentioned Percy Johnson, an ex-boyfriend of Violet's, who wouldn't take no for an answer."

Interesting. Dana hadn't mentioned Percy to me. I had also heard Wendy Washington was very vocal about wanting her spot as lead caroler this year. Now that Violet was out of the picture, the role had conveniently gone to Wendy. I made a mental note to look into all of those leads.

"Thank you for your time, Doctor," Holden said as he stood.

Dr. Greaves rose, too, and walked us to the door. "Lyra," he said softly, stopping me with just my name.

I looked at him.

"I know you carry this town on your shoulders. You always have. But don't carry this death alone."

My chest tightened, and I nodded. I did feel responsible for all of the citizens in town, but I wasn't worried about my health. I could heal myself. It was the town I was worried about. Holden's hand brushed the small of my back as we moved into the hallway, grounding, like a quiet reminder that I wasn't the only one standing in the cold.

We stepped outside into air that bit at my lungs. Snow had started falling again, light and steady, dusting the world in clean white like it was trying to erase what had happened. But the truth didn't erase that easily.

Holden's breath came out in a white puff, his gaze fixed on the street. "He didn't see anything in her history that explains her collapse."

"No," I said.

He looked at me, his voice low. "You think we should push Bellamy?"

I thought about Violet's warmth. Her steadiness. The way the town wanted to wrap her death in a neat ribbon and move on. And I thought about her sister who deserved to know the truth… whatever that may be.

"I think," I said carefully, "we can't afford *not* to."

Vex's tail flicked once against my coat collar. *Now we're moving.*

And as we walked back with Fenrin at our heels toward the glow of Winter WishFest, toward vendors and lanterns and a town that didn't know it had become a crime scene, I felt the shape of the next step solidify in my bones. We were done accepting the easy answer.

Now we were going to ask for the hard one.

The county medical examiner's office sat on the outskirts of town, a low concrete building that looked like it had been designed specifically to avoid drawing attention to itself. No wreaths or lanterns or cheer clinging stubbornly to the corners.

Just gray siding, a parking lot dusted with snow, and a sign in plain lettering that read: **COUNTY FORENSIC SERVICES**

I pulled my coat tighter as Holden shut off the engine. "This is where we find our answers," he said.

I nodded. "In the science."

Vex hopped lightly from my shoulder to the dashboard, peering out the windshield like he expected the building to peer back. *I dislike places where truth smells like chemicals.*

"You dislike most places," I replied.

Yes. But this one is honest about it.

Fenrin remained in the backseat, curled into a tight ginger loaf. Her tail swooped once, slow and watchful. She didn't move when we opened the doors, just opened one amber eye as if committing the place to memory.

Inside, the air was colder than I expected. Fluorescent lights hummed softly overhead. Everything smelled faintly of antiseptic and something metallic I didn't want to think too hard about.

Dr. Ethan Bellamy met us at the front desk. He was tall, lean, and composed, like someone who dealt with death daily without letting it calcify him. His white coat was immaculate, his red hair silver at the temples, and his expression professional without being unkind.

"Chief Thorn," he said, offering a firm handshake. "Ms. Wells."

"Thank you for seeing us," Holden said. "On short notice."

Bellamy nodded once. "I assumed you wouldn't be coming if it wasn't important."

That alone made my stomach clench.

He led us down a corridor that branched into rooms I didn't want to imagine in detail. We stopped in a small office with a metal desk, two chairs, and a filing cabinet that looked like it had been there since the seventies.

Bellamy sat and folded his hands. "I understand you're requesting an expanded autopsy and toxicology panel for Violet Snowe."

"Yes," Holden said. "Based on new information."

Bellamy's gaze shifted to me as if evaluating my role in this investigation.

"You ruled the death as natural causes," I said carefully. "Cardiac event."

"I did," he replied. "Based on presentation, environment, and initial screening. Sudden collapse during exertion in cold weather fits a cardiac scenario, especially in adults."

"But..." Holden said, holding up a finger.

Bellamy inclined his head. "But?"

I took a breath. "Her primary care physician confirmed she had no known heart condition. No family history. No medications that would complicate things."

Bellamy's eyes sharpened slightly. "Dr. Greaves is thorough."

"He is," Holden said. "We feel it's only right to do the same. For Violet's sake, as well as her sister's."

Bellamy listened without interrupting, his expression unreadable. "Her medical history does introduce uncertainty."

Relief flickered in my chest. "What does that mean procedurally?" I asked.

"It means," Bellamy said, "that I have justification to expand the scope of examination." He stood and moved to the filing cabinet, pulling a folder and setting it on the desk. "A full autopsy would involve a comprehensive internal examination," he continued. "I'll look for structural abnormalities, signs of disease, anything that could explain sudden cardiac failure."

"And toxicology?" Holden asked.

"We already ran a standard screen," Bellamy said. "That checks for common substances like alcohol, certain drugs, obvious toxins. It was negative."

I frowned.

"But," he continued, "an expanded panel looks deeper for less common compounds. Substances that can mimic natural causes. That takes more time."

"How much more?" I asked.

Bellamy considered. "Preliminary autopsy findings happen within a few days. Expanded toxicology can take anywhere from one to several weeks, depending on what we're testing for and lab backlog."

Weeks. I felt the weight of Winter WishFest pressing down on me. The lights, the crowds, and the way the town wanted to keep moving.

"And authority?" Holden asked. "What do you need from us?"

"In this case," Bellamy said, "your formal request as Chief of Police is sufficient. Especially with corroborating medical information. I'll document the justification."

Holden nodded. "You'll have it."

Bellamy's gaze returned to me. "I want to be clear," he said gently. "This does not mean Violet Snowe was murdered."

"I know," I said. "It just means we don't know yet."

"Exactly."

He slid a form across the desk. Holden signed it without hesitation.

"What happens now?" I asked.

"I'll let you know when I have something definitive," Bellamy said, closing the folder. "I'll begin the autopsy tomorrow morning."

Tomorrow. The word echoed louder than it should have.

As we stood to leave, Bellamy hesitated, then added, "For what it's worth, if the expanded tox shows something unusual, it may explain why the initial presentation looked cardiac."

"Something that mimics it," I said.

"Yes," he replied. "Which is why we don't rush conclusions."

"Thank you for your time," Holden said, and we left. Outside, the cold air had a bite to it. "That went better than I expected."

"Because you're the Chief," I said. "And because Violet didn't fit the story. So what should we do now?"

"Now we wait for science to do its thing," Holden said.

Vex leapt back onto my shoulder. *Waiting is intolerable.*

"I know," I murmured.

Fenrin jumped out of the car, stretched, then blinked up at me. I nodded, and she transformed into a hawk, then flew off toward the festival grounds in quiet surveillance of the town.

As we drove back toward town, Holden held my hand. The lights of Winter WishFest appeared in the distance, glowing stubbornly against the snow. The festival would go on. People would laugh. Vendors would sell sweets. The town would pretend it hadn't come close to something darker.

But now there was a clock ticking beneath it all.

Somewhere between autopsy results and lab reports, the truth was waiting. And when it surfaced, Wishville would have to decide whether it still wanted to carry on as usual, or finally stop and look at the facts.

ELARION DID NOT WELCOME YOU.

It *received* you, quietly and deliberately, like a place that had outlived the need to impress. The air cooled as I said the ancient incantation and stepped over the edge of the wishing well through the portal into another realm. Light thickened around me in layered currents that hummed beneath my skin. Stone formed beneath my slippers, smooth and faintly luminous, etched with ancient runes that pulsed slowly as if recognizing my presence and deciding to allow it.

Calderis was already there. He stood at the edge of the platform, tall and motionless, his silhouette cast against the soft glow of the city beyond. His ceremonial robes marked him instantly: deep obsidian layered with cobalt thread, the insignia of the Chief Enforcer woven directly into the fabric rather than stitched on later. The crest at his chest was water bound around a star, and it caught the light then held it, steady and severe.

He turned when he sensed me, his long silver hair hanging loose and flowing with his expression unreadable but intense. "You came alone," he said.

I had video messaged him through the crystal orb I had, Elarion's version of a cell phone. I had filled him in on everything that had transpired, and he'd asked me to meet with him and update the Elders.

"For now," I replied. My own ceremonial robes settled around me as the last of the transit magic faded. Wildflower-soft, moss and river-stone layered, with muted copper threads. The rose sash at my waist warmed faintly, as if reminding me why I wore it at all.

Calderis's gaze flicked to the emblem over my heart.

A sapling growing from a cracked stone, its roots entwining with a water current that looped into the shape of an eye. The leaves shimmered with silver, and the stone glinted with flecks of brown and green. It was a symbol of survival rather than status.

Without another word, we moved together into the inner ring. The path spiraled inward through the heart of Elarion's capital, the city unfolding in controlled beauty around us. Crystal spires rose like frozen lightning, their facets catching light from drifting lumina orbs overhead. Bioluminescent vines traced the arches, their glow subtle and restrained with nothing wasted or accidental.

This was not a place built for comfort.

It was built for continuity.

The doors to *The Council Chamber* awaited us. Twin arcs of moonstone veined with silver, curved inward as if the stone itself leaned toward the space beyond. Calderis placed his palm against the surface. The doors resonated with a low, bell-like tone that vibrated through my ribs before parting.

Inside, the chamber opened wide and high, shaped like the inside of a bell.

Twelve Elders sat in tiered arcs carved directly into the stone walls, their seats rising in a crescent that focused the eye toward the center dais. Each wore robes dyed to their domain: starlight silver, ember red, deep ocean teal, crystal white, shadow obsidian, rich earth umber. Memory orbs drifted slowly overhead, casting reflected light across faces that had learned patience the way mortals learned breathing.

And at the center sat Vaerion.

Chief Elder.

Calderis's father.

His silver hair was braided with strings of twilight blue, pulled back from a face carved in calm authority. The crest at his chest was an ancient whirlpool encircling a starburst that glimmered faintly, containing power rather than displaying it.

I bowed.

Calderis inclined his head.

Vaerion's gaze fixed on me immediately.

"Guardian Wells," he said. His voice carried without effort. "You return to Elarion bearing weight."

"Always," I said evenly. "That is the nature of my post."

A ripple of quiet murmurs passed through the chamber.

Vaerion lifted one hand. Silence returned at once.

"You requested this audience," he said. "Speak."

I stepped forward. "The rebels are no longer in the mountain caverns. Their enclave has been abandoned." The Elders knew of my encounter with the rebels during the Fall WishFest, but I hadn't fully updated them since as I had been struggling with my mother's last message to me.

This time, the murmurs were louder.

Vaerion's eyes narrowed slightly. "And their leader?"

I met his gaze. "Serena."

The name landed like a dropped blade. Several Elders stiffened. One leaned forward. Another turned sharply to Vaerion. Calderis's posture went rigid beside me.

"My mother," I continued, my voice steady despite the tension tightening in my chest, "has confirmed her role. She is leading the revolution. Their current location is unknown."

Vaerion studied me for a long moment. "You are certain."

"Yes."

"And you bring this to us now," he said, "because—"

"Because the surface has suffered a fatality connected to

ongoing instability," I said. "And because we don't think the death was accidental."

The temperature in the chamber dropped.

"A human?" asked the Elder in crystal white.

"Yes," I said. "Violet Snowe. A respected member of the town."

Vaerion's gaze sharpened. "Cause of death?"

"We're not sure, but we've ordered further testing," I replied. "She appears to have had a heart attack without any medical issues."

Several Elders exchanged looks.

"And why is this of concern to Elarion?" Vaerion asked.

"Because if she was murdered, then Winter WishFest could be compromised. A wish might not be granted which affects the stability of the treaty," I said. Two murders and one cold case had occurred during the festivals this past year. Another murder would raise considerable alarm and could lead to a permanent shutdown.

Calderis turned his head sharply toward me, though he already knew this part.

Silence fell again, deeper this time.

"Guardian Wells and Chief Thorn are looking into matters above," Calderis said formally. "I will secure the borders and hunt for the rebels below."

Vaerion's fingers tightened once on the arm of his chair. "Do you believe the rebels are involved with the murder above?"

"I believe," I said carefully, "that we cannot rule it out." Nor could we confirm it. "The investigation is ongoing," I added. "We will pursue all angles. Our allegiance as the Covenant Three is to protect the treaty at all costs and keep the peace between both realms." Even though my mother had planted a seed of doubt regarding the treaty and the Elders, but for now, my allegiance was firm.

Vaerion's gaze lingered on me. "And Serena?"

"We are searching," I said. "But she has learned how to disappear with ease." A familiar, painful truth.

Vaerion leaned back slightly, considering. "You will keep the Council informed."

"Yes."

"And you will not act unilaterally," he added.

I bowed again. "I will act responsibly."

It was not the same promise.

Vaerion studied me for a long, measuring moment, then inclined his head. "This Council acknowledges the loss of the human woman, and the threat to the treaty. We will remain… attentive."

Not supportive.

Or forthcoming.

Just attentive.

As we turned to leave, Calderis spoke quietly. "Father."

Vaerion's gaze shifted to him.

"The rebels are growing bolder," Calderis said. "And someone has crossed a line."

Vaerion's expression did not change. "Then see that the line holds."

Calderis nodded and we left. The doors sealed behind us with a resonant hush. Once we were beyond the chamber's reach, Calderis exhaled slowly. "They believe only what they are ready to believe."

"Yes," I replied. "And nothing more."

His gaze met mine, steady and grim. "You did not tell them everything."

"No," I said. "Not yet."

Some truths were dangerous. Not because they were false, but because of who controlled them. My mother had told me the treaty was not what I thought, and that the Elders had lied. I wasn't sure how much Calderis knew about that, so I hadn't even told him everything.

It was time I did a little digging on my own.

~

Elarion never felt empty.

Even when it was quiet, even when its streets were sparsely traveled and its halls echoed instead of hummed, the realm carried memory like stone carries heat long after the sun has set. Light lived here differently, soft and diffuse, filtered through bioluminescent veins in the cavern walls and drifting motes that pulsed faintly like a living heartbeat.

I had stayed with the promise to follow shortly, after I stopped by my mother's house…my house now.

Calderis had reluctantly returned topside to update Holden and LuLu since it was nearly dawn and they would be waking, wondering where I was. Calderis made me repeat a promise twice: *Do not go looking for trouble alone.*

I promised…with my fingers crossed behind my back.

Besides, I wasn't alone. Only, I didn't go to my mother's house. I put myself in my mother's shoes and thought about the places she used to go. Because I wasn't looking for trouble…I was looking for my mother.

Unfortunately, these days, they were one and the same.

Vex paced the curve of my shoulder, his tail flicking as his gaze swept the wide causeway leading into the lower districts of Elarion. Fenrin padded beside me in her ginger cat form, silent and intent, her ears angling toward every whisper of sound like she was mapping the realm in real time.

You are walking like someone following a ghost, Vex observed.

"She's not a ghost," I said quietly. "She's very much alive." Which was the problem.

Serena Wells, Guardian before me and rebel leader now, had vanished into the world beyond Elarion a century ago, taking others with her. We'd searched the mountain caverns. We'd searched the outskirts. We'd searched every place that made sense.

Which meant she hadn't gone anywhere sensible.

I followed instinct instead.

Her favorite places.

The Spiral Terrace was first. It lay along the inner ring of Elarion, where the stone curved outward into layered balconies carved centuries ago by Dweller artisans who believed beauty itself was a form of defense. The terraces were quiet now, many of the dwellings dark, their occupants relocated deeper into the city after the rebellion fractured trust.

I remembered being small here, smaller than I'd wanted to be, my mother's hand warm and steady in mine as she pointed out constellations etched into the ceiling stone.

"She loved this place," I murmured.

Fenrin leaped lightly onto a low wall, her tail curling. She smelled the air, then shook her head.

No fresh trail, Vex translated. *But echoes linger.*

Echoes were better than nothing.

The first person I sought was Caelvar. He was ancient even by Dweller standards, his silver-white hair worn long and braided with copper thread, his robes layered in blues and greens that shimmered faintly when he moved. He'd been a historian once. Then a teacher. Then a confidant to my mother.

He sat where I remembered him, hunched over a low stone table etched with maps that shifted slowly beneath his fingers.

"Lyra Wells," he said without looking up. "You walk like your mother when you are worried."

My heart squeezed. "She taught me."

He finally lifted his gaze, with his eyes pale and piercing. "Then she taught you too well."

I sat across from him. "Did she come to you?"

He didn't pretend not to understand. "Before she left? Yes."

Vex went still.

"What did she say?" I asked.

Caelvar's fingers paused over the map. "She asked me a question she'd asked many times before."

I waited.

"Where does a truth go when no one is allowed to speak it?"

Cold slid down my spine. "What did you tell her?" I asked.

"That truths don't disappear," he said softly. "They retreat. They wait. And they gather strength in places no one claims."

Fenrin's ears pricked.

"Places like where?" I pressed.

Caelvar met my gaze steadily. "Not Elarion."

I swallowed. "Outside the realm?"

"Yes," he said. "But not the mountain caverns you searched. Not the wild edges, either. She has spies everywhere. She knew you would look there."

Of course she had.

"She asked about *The Badlands*," he continued.

The word sounded heavy and old. I hadn't heard it spoken aloud in decades. "*The Badlands* aren't real anymore," I said automatically. "They collapsed. The magic bled out."

"That is what we tell the young," Caelvar replied. "And what the Elders prefer."

I stiffened. He noticed.

"They exist," he said. "Changed. Scarred. A no-man's land between realms where magic doesn't flow cleanly and time behaves badly."

Fenrin made a low sound in her throat, something uneasy.

Why would she go there? Vex asked.

Because no one else would. I stood slowly. "Did she say when?"

"Only that she was done pretending lies didn't exist," Caelvar said. "And that if the truth could not live in Elarion, she would take it somewhere it could not be erased."

I left him with a nod that I didn't trust myself to speak through.

The second place was quieter.

A narrow bridge of living crystal arched over a dark chasm, its surface faintly warm beneath my boots. My mother used to bring me here when I was overwhelmed, when Elarion felt too loud, and too watched. We'd sit at the center and listen to the silence.

That was where I found Nythea. She was old too, though her hair remained iridescent, her eyes bright and sharp. A healer once. A friend always. She didn't pretend surprise when she saw me.

"I expected you would come one day," she said mildly.

"I was waiting for the right time," I replied.

She smiled faintly. "So did she."

My breath caught. "She came back here with you?"

"Yes," Nythea said. "Right where you are now. She said the city felt…hollow."

I swallowed. "Did she leave anything?"

Nythea reached into her sleeve and withdrew a small object. A shard of stone, dull and gray, its surface etched with a faint spiral. Not Dweller made. Not Elarion stone at all.

"This fell from her pocket," Nythea said. "She said you'd know what it meant."

My fingers trembled as I took it. The spiral wasn't decorative. It was a map marker. "She's not hiding," I whispered. "She's waiting…and she's not alone.

Fenrin leapt to my shoulder, her claws gentle but firm.

Waiting for you, Vex finished.

I closed my fist around the shard and stared into the chasm below, its depths swallowing light. Serena hadn't fled. She had chosen exile. A place beyond rule, beyond erasure, and beyond control. A place the Elders didn't patrol. A place no one wanted to go.

The Badlands.

I exhaled slowly, my resolve settling like armor beneath my skin. "Okay," I murmured to the quiet realm. "I hear you."

And somewhere far beyond Elarion's glowing halls, in a land scarred and forgotten, I knew my mother was watching too.

CHAPTER
Five

THE *TOWN HALL* smelled like burned coffee and winter coats that had never quite dried.

Rows of folding chairs filled the room, arranged in careful lines that suggested order even as people clustered in the aisles, whispering, shifting, scanning faces for reassurance or confirmation of their worst fears. Someone had set out a tray of store-bought cookies on a side table, untouched except for one broken chocolate chip that looked like it had been snapped in half out of nervous habit.

I stood near the back with Holden and LuLu, my clipboard tucked under my arm like a shield I didn't entirely trust anymore. I kept my face calm and neutral, but inside, my thoughts were a chaotic mess.

Vex perched on my shoulder, his tail wrapped neatly around my collarbone like he was anchoring himself. Fenrin was nowhere to be seen, which meant she was somewhere she wanted to be, listening without being noticed. Ginger cats were excellent at that…or maybe she was a mouse today.

The mayor stood near the front of the room, conferring in low tones with two council members. Doug Delaney looked thinner than usual behind the podium, his boney shoulders hunched, tie crooked, and combover grayer than I remembered. Leadership was weighing on him.

A murmur rippled through the room as Trip Danderly took a seat in the front row, his sparkly badge attached to his coat, wand-shaped flashlight in its holster, and hat balanced on his knee like he expected to be deputized at any moment. The self-appointed Wish Sheriff had brought a notebook, per usual.

LuLu leaned toward me. "He's already live-posting," she murmured.

"That doesn't surprise me," I said under my breath.

Holden shifted slightly closer. A quiet line of support I was more grateful for than I wanted to admit.

Doug cleared his throat into the microphone.

The sound snapped the room into silence.

"Thank you all for coming," he began, his voice strained but steady. "We're here to talk about what happened the other night. And about how we move forward as a town."

I watched faces as he spoke.

Alistair was consoling the visibly upset Wellies. So much for his quiet retirement. Betsy Plum's jaw was set hard. Maisie Flint clasped her hands together like a vice. Willa Hartman sat rigidly upright. And Tasha Frimble sat near the aisle with her foot tapping just slightly too fast.

Violet Snowe had touched all of them in small, ordinary ways.

Doug paused, then said her name. "Violet Snowe was a valued member of our community."

The room nodded together.

"She volunteered year after year. She sang. She showed up. And her loss has shaken us," he continued.

Someone sniffed loudly.

Another person reached out to squeeze a neighbor's hand.

Doug nodded once, as if acknowledging the collective grief. "Originally, the medical examiner confirmed that Violet's death was believed to be due to natural causes like a sudden cardiac event."

There it was. The story everyone wanted. But he didn't stop.

"However," Doug continued, and the room leaned forward as one, "new information came to light that required further investigation."

The air changed.

Holden straightened beside me.

LuLu's hand stilled at her side.

Doug gestured toward Holden. "Chief Thorn will explain."

Holden stepped forward, his presence steadying the room even as tension crackled beneath the surface. He didn't raise his voice, but he didn't soften it either. "Based on information provided by Violet's primary care physician, there is no known medical history that would explain a sudden cardiac event."

A ripple moved through the crowd.

Bart muttered something under his breath.

"For that reason," Holden continued, "I formally requested a full autopsy and expanded toxicology testing."

The word *toxicology* landed like a dropped plate.

"What does that mean?" someone called out.

"It means," Holden said calmly, "we're being thorough."

Trip Danderly shot to his feet. "Are you saying someone poisoned her?"

Doug lifted a hand. "Trip—"

"No, no," Trip barreled on. "Because I've been saying for years this festival attracts bad energy. Outsiders. People with agendas—"

"Sit down," Doug snapped, louder than I'd ever heard him.

Trip subsided, grumbling, but he didn't look satisfied.

Doug took a breath. "The preliminary results from the expanded testing are not final, but they do indicate the presence of a compound that affects the heart."

A hush fell over the room so completely I could hear the hum of the lights overhead.

"A *compound*?" Maisie whispered.

Doug nodded. "One that can mimic the symptoms of a cardiac event after being ingested."

The words rearranged themselves in the air, reshaping the room.

"That means—" Willa started.

"It means," Holden said with authority, "that Violet Snowe may have ingested something that caused her collapse."

The reaction was immediate.

"No."

"That's impossible."

"From where?"

"You can't mean—"

Willa stood abruptly. "You are *not* suggesting it was one of us."

"No one is making accusations," Doug said quickly. "Please—"

"But you're implying it," Betsy shot back. "My kitchen is spotless. I feed my own family."

"So do I," Maisie said, her voice trembling but firm. "I keep records. I know what goes into everything."

Dot finally looked up, her eyes brimming with unshed tears. "This was supposed to be a festival, not a witch hunt."

"Then maybe we shouldn't have secrets," Trip muttered, eying everyone in the room suspiciously.

"Trip," LuLu said firmly, and for a moment every head turned toward her. "If you don't have facts, sit down."

He did, looking offended.

Doug raised both hands. "Please, everyone, this is exactly why we're here. To stop rumors before they spiral. Violet told the choir director she purposely didn't eat before the festival because she wanted to sample everything." He looked directly at me then. "Lyra, as Festival Chair, you sampled the food, correct?"

"Actually, no. I was delayed when the generator malfunctioned, which took longer than expected. I didn't make it back to the festival stage until the show was about to start."

Vendors started speaking all at once, saying Violet came by

when Lyra was supposed to, so they offered her those samples, intending to make fresh ones for Lyra later.

The room turned toward me, horrified.

I nodded. "That is correct." I felt the weight of it hit all at once—the implication, the guilt, the sudden realization rippling outward like a shockwave.

Someone whispered, "Someone was trying to kill Lyra."

"No," Doug said quickly. "We don't know that."

But it was already out there.

Betsy's face went pale. "No one else ate those samples except Violet."

Maisie pressed a hand to her mouth. "Oh, my goodness, did someone tamper with my food?"

Willa shook her head slowly. "Why would anyone want to harm our Festival Chair?"

I swallowed, forcing myself to speak. "We don't know for sure that someone wanted to harm me or Violet," I said, my voice steady despite the way my hands shook.

"If Violet only ate at the festival, and the poison was ingested, then someone had to put it in one of the samples," Holden said quietly, "and that someone is still out there."

The room fell silent again.

Doug cleared his throat. "I'm sure Chief Thorn will thoroughly investigate all angles. Until the investigation is complete, we ask that everyone cooperate. Provide timelines. Be honest. And remember, we all deserve the truth."

A murmur of agreement followed, subdued but resolute.

As the meeting adjourned, people lingered, huddling in small groups, their voices low and urgent. Fear had replaced grief. I stood rooted in place, staring at the podium where Doug had stood moments before.

Vex shifted. *We need to know who that someone is.*

"Yes," I whispered. "We do."

And as the town hall slowly emptied, one truth settled deeper than the rest, Winter WishFest had stopped being a celebration. It was now a murder investigation. And I wouldn't rest until we knew for sure who the intended target really was.

The *Town Hall* didn't empty so much as unravel.

People lingered in clusters, their voices low and edged, the air buzzing with a nervous energy that wasn't there when the meeting began. I stayed where I was, near the back, with my clipboard pressed flat against my ribs like it could anchor me.

Vendors gathered instinctively, the way people did when they needed to reassure one another that the ground was still solid. Bart and Gus had their heads together, in tense discussion. Betsy stood with her arms crossed and jaw set so tight I worried she might crack a tooth. Maisie Flint hovered nearby looking pale, but upright with one hand clenched around the strap of her bag. Willa Hartman spoke in quick, clipped sentences to Tasha Frimble, who nodded but didn't say much as her eyes darted toward the door like she was considering escape.

Dot lingered a few steps away, staring at nothing as Tilly and Belle tried to console her.

Trip Danderly prowled the perimeter, his notebook tucked under his arm, clearly itching to corner someone. Every time he opened his mouth, Doug Delaney shot him a look hard enough to cut glass.

Dana came to a stop beside me, looking pale and devastated. Fragile, even. "Do you really think someone poisoned my sister?"

"We don't know anything for sure, but it's looking that way."

"I just want to bury her so she can rest in peace. This is all a mess now. I seriously can't take much more." Her eyes welled with tears.

"I know, and I'm so sorry. We really are just trying to get at the truth for you."

She nodded, dabbed at her eyes, and then left.

Holden leaned in close to me. "You okay?"

I nodded automatically. Then, after a beat, I shook my head. "Ask me again later."

"That was a lot," he said gently, rubbing my back.

"That was the town realizing there's a murderer on the loose… again," I replied, leaning into him. "It feels *bigger* than a lot."

LuLu slipped in on my other side, her voice low. "You handled it well."

"I didn't do anything," I said.

"You didn't fall apart when you realized you might be the target," she corrected. "That counts."

Across the room, Betsy spotted me and broke away from the group. She moved fast, her anger giving her momentum. "Lyra," she said, stopping short of me. "Those samples—"

"I know," I said quickly. "And you didn't do anything wrong."

Her eyes searched my face, fierce and glossy. "If someone tampered with my food—"

"We don't know if it was yours," I said. "Violet ate all the samples. There's no way to tell which food it came from."

Maisie joined us then, her voice trembling despite the way she squared her shoulders. "I keep my cider locked down. I don't leave it unattended. Well, except for your sample, I guess."

"I know," I said again. "You're meticulous."

Willa stepped closer, her arms wrapped around herself. "People are going to look at us differently now."

The truth of that settled heavy in my chest. "They shouldn't, but they might. And I'm sorry."

"For Violet," Dot said suddenly.

We all turned to her.

She pushed her glasses up with a shaking finger. "I'm sorry for *Violet*. She didn't deserve to be part of this."

"No," I agreed softly. "She didn't."

Silence stretched between us, thick and uncomfortable.

Doug approached then, his expression weary. "We're going to keep this contained as much as possible. Holden and I will coordinate statements. No one here is being accused of anything."

"Yet," Trip muttered from behind him.

Doug spun. "Trip, go home."

Trip bristled. "People deserve to know if one of our own is a killer."

"And people deserve not to be terrorized by speculation," Doug snapped. "This town doesn't eat its own."

Trip scoffed but backed off, muttering about vigilance and justice as he retreated toward the door.

Doug turned back to me, lowering his voice. "Lyra, I need you to consider stepping back from public appearances for a bit."

My stomach dropped. "You want me to hide?"

"I want you safe," he said. "At least until we know more. What if you really were the target and not Violet?"

I glanced at Holden. His jaw tightened.

"It doesn't matter who the target was. I can't step back," I said. "Winter WishFest is still running. People need to see that it hasn't broken us."

Doug sighed. "I was afraid you'd say that."

"Besides," I added quietly, "if someone wanted to hurt me, disappearing won't stop them. It'll just make everyone else more nervous."

Doug studied me for a long moment, then nodded reluctantly. "We'll increase patrols."

Holden didn't comment, but I felt the tension radiating off him like heat.

The crowd thinned slowly after that. Chairs scraped. Coats were pulled on. People avoided my eyes or held them too long, like they were trying to memorize me just in case I was next. When the room finally cleared, the quiet felt wrong. Too abrupt after the storm.

We stepped outside into the cold night, snow drifting lazily from a sky that looked far too peaceful for what had just happened. The festival lights glowed in the distance up the hill, steady, as if nothing had changed.

Everything had changed.

We walked in silence for a few steps before LuLu spoke. "Someone planned this."

"Yes," I said.

"And they knew you," she added.

I stopped walking.

Holden and LuLu both turned to face me.

"They didn't just know my schedule," I said slowly. "They knew my habits. That I sample everything. That vendors set things aside. That I'd be pulled in a dozen directions before the singing."

Vex shifted on my shoulder. *They knew how to wait.*

A chill slid down my spine that had nothing to do with the cold. "They also knew I wouldn't think twice about it," I continued. "Because it's never been dangerous before."

Holden clenched his jaw. "We'll treat this like any other case."

"Except it isn't," I said. "Because Violet died in my place."

"Allegedly." LuLu reached out and squeezed my hand. "We need to look into possible enemies for you both."

"I know," I said, uncomfortable with the thought that I could have enemies.

We reached the edge of the square and paused, looking up at the path that led back to the festival grounds. Laughter drifted down, faint but determined.

"They're still celebrating," LuLu said softly.

"They need to," I replied. "So do we."

Holden nodded. "I'll talk to Bellamy tomorrow. See if there's anything new."

"And I'll start retracing Violet's day," I said. "Every stop and interaction she had."

"Carefully," Holden said.

"Always," I lied.

Vex's tail flicked. *You're already planning something.*

"I don't know what you're talking about," I said.

Fenrin appeared then, padding out of the shadows in her ginger cat form, snow dusting her whiskers. She wove between my legs once, then sat and looked up at me, her gaze steady and intent.

"I know," I murmured, crouching to scratch behind her ears. "I'll be careful."

She bumped her head against my hand, a silent promise or warning, I wasn't sure which.

As we started back up the hill toward the glow of Winter WishFest, I felt the weight of the night settle into something more than fear. Resolve. Someone had possibly tried to kill me. They'd failed. And now, for Violet Snowe, for this town, and for the truth buried beneath lights and lanterns and tradition, I was going to make sure they didn't get another chance.

That started with asking the question, *Why me?*

CHAPTER
Six

MY HOUSE WAS AN ANCIENT, two-storied, old clapboard that sat hidden in a nook of trees away from town. It had been my father's house three hundred years ago, and mine for the last century, having gone through numerous renovations. For a long time I had lived alone, hesitant to make friends because I would outlive them.

My human father had died when I was little, and my mother vanished one hundred years ago. It had been a lonely existence taking over her role as Guardian of the Well, but then I'd met Holden. After he fell in the well, trying to save me, Calderis's father Vaerion had wanted me to erase Holden's memory. But after he proved useful, Vaerion made us The Covenant Three, tasked with keeping the peace between both worlds.

Then when LuLu arrived and followed us into the well, I once again was told to erase her memory, but LuLu's psychic gift prevented that from happening. She too had proven her worth and was an unofficial member of our team now. Vaerion didn't like it, but she was under Calderis's protection. LuLu, Vex, and Fenrin lived with me now, and for the first time, I didn't feel so alone anymore.

That evening, snow piled along the porch rails like frosting, and a single wreath hung on the door because Wishville expected it, not because I felt festive. Warm light glowed through the windows, soft and domestic, the kind of light that promised safety.

But I was discovering safety was a lie.

Inside, the air smelled like cinnamon from the simmer pot I'd set on the stove out of habit. Orange peel and clove, with a stick of cinnamon bobbing like it was trying to escape. My living room was tidy because I cleaned when I was anxious. Blankets were folded, pillows fluffed, and everything aligned like I could organize the chaos out of the world if I tried hard enough.

I couldn't.

Vex prowled the back of the couch like a tiny, judgmental panther, his tail flicking, and blue eyes sparkling with the restless energy he got when something didn't make sense. Fenrin, in her ginger cat form, had claimed LuLu's scarf in the armchair and was kneading it with serious intent, as if she planned to make a sweater by midnight.

Holden stood near the window, his six-foot-four-inch frame tense as he half watched the street through the curtains, half pretending he wasn't. He'd taken off his sport coat but kept the holster, posture, and weight of being the person everyone expected to hold the line. His neck looked tense, his jaw clenched, and his storm-gray eyes tracking headlights that passed too slowly.

My heart melted at the sight of him...my rock.

LuLu sat cross-legged on my rug with a legal pad in her lap, her pen tapping against her bottom lip. She'd moved into investigative mode the second we stepped through the door, like she could outwork fear if she gave it nowhere to settle. She swept her long, wavy black hair out of her face and squinted her almond-brown eyes as she studied her notes.

And then there was Calderis.

He didn't knock. He *never* knocked. One moment the kitchen

doorway was empty, and the next he was there, standing six-foot-ten-inches tall and deathly still, as if the shadows had decided to take shape and become a person.

He wore a black leather jacket over a burgundy sweater and black jeans instead of his long ceremonial robes. His silver hair was a pale blond and pulled back into a man bun, his chiseled face clean-shaven. While his clear-glass eyes were pale blue as they swept the room once, taking everything in with the calm precision of someone trained to assess threats.

To Wishville, he was Detective Cal Deris, Holden's buddy from Boston. To me, he looked like my childhood. He looked like Elarion. He looked like the part of my life I couldn't explain without breaking everything.

His gaze landed on my face and held there for a beat too long, his expression unreadable but intent. "You're alive," he said.

"Shocking, I know," I replied, trying for lightness but missing by a mile.

Holden's head turned sharply, nodding once when Calderis appeared. They were civil and knew how to work well together with a level of respect, but they were not friends. LuLu, on the other hand, brightened instantly as they were now an official couple like Holden and me.

LuLu bounced to her feet, ran over, and gave Calderis a big hug. "Hi, babe."

He frowned. "I keep telling you I'm no child."

"Oh, silly." She hugged him tighter. "It's a term of endearment."

He tilted his head, allowing the hug and even semi-hugging her back. His lips tipped up ever so slightly before he went back to all business and stepped farther inside. His boots made no sound on my wood floors. "You said it was urgent."

"It is," LuLu said, resuming her seat. "We have updates."

Vex yawned dramatically from the couch. *Oh good. Group trauma.*

Fenrin flicked one ear, continuing to knead the scarf like she was preparing it for battle.

I moved toward the kitchen and grabbed four mugs, because I was still pretending hot drinks could solve murder, and poured mulled cider with a shot of brandy into each. My hands shook only a little. I set them down on the coffee table, then sat on the couch beside Vex.

Holden took the armchair. LuLu stayed on the floor. Calderis remained standing until I gave him a look that said *sit down or I will throw a pillow at you,* and even then, he only perched on the edge of the second chair like his body refused to fully relax.

"You're tense," Holden said to him.

Calderis's eyes shifted to Holden. "So are you."

Holden didn't deny it.

LuLu cleared her throat, loudly. "Drink up, boys. Clearly you need it. Let's focus before the testosterone turns this into a gladiator match."

"That's beyond testosterone," I muttered.

Vex's tail swished. *It's ego.*

I took a slow breath and updated Calderis to bring him into the loop. "The preliminary results for Violet Snowe's toxicology screening are in."

Calderis didn't blink. "Confirming her death wasn't natural, I presume."

Holden's brows drew together. "It gets worse than that."

"I'm listening," Calderis said calmly.

LuLu slid her notepad closer and spoke quickly, like she could outrun the tension. "Preliminary results indicate a compound that affects the heart, something that mimics a cardiac event."

Calderis's gaze snapped to mine. "Cardiac Glycoside."

I froze.

Holden leaned forward slightly.

LuLu's pen paused midair.

"That's...specific," Holden said.

Calderis's eyes stayed on me. "It presents like heart failure. Collapse. Shallow breathing. A body that looks as if it betrayed itself."

The way he said it made the memory crystal clear. Violet's candle falling into the snow, and her mouth opening like she couldn't get enough air. "How do you know that?" I asked quietly.

Calderis's jaw tightened once. "Because, as you know, Elarion has poisons too."

I hadn't thought about a threat from Elarion.

Holden's gaze snapped to Calderis's. "So now we're talking about—"

"Not yet," I cut in quickly. "We can't be sure of anything. This is just another possibility to explore."

Holden held my gaze, his jaw tight, then he nodded once. "Fine. But we'll need facts to proceed. Bellamy doesn't have anything concrete yet, either."

Calderis didn't look away from me, the worry etched in his features visible.

"Tell him what happened at the meeting," Holden added.

I did. I told him about Doug's announcement. The room turning toward me. The whispered sentence that still felt like a bruise, *Someone was trying to kill Lyra*. I told him what Holden had learned, how the vendors had set aside samples for me, and Violet had been given them when I was delayed by the generator crisis.

Calderis went still in a way I recognized. Controlled anger. The kind that didn't flare; it ignited. "The killer knew," he said softly. "They anticipated your pattern."

"Yes," I said. "Which means the target wasn't random. And Violet..." My voice caught. I forced it to steady. "Violet died because she was in the wrong place at the wrong time."

Vex shifted closer to my thigh, pressing his warm weight against me. *Wrong place and time is hazardous in Wishville.*

Holden's expression softened for a moment. "We still don't

know for sure that you were the target, Lyra. We're going to look into all possibilities until we find out who did it."

LuLu nodded, then looked at me. "Which brings us to motive."

I stared into my mug, watching steam curl upward like a question. "Why would someone want either me or Violet dead?"

No one answered immediately, because no answer was simple.

"Violet had a few enemies, remember?" LuLu said, checking her notes. "Her estranged cousin, Ozzy Snowe, came back demanding part of their Granny's inheritance. Violet's ex-boyfriend, Percy Johnson, who won't take no for an answer. And let's not forget her rival, Wendy Washington, who was heard saying she would do anything to land the lead caroler role."

Holden nodded. "As for you, Lyra, you've got power. Not official political power, but influence. You decide vendor placement. You approve events. You can shut someone down if they break safety rules."

"I don't," I said.

"But you *could*," he corrected. "And some people might resent what you represent. Tradition, the well, WishFest itself."

LuLu tapped her pen. "Any past conflicts? Someone you kicked off a committee? Denied a vendor spot? Public arguments?"

My mind ran through faces, voices, complaints. Betsy's loud fury over rules. Maisie's protective pride. Dot's dramatic opinions, and Tasha's righteousness. Not to mention, Trip Danderly's endless crusades for attention.

"No one who'd jump to murder," I said. "Not from the human side."

Holden's eyes narrowed slightly. "People might surprise you. It's happened before."

I didn't like how true that was.

Calderis's voice cut through, low and even. "You are still thinking in one world."

I looked up.

His pale eyes held mine like a tether. "We now know your mother didn't just vanish. She switched to the rebel side as their leader. She wanted you to join her, but you refused. And now an attempt is made on your life."

The simmer pot on the stove bubbled softly. He knew, just like the Elders did, that the rebels had vacated the mountain cavern. I didn't tell him, or anyone yet, that I went to see her old friends and that I thought she was in *The Badlands*. I needed a clear head before deciding what to do. My chest tightened as Serena's face rose in my mind. My mother standing in the cavern, her eyes fierce and voice steady as she told me the treaty wasn't what I believed.

I set my mug down with careful precision, because my hands were suddenly too unsteady for heat. "The last thing she told me during out standoff was that the Elders lied," I said carefully, studying Calderis. He might not have the best relationship with his father, but he trusted him. "That the treaty is…curated. That there's something in its foundation that isn't true."

Calderis's jaw set. "Your mother betrayed you. She is the rebel leader. My father is the Elder Chief, upholding what we've been fighting to protect for over centuries."

"She's still my mother," I snapped, sharper than I meant to.

His gaze didn't waver. "And she is still capable of manipulation."

"As is your father." I thrust my chin in the air.

LuLu lifted a hand. "Okay, pause. We're not doing 'Team Serena' versus 'Team Vaerion' tonight. We need to look at the reality. Someone used a compound that mimics cardiac failure."

Holden's eyes cut to Calderis. "You said 'Cardiac Glycoside' like you'd seen it before. Is that something humans use, or—"

"Humans have them," Calderis said. "Plants contain them. Foxglove. Oleander. Lily of the Valley."

My stomach sank. Real, ordinary, and plausible. That meant the killer didn't need magic to do this.

But Calderis continued, his voice calm. "Elarion has a refined variant that acts faster, is cleaner, and harder to detect."

Holden's jaw tightened. "That's convenient."

"It is dangerous," Calderis corrected.

Vex's ears angled forward. *I dislike refined danger. It's showy.*

I looked between them, then to LuLu. "If this was Wishville, I get it. But Elarion...why?"

LuLu's pen scratched across her notepad. "Because of Serena's claim." Her gaze locked onto mine. "Because you've been snooping around on your own, asking questions you weren't supposed to ask since Fall WishFest."

I should have known nothing got by LuLu.

Holden's gaze snapped to me. "You've been asking questions on your own?"

I hesitated just long enough.

His eyes hardened. "Lyra."

"I've been careful," I said. "I've been...discreet."

Calderis's expression hardened. "Discreet is not invisible. Discreet is careless."

I swallowed. "At the end of the last case, when Serena told me the treaty was based on a lie and the Elders were corrupt, she said it like she expected me to already be suspicious. Like she knew something I didn't."

LuLu nodded. "So, of course that made you want to dig into it." She shrugged. "It's what I would have done."

"I've been looking into the matter in small ways," I admitted. "Questions in Elarion. Looking at old references. Comparing stories."

Holden looked like he wanted to say ten different things at once, and none of them were polite. "That puts a target on you," he said finally. "Human or not."

"We are in agreement." Calderis's gaze shifted from Holden's to mine and then locked. "If an Elder or another Dweller or even a rebel wanted you silent, they would not strike directly. They would strike through misdirection."

"By using a human festival," LuLu said.

"By using your role," Calderis added. "Festival Chair. Guardian. You stand at the hinge between worlds even if the town doesn't know it."

He was right. I stared at the flicker of light in my window, the reflection of Winter WishFest glow bleeding faintly into the night. "So, what do we do?"

Holden's voice was immediate. "We treat this like a human case, because it might still be just that. We keep the suspect list grounded in who had access from both realms. Who could have slipped something into those set-aside samples."

LuLu nodded. "Then we interview everyone, both Violet's enemies and Lyra's. We map Violet's timeline again. We look for anyone who hovered near the 'Lyra samples' more than once."

Calderis spoke last. "And we look in Elarion quietly, without alerting the Elders."

Holden's gaze cut to him. "We're in agreement again. Will wonders never cease."

"Wonders have nothing to do with this," Calderis said, his tone flat. "Facts do."

LuLu exhaled. "Here's a fact for you. If this is connected to the treaty lie, we need to know why so we can stop it before the next attempt on Lyra's or someone else's life."

"The Covenant Three," I murmured.

Calderis's eyes shined with approval. "Yes."

"And your plus one," LuLu added. "Don't forget that."

"I could never," Calderis said, his gaze softening on her for a brief moment.

LuLu patted his arm. "Holden is the shield in town. Calderis is the blade in Elarion. And I'm the savvy sidekick."

Calderis frowned but said nothing.

Holden blinked. "Did you just assign us fantasy roles?"

LuLu smiled sweetly. "Yes. I mean, think about it. Our *lives* are a living fantasy."

Vex hopped down from the couch and stalked across the coffee table, his tail high. *And I am the commentator. Fenrin is the —*

Fenrin lifted her head from the scarf, her amber eyes narrowing, and swatted his tail with one paw.

Vex hissed. *The menace.*

Fenrin yawned and settled back down as if pleased with herself.

Despite everything, a small, startled laugh escaped me.

Holden's gaze softened briefly when it met mine.

I cleared my throat and forced the moment back into focus. "Okay, here's the plan." I looked at each of them in turn. "Tomorrow, Holden, you start formal interviews with the vendors and anyone who had access to the set-aside area. Not accusatory, more like procedural so you won't raise any red flags. We don't want to scare the culprit away."

Holden nodded once. "Done."

"LuLu," I continued, "you dig into Violet. Quietly. Use your gift. See if any of her enemies had access or connections to the compound poison. Someone must know something."

LuLu's eyes sharpened. "Already on it."

"And Calderis," I said, my voice lowering, "you go to Elarion and look into any possible enemies I might have there and who might have had access to Cardiac Glycoside."

Calderis's gaze held mine, steady as stone. "And what will you do?"

"I'm going to check in with Weylan and Sparks. See if they saw anything in the sky or on the ground."

I inhaled slowly, feeling the truth of it settle. We were no longer dealing with a tragedy.

We were dealing with intent. And somewhere between a human festival and a hidden realm, between a lie buried in an ancient treaty and a woman who died singing under lantern light, someone had decided one of us was a problem that needed to be removed.

I leaned forward, my hands braced on my knees, and let my

resolve harden into something clear. "Whoever the killer is," I said quietly, "made one mistake."

Holden's eyes narrowed. "What's that?"

I looked at the warm glow of my living room, at the boyfriend and friend I trusted completely, at the two cats who were my secret weapons with whiskers, and at the Dweller enforcer who'd crossed worlds to stand by my side.

"They missed," I said. "But rest assured...I won't."

CHAPTER
Seven

BY MORNING, Winter WishFest had recovered like putting makeup over the bruise. Fresh snow had fallen overnight, smoothing the hill path into a clean ribbon of white, and the festival clearing looked almost innocent again. Lanterns still hung in rows, vendor tents sat in neat lines, and someone—probably Belle—had already marched through with a shovel and a sense of moral superiority, scooping up last night's snowflakes as if tidiness could rewrite tragedy.

It couldn't.

I climbed the hill with my clipboard tucked under my arm, my breath making soft ghosts in the cold. Vex rode my shoulder, unusually still, his blue eyes scanning the clearing like the festival itself might blink and reveal teeth.

You're doing it again, he said.

"Walking?" I asked.

Pretending that because the snow is pretty, nothing underneath it is rotten.

I didn't answer because he wasn't wrong, and I didn't have the emotional bandwidth to argue with a cat who technically wasn't a cat.

At the top of the hill, Weylan's hot air balloon hovered above the clearing like an oversized ornament someone had accidentally let go of. The envelope was a deep midnight blue spattered with pale silver stars, and the basket was wicker reinforced with something that looked like brass, swaying gently in the wind. People pointed up, distracted for a moment by the spectacle. The hot air balloon had become part of WishFest recently as if it had always belonged.

Weylan belonged too, in his own impossible way. He stood near the basket with a pair of goggles pushed up into his blond hair, his scarf flung over one shoulder like it had been styled by a dramatic weather god, and his hands tucked into fingerless gloves. He looked like someone who'd wandered out of an antique travel poster and decided to stay.

"Festival Chair!" he called when he spotted me, his voice too loud for the morning's careful mood. "Guardian of Merriment! Keeper of Clipboards! The Hill's Most Determined Marcher!"

I grimaced. "Please don't narrate me."

"It's not narration," he said seriously. "It's ambiance."

Vex's tail snapped against my collar. *He is exhausting.*

"I know," I muttered. "But he's useful."

Weylan's grin widened. "I heard the town held a meeting last night."

News traveled fast in Wishville. I stopped beside the basket, letting my gaze sweep the clearing out of habit. Vendors were setting up with stiff movements, volunteers were adjusting strings of lights, and a few early visitors were clutching cocoa cups like talismans.

"We did," I said carefully. "It was...necessary."

Weylan's expression sobered, the excitement dimming into something more watchful. "Violet Snowe."

My throat went dry at her name. It still felt unreal, like saying it made it true again. "Yes," I said. "Poor woman."

He nodded once, then lowered his voice. "Her poor sister."

The sincerity in it surprised me, landing softly like a feather. "Thank you. I'll pass your condolences on."

Weylan glanced around, then tipped his head toward the far side of the clearing where the generator shed sat half hidden behind a stack of salt bags and extra extension cords. "You didn't come up here for condolences, though."

No, I hadn't.

I followed his gaze and spotted Sparks crouched near the shed, one knee planted in the snow, a toolbox open beside him like a black mouth full of metal. He was the opposite of Weylan in every way. Muscular where Weylan was lanky, quiet where Weylan was theatrical, and grounded where Weylan seemed made of wind.

Sparks wore a worn canvas jacket dusted with snow and grease, his blond hair tucked beneath a knit cap. A smear of engine oil streaked one cheekbone like war paint. He didn't look up as he worked, his hands moving with calm precision over the generator housing.

He belonged here too.

Sparks was the eyes on the ground in the way Weylan was the eyes in the sky. Calderis had let him stay in Wishville—*allowed* was the better word—because Sparks could fix anything. And because sometimes the line between "accident" and "someone made this happen" was an electrical cord.

I'd learned that the hard way.

I headed toward the shed, my boots crunching over snow. Weylan fell into step beside me, his scarf trailing behind like a banner. Vex stayed rigid, his gaze traveling from face to face and movement to movement. Sparks looked up as we approached, his eyes steady and alert. Pale blue flecked with gold sizzles, like he could see a problem before it happened.

"Lyra," he said simply.

"Sparks," I replied. "How's the generator?"

His mouth flattened. "Holding. For now."

"Translation?" I asked.

"It's fine," Weylan offered helpfully. "But it's also not fine."

Sparks shot him a look.

Weylan lifted both hands. "I'm practicing being part of a team."

You're practicing talking, Vex muttered.

Sparks pushed up from his crouch and wiped his hands with a rag. "Turns out, someone tampered with it."

The cold in my veins didn't come from winter. "What do you mean tampered?" I asked. I had thought the first breakdown had been accidental.

He nodded toward the panel. "The wiring wasn't just loose like we first thought. It was pulled. Someone yanked the main line just enough to arc, then shoved it back in so it looked like a vibration did it."

My brain tried to instantly tie it to Violet, or to myself, or to the way Night One had spiraled, but something snagged. If someone wanted me dead, they didn't want me *busy*. They wanted me predictable. They wanted me doing exactly what I always did, showing up to taste the samples set aside for me.

A diversion that kept me away didn't feel like a murder plan. Unless Violet had been the target after all. I stared at the generator, and for the first time since this all started, I let myself hold two truths at once.

Violet had been poisoned.

And this generator tampering might be something different.

Holden's voice cut through my thoughts as he approached from the path, his breath visible in quick puffs. He looked like he'd slept in his clothes, dark circles beneath his stormy eyes and his posture locked tight like his body didn't trust the world anymore.

LuLu trailed behind him, with her phone in her hand and hair tucked into a messy knot like she'd decided sleep was optional and facts were oxygen.

"Hey," Holden said, stopping beside me. His gaze shot to Sparks, then Weylan, and he nodded. "Weylan. Sparks."

Weylan offered an enthusiastic two-finger salute. "Chief Thorn! Still tall! Still grim! Excellent brand consistency."

Holden blinked once. "Thanks."

LuLu leaned in and murmured, "I like him more and more every time I meet him."

Holden muttered, "Of course you do."

Sparks ignored the commentary and looked directly at Holden. "Thanks for coming, Chief. I can show you where it was pulled."

Holden's face tightened. "What have you got?"

"I thought the generator broke down on its own," Sparks said. "We repaired it briefly before the show, but after inspecting it closer, I found it like this." He was smart, quiet, and controlled. Everything Wishville wasn't.

"Show me," Holden said.

Sparks crouched again, pointing to the panel with a gloved finger. "Here. This line feeds the gazebo lights and the mic system. When it arcs, it flickers, trips half the strings, and throws the audio."

LuLu crouched too, her eyes narrowing. "So that's why the choir director said the mic cut out for good a second right before—"

"Before Violet collapsed," I finished.

Holden blew out a breath slowly. "Any idea who could've done it?"

Sparks's gaze shifted briefly across the clearing, landing on the Vendor Row where people were setting out pastries and simmering cider like their hands weren't trembling. "Anyone who walked past. Anyone who knew what they were looking at. Maybe even Finch."

My stomach tightened at Finch's name. I didn't think he'd poisoned anyone, but I didn't know him all that well. Could he be the kind of person who'd pull a wire for reasons that had nothing to do with murder? The generator angle still felt off.

"Or," I said carefully, "someone who wanted something dark for a minute."

Holden's eyes cut to me. "Like what?"

I didn't answer yet.

Weylan leaned down slightly, his voice lowering in a rare moment of seriousness. "Not anyone."

We all looked at him.

He lifted his chin toward the sky. "I was up."

"Up?" Holden repeated.

Weylan nodded once, and for the first time, his usual theatrical glow was gone. "Test flight. I always do one on opening day. Wind check. Burner check. Make sure I'm not going to drift into the treeline and become a winter cautionary tale. Wouldn't want to give myself away by having to use magic to get back on track."

Sparks's fingertips buzzed with electricity. "That's never stopped you from manipulating the winds before."

Weylan ignored him. "I was above the clearing around late afternoon. When the lights first started to stutter."

"What did you see?" I asked.

Weylan's eyes narrowed, his gaze losing focus slightly like he was replaying a memory. "I saw someone near the generator shed."

Holden went very still. "Can you describe them?"

Weylan hesitated, then spoke carefully. "They were bundled. Dark coat. Hood up. Moved like they didn't want to be noticed, but...they didn't move like a tourist either. They moved like someone who knew where they were going."

LuLu's pen appeared in her hand like magic. "Height? Build?"

"Average," Weylan said, frustration traveling across his face. "Not tall like you, Chief. Not short. Just...normal. But they had something in their hand."

"What?" I asked.

Weylan swallowed. "A small tin. Or a case. Hard to tell from above. And they kept opening it and closing it. Like they were checking something inside."

My mind flashed to a vial. A powder. A paste. A compound you could shake into a food sample or wipe onto a cup rim and never look back. But it still didn't solve the part that mattered. If that person was the poisoner, why sabotage the generator and risk making me miss the tasting?

Unless…they didn't. Unless the target *was* Violet. Or they expected me to arrive anyway. Or the person by the shed was there for something else entirely and the timing was just… convenient.

Holden's voice was low. "Did they do anything to the generator?"

Weylan's jaw hardened. "They crouched. They were there less than a minute. Then they stood and looked up."

A shiver crawled over my skin.

"Looked up?" I repeated.

Weylan nodded slowly. "Right at me. At the balloon."

"You sure?" LuLu asked.

"I'm sure," Weylan said, and his voice had lost its whimsy entirely. "It was like…they felt me watching. Like they knew the sky had eyes."

Vex's claws flexed gently against my coat. *That is the kind of awareness I dislike.*

Sparks's gaze slid to Holden. "After that, the generator was pushed back into place. It would've looked like a normal malfunction."

Holden's jaw worked once. "So, someone messes with the wiring. Creates a flicker. A little chaos." He looked at me, and I could tell he was trying to force the story into a single line that made sense.

But I shook my head slightly. "No," I said quietly. "Not necessarily."

LuLu's eyes snapped to me. "What do you mean?"

"I mean," I said, choosing my words carefully, "Violet's poisoning was intentional. But this feels like someone who wanted the lights to go out for a minute. Not to distract me. To cover something."

Holden went still.

Sparks's expression didn't change, but his eyes narrowed like he'd been waiting for someone to say it out loud.

Weylan's voice dropped. "Exactly."

"What could they cover?" Holden asked.

Sparks snapped his toolbox shut with a decisive click. "Depends on what they were doing when the lights flickered. And who wanted to move unseen."

LuLu looked from the shed to the vendor line. "Or what they wanted to move."

The cold moved deeper into my bones. Could this be the work of the rebels? Or maybe something else entirely.

Holden straightened, his shoulders squaring like he was putting on his Chief hat. "You two need to give formal statements."

Weylan winced theatrically. "Paperwork. The true villain."

Holden didn't smile. "Today."

Sparks nodded once. "Fine."

LuLu looked at me, her eyes wide. "This is big."

"It's...a lead," I said, and my voice sounded steadier than I felt. "Maybe not the murder thread. But a thread."

Vex's tail flicked. *Threads make nets.*

I stared out at the festival clearing, at the tents, the lights, and the people trying so hard to be normal. Violet Snowe had collapsed under lantern light while a town held its breath and then told itself it was winter's fault. Winter or poison? Neither pulled wires.

But whoever did might have been counting on everyone looking the other way.

I swallowed hard and lifted my clipboard like it could shield me from the truth. "Okay," I said quietly. "We have a direction now."

Holden's eyes were hard. "We have a person."

Weylan's gaze drifted skyward, his face tightening as if we were standing in that hooded person's shoes. "And that person knows they were watched."

Which meant two things at once. We weren't blind anymore. And someone in Wishville had realized the sky was paying attention.

~

The *Festival Office* smelled like paper, coffee, and anxiety. It was a narrow room tucked behind the old maintenance shed, a space that only came alive during WishFest season. The rest of the time it sat quiet and forgotten, housing clipboards, folding tables, and a battered metal filing cabinet that predated indoor plumbing.

During festivals, it became the nerve center. The *Festival Office* was the place where official deposits were logged, incident reports filed, and everyone pretended numbers always added up. Today, the pretending was thinner.

I stood near the scarred wooden desk with my clipboard pressed to my chest, watching Doug Delaney rub his temples like he could physically knead the problem smaller. Holden leaned against the wall near the door, his arms crossed, posture deceptively casual as if he was clocking every movement, every tone shift. LuLu hovered near the filing cabinet, flipping through deposit envelopes with a focus that bordered on predatory.

Betsy Plum sat stiff-backed in a folding chair, her arms crossed, and her jaw tight. Maisie Flint stood beside her, one hand braced on the table, her knuckles white. Willa Hartman lingered near the doorway, her coat still on and eyes darting between faces like she was deciding whether staying or leaving was the safer option.

No one wanted to be here.

"I counted twice," Betsy said, breaking the silence. Her voice was sharp but controlled, like a blade she was gripping too hard. "Three times, actually. I don't miscount."

Doug sighed. "No one's accusing you of that, Betsy."

"Well, someone's short," she snapped. "And it's not *my* math."

Maisie swallowed. "I'm missing seventy-eight dollars from my booth," she said quietly. "That's not a rounding error. That's someone deciding seventy-eight dollars won't be noticed."

Willa nodded stiffly. "Mine's less. Twenty. But it's still wrong. I check my cash multiple times throughout each day, so I know when my box comes up short."

My stomach turned over, not in panic, but in recognition. Patterns. "How many vendors have shortages?" I asked.

Doug hesitated.

Holden pushed off the wall. "Doug."

Doug exhaled. "Four so far. Out of twelve. And that's only the ones who've checked already."

LuLu looked up with a puckered brow. "And the others?"

"Some haven't reconciled yet," Doug admitted. "Some assume it'll shake out."

It wouldn't.

LuLu slid a ledger across the desk toward me. "Look at the incident notes."

I leaned in. The ledger had a neat handwritten explanation on the front. *Crowd surge near stage during singing. Possible miscount due to distraction.*

I frowned. "This one too?"

LuLu nodded and pointed to another entry. Same handwriting. Same phrasing.

Another. Same again.

My chest tightened. "Doug," I said carefully. "Who writes these notes?"

Doug shifted uncomfortably. "The finance volunteers rotate each season. Whoever's on intake."

Each WishFest, the local vendors who have a booth in the festival have to give a percentage of their profits to the town.

"Which is?" Holden asked.

Doug named two people then hesitated. "But mostly... Edward. He's been helping me coordinate deposits this season."

LuLu's eyes flicked up. "Edward Langley?"

Doug nodded. "He offered. Said he had experience with nonprofits. Grant accounting."

I didn't like the way LuLu's pen paused mid-scratch. "Has Edward been present during all the reported shortages?" she asked.

Doug frowned. "I—I'd have to check."

Holden stepped forward. "We'll check."

Betsy leaned forward suddenly. "Are you saying someone stole from us?"

"No," Doug said quickly. Too quickly. "I'm saying there may have been confusion. A procedural issue."

"Someone stole from us," Betsy repeated, louder now. "During a festival where a woman died."

The room went still.

That was the thing Wishville hated most...overlap. One bad thing was survivable. Two at once meant the story couldn't be kept neat.

I took a slow breath. "This doesn't mean any of you did anything wrong," I said, meeting each vendor's eyes. "And it doesn't mean these things are connected."

Holden's gaze slid to me briefly. He knew what I was doing. Separating leads before they tangled beyond repair.

"But," I continued, "it does mean someone exploited the chaos."

LuLu tapped the ledger. "And they were comfortable enough to do it more than once."

Willa's voice trembled. "During the singing?"

"During distractions," Holden said. "Lights. Sound. Crowd movement."

My mind jumped back to the generator shed. The pulled wire. The flicker that had sent me sprinting away from the vendor row and later during the choir's song.

"That flicker," I said quietly. "It wasn't random."

Doug looked at me sharply. "Lyra—"

"It wasn't about the lights," I continued. "It was about pulling attention."

LuLu nodded. "Classic misdirection."

Betsy's face went pale. "You mean while everyone was looking at the stage…"

"Someone was moving through the booths," Holden finished.

The words settled heavy and cold.

Maisie wrapped her arms around herself. "I remember someone bumping my table. I thought it was just the crowd."

Willa swallowed. "There was a person asking about donations. With a tin. Said it was for the winter fund."

My pulse spiked. "What did the tin look like?" I asked.

Willa frowned, thinking. "Small. Metal. Blue, I think. Or gray. Hard to tell. It had a latch."

LuLu's eyes snapped to mine. The tin. The one Weylan had seen from the sky.

Doug looked stricken. "We don't have a winter fund."

"No," I said softly. "But someone wanted it to look like we did."

Holden straightened. "Okay. New protocol. No one leaves this room until we document exactly what you saw. Times. Faces. Conversations."

Doug looked overwhelmed. "Holden—"

"This isn't public," Holden said firmly. "This is theft, and we're stopping it."

The word *theft* seemed to ground the room in a way *murder* hadn't. Theft was something Wishville understood. Theft had rules. Theft had perpetrators who weren't mythic or unknowable. But I knew better. Because the theft explained the flicker. And the flicker explained my absence.

Which meant…this wasn't the killer's plan.

I stepped back slightly, the realization clicking into place with brutal clarity. If I was the target, the killer would have wanted me at the vendor row. They would have planned for me to eat. They wouldn't have counted on chaos. Someone else had created it.

Two crimes.

One moment.

LuLu met my gaze, and her eyes sharpened.

Holden followed my expression. "Lyra?"

"This wasn't connected," I said quietly. "Not intentionally."

Doug looked confused. "What wasn't?"

"The generator issue," I said. "The theft. They weren't meant to pull me away. They were meant to pull eyes."

"And the poison?" Holden asked, already knowing.

"That was separate," I said. "One scenario is the person who poisoned the samples expected me to show up since the samples were meant for me to taste as Festival Chair...but I don't know why someone would want me dead."

Silence fell again, this time heavier and more dangerous.

LuLu exhaled slowly. "And the other scenario is the timing is coincidental. The person was following Violet and she was the target all along. Again, we don't know why."

My throat tightened. "We'll keep looking into both."

Betsy covered her mouth.

Maisie whispered, "Oh God."

Holden's jaw set hard. "Okay," he said, his voice steady but lethal. "Then we treat this as two investigations."

Doug blinked. "Two?"

"Yes," Holden said. "One theft operation under festival cover. And one homicide."

My stomach twisted, but my resolve deepened. "And they just collided."

Laughter drifted faintly from the hill. Music. Lantern light. Wishville insisting on joy because the alternative was unbearable. I straightened my clipboard against my chest. Somewhere between stolen cash and a poisoned sample, someone had gambled on chaos.

But they'd lost control of the board, and now we were watching every move.

Eight

THE NEXT MORNING, Winter WishFest went on as if nothing was wrong. Lanterns swayed gently overhead, their amber light warming the snow into something almost magical. Music drifted from the gazebo again, lighter today and instrumental only, while the scent of cinnamon and sugar wafted through the air as if the festival itself were determined to overwrite memory.

I let it.

Because watching people reclaim joy was part of my job.

And watching for cracks beneath it was the rest.

Holden was patrolling the perimeter, as I moved through the center of the clearing slowly with my clipboard tucked against my side, and my eyes scanning hands instead of faces. Who lingered too long. Who doubled back without reason. Who moved *against* the flow instead of with it.

Vex rode my shoulder like a living radar dish, his tail flicking once every time something felt off.

You are vibrating, he informed me.

"I am observing," I said quietly.

You are vibrating observationally.

I ignored him and paused near Maisie's cider stall, pretending to check lantern spacing while my attention tracked the crowd. A cluster of tourists laughed near the maple taffy station. A volunteer refilled paper cups. Somewhere, a bell chimed cheerfully, unaware of how inappropriate it felt.

That was when it happened.

Someone bumped into me harder than necessary. "Sorry!" a voice said quickly, already moving past.

Too fast.

My clipboard slipped from my grip. Vex hissed under his breath. I twisted just in time to see a dark-coated figure vanish between two stalls, their hood pulled low despite the mild snowfall.

At the same moment, Maisie gasped. "My box," she said. "That was heavier a second ago."

I was already moving.

"Holden," I said into my phone, keeping my voice steady. "We have a live one."

Across the clearing, I saw him straighten instantly, his gaze snapping to mine. He followed my line of sight, his hand lifting to his radio, but whoever it was didn't run.

They melted into the crowd.

The crowd closed in like water, laughter and movement swallowing the gap where the figure had been. No chase or dramatic reveal. Just absence.

Vex's claws flexed against my coat. *That was practiced.*

My stomach clenched. This wasn't the poisoner. This was something else.

The Wellies found me before I could find them.

"Lyra!" Tilly announced, emerging from the crowd with Belle and Dot in tow like a tribunal on sensible shoes. "We have observed a suspicious energy."

"Of course you have," I said.

Dot pushed her glasses up, her eyes enormous. "Someone just brushed past Belle and apologized *twice.*"

"That's not illegal," I said.

"It is emotional dishonesty," Dot replied.

Belle sniffed. "And they were walking the wrong way. Sent my poor pigeons scattering everywhere."

I stilled. "Wrong how?"

"Against the music," Belle said. "People move with rhythm, even unconsciously. They were cutting through it."

Tilly leaned in conspiratorially. "Also, they smelled like metal."

Vex purred faintly. *I like her.*

I leaned in. "Did any of you see their hands?"

Dot nodded immediately. "Yes. Gloved. But holding something boxy. Like a tin. Or a—"

"Cash box," I finished.

All three Wellies went very still.

Belle's voice dropped. "Oh."

"Stay together," I said firmly. "And if you see anyone circling stalls without buying anything, you come find me or Holden. Immediately."

Tilly saluted. Dot squared her shoulders. Belle looked offended someone else had issued instructions before she could.

As they marched off, Vex murmured, *They are alarmingly effective when motivated by righteousness.*

Weylan descended five minutes later. Not the balloon...just Weylan, his boots crunching softly as he joined me near the edge of the clearing. I glanced around to make sure no one saw him manipulating the wind. He was taking a chance by using his magic in pubic. His usual theatrical glow was dimmed and eyes icy as frost.

"Sorry, boss," he said. "I sometimes forget myself when I'm excited."

"Just be careful," I replied. "Did you see anything?"

He nodded. "From above. Same person as before. Same drift pattern. They avoid lantern light and stay close to cash flow."

"That confirms it," I said.

Sparks appeared from the opposite direction, wiping his hands on a rag. "Second stall. Different vendor. Same light touch."

Holden joined us, his jaw tight. "Two theft attempts. Same MO. Nothing to do with poison, it seems."

"No," I agreed. "This is a different predator, just like we suspected. They wanted me here. Visible. Distracted. Doing Festival Chair things."

Holden's eyes darkened. "And while you were, someone else was stealing."

Wishville was old-fashioned. Festival vendors used old-school cash boxes for their sales instead of registers like in their permanent business establishments. They weren't locked during festival hours for the ease of taking payment and making change, which left them vulnerable to theft. This wasn't coincidence. This was cover. I forced myself to breathe and approached Finch and Elliot near the hot cider line, fixing the heater.

"Hey," I said lightly. "Quick question. Did you notice anyone hovering near the cash boxes tonight?"

Finch rubbed his jaw. "Now that you mention it, there was a guy? Or maybe a woman? I asked if I could help them. They said they were checking totals for the day, but said they would come back later when the vendors weren't so busy."

My chest tightened. "Did they have any credentials?"

"I didn't ask," he said slowly. "But they sounded confident."

Confidence. The easiest costume.

"Thank you," I said. "Keep your eyes peeled and let me know if you guys see anything more."

He nodded once. "Will do, right, Elliot?"

Elliot was probably twenty. I'd watched him grow up. He kept to himself and was quiet but had always been a hard worker. "Yes, ma'am," he said, looking away when his eyes met mine.

"How's your mother, Elliot?"

"Not too well." He shrugged. It was just the two of them.

"I can set up a food train if that would help."

He straightened his back. "We don't take charity, Ms. Wells."

"Well, then at least let me send over some soup. I made far too much, and I would hate to see it go to waste."

He nodded once. "I guess that would be okay. Thank you, ma'am."

I moved on and Vex looked up at me. I could swear he raised an eyebrow he didn't have. *You don't cook.*

"Trust me, I'm not even going to try. I'll have the Wellies make a batch. They live for a crisis that involves broth."

As we walked, the truth settled heavily in my bones. Someone had used my festival. Someone had used chaos. And someone else, someone quieter and more deliberate, had possibly tried to kill me. I came to a stop and stared out over the clearing, the lanterns glowing like nothing beneath them had changed.

I felt exposed.

For the first time since Violet died, fear slipped past my resolve and took root, fear of what my visibility made possible. Being Guardian meant standing in the open. Being Festival Chair meant smiling while predators watched. I hated that they knew my habits. I hated that Violet had paid the price. And I hated most of all that part of me wanted to retreat.

But retreat wasn't an option.

I sighed and made my way back to the group. "Okay," I said quietly. "Here's what we're doing."

Holden met my gaze. "You sure you want to be involved?"

"No," I said honestly. "But it's necessary."

"We keep the festival running," I continued. "Longer hours tomorrow. Extra events. We *invite* the thief to keep stealing."

Sparks nodded immediately. "I can tag boxes. Quietly."

Weylan smiled without humor. "I'll stay airborne."

And I, Vex said smugly, *will judge everyone.*

Holden exhaled. "And the poisoner?"

"That's a different hunt," I said. "One we don't announce."

As the music swelled again and laughter cautiously returned, I lifted my clipboard and stepped back into the glow. The thief thought chaos was cover. The poisoner thought fear would stop me. They were both wrong. The festival would be our bait.

And this time, I would be watching.

The Wishbone Café was packed in that peculiar Winter WishFest way. Half the room was made up of locals who "just needed something warm," and the other half made up of visitors who treated every mug of cocoa like it came with a souvenir certificate.

Snow clung to boots near the entryway. Scarves draped over chair backs like colorful surrender flags. Someone's kid was licking powdered sugar off a scone with the focus of a scientist. And under all of it, woven through the cinnamon and clove and forced cheer, was something new in Wishville's air.

Suspicion.

I slid into the back booth with LuLu and tried not to look like the Festival Chair who might've been the intended target of a poison assassination. Holden arrived a moment later, tall enough that he had to duck instinctively under the hanging wreath someone had insisted on attaching to the booth divider. He didn't take off his coat. He didn't sit like he was here to eat.

He sat like he was here for a case.

Vex hopped onto the seat beside me, his tail neatly tucked around his paws and blue eyes scanning the café the way Holden scanned a crime scene.

Calderis arrived last. One moment, the space at the end of the booth aisle was empty. The next, Detective Cal Deris from Boston was standing there, tall and silent, his black coat dusted with snow that hadn't been there two seconds earlier. His silver hair, now blond, was pulled back, his expression carved into its usual careful neutrality. But his clear-glass eyes, now pale blue, found mine immediately, checking in.

Something tight in my chest eased by a fraction. Holden's jaw clenched like it always did when Calderis appeared like a shadow with a badge. He didn't say anything, but the tension of this case settled over the table like an extra place setting.

LuLu saved us all. "Okay," she said briskly, sliding her phone onto the table like she was slamming down a legal exhibit. "We are doing this like adults. No posturing or snarling or *'my world is more dangerous than your world'* nonsense."

Holden blinked once. "I don't snarl."

LuLu looked at him and arched a sleek black brow. "You *radiate* snarl."

Calderis didn't react, but I saw the faintest shift of his gaze toward LuLu that could've been amusement if he'd been a person who knew how to have it.

I blew out a slow breath. "Thank you, LuLu."

"You're welcome," she said. "Now for the updates. We start with Violet, because that's the reason this whole town feels like it's walking on broken glass. I retraced Violet's life like I was writing her obituary and prosecuting her enemies at the same time."

"That's...comforting," I said weakly.

"It should be," she replied. "Because her suspect pool is not imaginary. We were right about a few of these people."

Holden's gaze sharpened. "Go."

LuLu ticked off names on her fingers. "Percy Johnson," she said first. "Ex-boyfriend. Possessive. Boundary issues. He has a history of showing up uninvited and making scenes when he doesn't get his way. Nasty past."

Vex's tail swished once. *A man who thinks 'no' is a suggestion.*

LuLu nodded as if she'd heard him. "Percy was seen in the clearing before the singing. He handed Violet the cocoa sample from the vendor, insisting she take it."

Holden's eyes narrowed. "Who saw that?"

"Willa," LuLu said. "And she swears Violet didn't look happy about it. More like she was tolerating him because she didn't want a public confrontation."

My skin prickled. A cocoa cup was a simple thing, yet suddenly it felt like a weapon.

LuLu continued. "Second: Wendy Washington."

I grimaced. "The rival."

"The rival with a grudge," LuLu corrected. "She's been furious since Violet landed the lead caroler role again. Dot overheard Wendy say Violet was 'hogging the spotlight' and that she'd 'get what was coming.'"

Holden leaned back a fraction, his eyes hard. "Furious enough to murder her?"

"Maybe." LuLu shrugged. "Third: Ozzy Snowe."

My stomach turned over. "Violet's estranged cousin."

LuLu said, "Dana confirmed the inheritance situation. Grandmother left everything to Violet and Dana. Ozzy was cut out. He came to town two nights ago. Checked into the *Mountain Pine Inn* under his own name."

Holden's voice went low. "He wanted to be seen."

"Exactly," LuLu said. "And Lyra saw him confronting Dana by the gazebo."

All eyes turned to me.

"He was aggressive," I said quietly. "Not physically, but he wanted to provoke her. He was furious. And he said Violet being gone 'changes things.' He only left when he spotted two large, scary-looking men. The kicker is, the men followed him as if they knew him."

LuLu tapped her phone. "So, Violet has three human suspects with clear motives: obsession, resentment, and money mixed with desperation."

Holden nodded once. "Good work, Morales."

"Thanks, Thorn." She winked.

Calderis frowned.

"Now the vendors." Holden pulled out a small notebook and flipped it open. "First, everyone is panicked. Makes me wonder if they are lying to themselves about how much they noticed."

"Welcome to Wishville," LuLu muttered. "Where people live in a fantasy because they can't face reality."

"Facts." Holden snorted. "So, Violet made the rounds. She sampled. She talked. She was seen at nearly every booth because she told Thomas Whitaker she purposely didn't eat before Wish-Fest because she wanted to taste everything."

"So, basically she could have ingested the compound anywhere in the festival," I said.

"That's the working assumption, but here's the other piece." Holden looked at me, then at LuLu, then at Calderis. "More vendors have come forward to report even more cash shortages."

LuLu's eyes narrowed. "Then, theft is still in play."

"It is," Holden confirmed. "And multiple witnesses confirmed a hooded person moving against the crowd flow, approaching booths during distractions."

My pulse ticked faster. "The figure with the tin."

Holden nodded.

LuLu leaned back, her eyes sharp. "Two predators. Same hunting ground. Just like we thought."

Calderis's pale eyes held mine. "I went to Elarion."

LuLu angled her body toward him, suddenly all focus. "And?"

"There has been no official notice of Dweller movement to the surface," Calderis said. "No sanctioned crossings. No Elder decree."

"Sanctioned," Holden repeated, his tone flat. "Meaning there could be unsanctioned movement."

Calderis didn't deny it. "Yes."

"And?" I pressed, because the most important part was still hanging there. "Did you find anyone who would want to harm me?"

Calderis went still in that controlled way I recognized, like he was angry but trying to control himself. "There are whispers about your mother. About the rebels. About the treaty."

My chest tightened so sharply it hurt. "Whispers from where?"

"The outer districts," Calderis said. "The places the Elders don't control as tightly. Some believe the Guardian is…a hinge. That if you fall, the treaty weakens. And if the treaty weakens, the Veiled Vault's binding could be weakened. We can't risk the Entity escaping again."

LuLu's pen stilled midair.

Holden's eyes narrowed. "You're saying someone might want Lyra dead to destabilize the treaty?"

"I'm saying it is a possible motive," Calderis replied. "Not proven."

My hands went cold around my mug.

Vex's mind-voice slid into mine, quieter than usual. *Predators choose targets that create chaos.*

"Okay," LuLu said, her voice brisk again like she'd snapped us back on track. "So, we have three lanes."

Holden blinked. "Three?"

"Yes," LuLu said, counting on her fingers. "One: Violet's personal suspects—Percy, Wendy, Ozzy. Two: festival access suspects—anyone who could tamper with food or drinks and knew Lyra's pattern. Three: Elarion-related suspects—any Dweller with knowledge of refined compounds or a motive tied to the treaty."

Holden exhaled through his nose. "That's not three lanes. That's a highway."

I stared out the café window at the hill leading up to the festival clearing. Even from here, I could see the glow of lanterns through the trees. The town was trying so hard to keep celebrating. To keep tradition intact. And I was sitting in a booth mapping out who might've decided my death would be useful.

I shook my spinning head to clear it. "What do we do first?"

Holden answered immediately. "We lock down your routine. You don't walk alone." His expression softened, but his voice stayed firm. "We make sure you don't become an easy target."

LuLu leaned forward, her eyes fierce. "And I'm going to talk to Dana again. About Violet's last conversations. Who she was *most* worried about. What she didn't say out loud. Maybe I can even get a reading off her."

Calderis's gaze stayed on me. "And I will return to listen in Elarion once more. Quietly. For any mention of crossings or compounds or murder plots."

"And the thefts?" I asked.

Holden's jaw tightened. "We use them."

LuLu's eyebrows lifted. "We use them?"

Holden nodded. "We put our bait plan into motion and catch the thief without announcing it. Then we see if the thief is connected to the poison."

It was a cold, practical plan. It was also the first plan that felt like we were moving forward instead of drowning.

LuLu covered my hand with hers, warm and steady. "You're not alone in this, Lyra."

I nodded, unable to speak for a moment. Holden's boot moved beneath the table until it connected with mine, close enough to anchor me without making a scene. Calderis didn't touch me, but his gaze held mine with the same message anyway.

You are not unguarded.

Winter WishFest continued to glitter like a lie people needed to survive. Inside *The Wishbone Café*, we finally admitted the truth. Someone had turned the festival into a hunting ground.

But now…so had we.

CHAPTER
Nine

THE NEXT MORNING, I stood at the bottom of my front steps with my coat half-zipped, listening to the distant hum of early music and the faintest drift of laughter. Holden had already been at work for hours. He'd left before dawn with that tight, controlled focus that meant he'd turned his fear into a plan. Bait boxes. Marked bills. Volunteers placed strategically like harmless little angels who just happened to have excellent peripheral vision.

LuLu had gone a different direction. She'd set out with her phone, her notebook, and that particular expression she got when she was about to charm information out of people who didn't realize they were being interviewed.

Violet's enemies.

Violet's orbit.

Violet's last conversations.

My job today was the one that made my stomach feel like it was packed with ice. Elarion.

I didn't want to leave the surface while Winter WishFest was still running, but I had to look harder in both worlds. If there was even a chance the poison had come from beneath the well, then I had to find proof.

I couldn't ask the Elders. Not while Serena's words still burned behind my ribs, *The Elders are corrupt. The treaty protects power, not balance. We're bigger than the Rebel Five. We're the Rebel Revolution. These Dwellers were erased. Silenced. Buried beneath rules written by those who never bled for them. And they're not the only ones. This affects both realms.*

The rebels' shadow stretched longer than anyone wanted to admit. So, I did what I always did when I couldn't trust the official channels.

I went sideways.

Calderis met me at the treeline behind my house, where the snow went untouched and the air smelled like pine and secrecy. He wore dark winter clothes that made him look human if you didn't look too long, with his black coat, gloves, and the kind of boots people wore to look practical. His pale hair was tucked beneath a knit cap, but we wouldn't need to worry about what we looked like because no one would see us. He'd brought invisibility cloaks that the Weaver Sisters had made for him at *The Starlit Loom.*

He glanced at me. "You are certain you want to do this now?"

"I'm certain I don't want the next person who eats a 'sample' to die," I said. My breath came out like white clouds. "And I'm certain that if the refined Cardiac Glycoside compound was made, someone in Elarion knows who asked for it."

His jaw tightened. "Then we go to the source now."

"The Elixiria Gardens," I said.

He nodded once with no hesitation or argument, just that quiet, lethal agreement that always reminded me he'd been trained to move toward danger, not away from it. We donned our invisibility cloaks and made our way up the hill to the Festival Clearing, through a crowd of people who had no idea we were there. No one was at the well making wishes at the moment, so we made our move.

At the well's edge, I said the ancient incantation and the portal opened like it always did, quietly and impossibly, as if the well water exhaled and reality stepped aside. Cold air became something else on the other side: mineral-rich, faintly sweet, and scented with glowing flora and distant waterfalls.

My boots hit moss, and then we stepped onto crystal-laced stones, humming softly underfoot like a heartbeat you could feel through your soles. Elarion unfurled around us in luminous layers. Floating lumina orbs hovered in gentle clusters, adjusting their brightness as we moved, as if they could sense the tension in my body and decided I needed more light. Glowing ivy draped across archways, petals releasing more of their fragrance that should have calmed me.

It didn't.

The star river ran nearby, a ribbon of constellations unspooling beneath bridges that sang when crossed. Far above, a flock of glasswing butterflies drifted, translucent creatures that looked like leaves and sounded like bells. It was beautiful. It was my home. Yet right now, it felt different.

Dangerous.

Calderis angled his body slightly closer to mine as we walked, a subtle shield that told me he was watching every shadow and every passerby. Dwellers moved through the paths with their graceful, otherworldly elegance. Tall and slender, with luminous eyes like gemstones. Their hair glimmered in shades of silver, pale lavender, and light blue, flowing like underwater currents even in still air. Their garments shifted with ambient magic, catching light and intention in equal measure.

And somewhere among them, there were whispers.

Not ones spoken loudly. Or even the kind you could catch by eavesdropping. They were the kind that lived in the angle of a gaze, the half-second pause when someone recognized me as the Guardian, the hinge...

The problem.

We didn't take the main starlit path. Calderis led me along a narrower route that wound behind cliff-built dwellings and floating platforms. The air warmed and cooled in subtle shifts, as if the cavern itself regulated temperature by mood. We passed a stall where a Dweller traded a vial of shimmering liquid for a woven band of protective thread. Goods weren't exchanged for money. They were traded for value measured in skill and consequence.

The Elixiria Gardens rose ahead like a living cathedral. Terraced levels bloomed with plants that glowed from within. Fruits pulsing like lanterns, herbs veined with light, and blossoms opening and closing in time with the lumina orbs drifting overhead. Water wove through the gardens in whispering streams, chiming softly as it flowed over crystal beds. The air smelled intoxicating with a scent that encouraged forgetting why you came.

I tightened my grip on my coat sleeves.

At the entrance, braided living vines parted as we approached, their petals trembling and releasing a faintly clarifying fragrance. A Dweller stepped out from between two luminous fruit trees. He was tall, even for a Dweller, his skin holding a pale lavender sheen that caught the garden's glow like moonlight on frost. Subtle markings traced his wrists and collarbones, glowing faintly as if inked by bioluminescence rather than pigment. His pale hair was pulled back at the nape of his neck, and his eyes were clear, observant, and uncomfortably intelligent.

His gaze traveled from Calderis to me with immediate recognition. "Chief Enforcer Calderis," he said, his voice as smooth as water over stone. "And Guardian Lyra Wells."

Calderis inclined his head. "Eryndel."

So this was him. Senior alchemist of *the Elixiria Gardens*. Ethical to a fault, if rumor was to be believed. I watched him closely, looking for signs. Because if he was uneasy, we all should be.

"We need to speak privately," Calderis said.

Eryndel's expression tightened almost imperceptibly. "That is not how the Gardens operate."

"Consider it a courtesy request," Calderis replied.

I stepped forward before Calderis could push. "We aren't here to accuse anyone," I said gently. "We're here because a human woman died on the surface. And the symptoms match something I was told exists down here."

Eryndel studied me for a long beat. Then something shifted, subtle but real. "Surface matters are not the Gardens' concern."

"They become your concern when they threaten the treaty," I said evenly. "And when there are whispers that harming the Guardian could weaken it."

Eryndel's gaze narrowed. He breathed out once, slow and controlled. "Come." He led us along a winding path deeper into the Gardens, past glowing herb beds and hanging vials of liquid light. The farther we went, the quieter it became, until the sounds of Elarion beyond the gardens faded to nothing.

We stopped at a sheltered alcove where a table had been grown from living wood and crystal, its surface etched with botanical sigils. Eryndel folded his hands. "Speak," he said.

Calderis didn't waste time. "Cardiac Glycosides. The refined variant."

Eryndel went very still. "It is not commonly requested," he said carefully.

"But it has been recently," Calderis pressed.

Silence stretched.

Then Eryndel spoke, his voice lower. "There was an inquiry."

My stomach dropped. "From whom?"

Eryndel's gaze slid aside, toward a cluster of luminous herbs swaying faintly. "Not anything sanctioned."

"A rebel," Calderis said flatly.

Eryndel didn't confirm it. He didn't deny it either. "They asked for something that could stop a heart without violence. Something that would pass for nature. They spoke of hinges. Of weakening foundations."

My breath caught. "They meant me."

Calderis's voice turned razor-sharp. "Did you provide it?"

"No," Eryndel said immediately. "The Gardens do not craft death for ideology."

"But someone does," I said. "If not you, then who?"

Eryndel hesitated, conflict written into every careful line of his posture. Then he sighed. "There are brewers beyond the Gardens. Those who believe the Elders hoard knowledge and call it protection. They trade in compounds the way humans trade in stolen coin."

A chill slid down my spine.

"Where?" Calderis demanded.

"The lower terraces," Eryndel said quietly. "Past the lumina groves. Where the ivy glows too bright and the air smells like sweet metal. A place called *Blackroot Hollow*. They call themselves *Veinwright Brews*. They believe the treaty is a cage."

A cage. A hinge. A Guardian in the way.

"If someone wanted to bring the compound to the surface," I asked, "could they?"

Eryndel met my eyes with grave ones. "There are unsanctioned crossings. Old fissures. Smuggler paths. If someone was willing to risk widening the breach…yes."

The weight of it pressed into my lungs. "Thank you," I said, even though the words tasted bitter.

"Be careful, Lyra Wells," Eryndel replied softly. "You stand where pressure gathers."

We left the Gardens with the glow still humming behind us, and Elarion unfolding serenely around a truth that was anything but. On the surface, Holden was laying traps for thieves. Below it, I'd just confirmed someone believed my death would be useful. And for the first time since Violet Snowe collapsed beneath lantern light, I understood the full shape of the danger. This wasn't about grief.

It was about leverage.

∽

The Wishbone Café was loud in the way only lunchtime during Winter WishFest could be. Chairs were scraping, mugs were clinking, and laughter was layered over low conversation like someone had turned the volume knob just a little too far to the right.

I slid into the booth by the front window and set my scarf beside me, letting the warmth soak into my hands. Outside, the hill toward the festival clearing glittered with lantern light even in daylight, stubbornly cheerful, like the town had collectively decided joy was an act of defiance.

Vex hopped onto the seat next to me, his tail curling neatly around his paws, and his eyes alert. *This is where humans refuel and gossip,* he observed. *A dangerous combination.*

"Tell me about it," I murmured.

LuLu arrived exactly thirty seconds later, her cheeks flushed from the cold and phone already in her hand like it had grown there. She slid into the booth across from me, shrugged out of her coat, and leaned in before I could even say hello.

"Okay," she said. "You're going to want coffee for this."

"I already do," I replied.

Jenna appeared as if summoned, dropping two mugs on the table without asking. "On the house," she said quietly. "Rough week."

"Thank you," LuLu said sincerely.

Jenna gave us a look that said *I'm pretending I don't know you're discussing murder,* and moved on.

LuLu wrapped her hands around her mug, took one bracing sip, then sighed. "I started with Ozzy."

My stomach soured immediately. "That was fast."

"I have good sources, and he's sloppy," LuLu said flatly. "Men with entitlement issues usually are."

I leaned back slightly, preparing myself. "What did you find?"

LuLu pulled up a note on her phone. "Ozzy Snowe is drowning. Metaphorically. Not literally."

"Gambling?" I guessed.

"Gambling," she confirmed. "Online sports betting, underground poker rooms, and at least one very sketchy backer who does not strike me as the forgiving type. Probably the one who sent the two giant goons you saw following him."

Vex's ears flicked forward. *Debt makes people inventive.*

LuLu nodded as if she'd heard him. "He's behind by six figures. Not all to one place, either. Which means he's juggling threats."

My throat went dry. "I wonder if Violet knew?"

"Lucky for us, I have sources everywhere. According to Violet's phone records, it appears she did know," LuLu said. "And here's the part that made my skin crawl." She scrolled, then read aloud softly. "'If you don't help me, I'll ruin you. You owe me after everything Granny did for you.'"

I stared at her. "He threatened her?"

"Repeatedly," LuLu said. "Dana confirmed Violet told her Ozzy was 'panicking' and 'not thinking clearly.' Violet refused to give him money."

"Because she knew it wouldn't stop," I said.

"Exactly," LuLu replied. "And Ozzy escalated. He showed up in Wishville earlier than he told Dana. He wanted to confront Violet in person."

My pulse kicked harder. "At the festival."

"Yes," LuLu said. "And here's the kicker. Ozzy didn't just want money. He wanted leverage. He asked Violet to co-sign something."

I sucked in a breath. "What?"

"A loan," LuLu said. "Or at least, that's what he called it. The paperwork was vague enough to be dangerous. Violet said yes, thinking he would go away after that."

"But he didn't." I shook my head slowly. "So, Ozzy had motive, opportunity, and desperation."

"And a temper," LuLu added. "Multiple people told me he was shouting in his hotel room the night before WishFest started. The front desk clerk remembered because he knocked over a lamp."

That image lodged itself in my mind. Ozzy pacing. Raging. Spiraling. "And after Violet died?" I asked quietly.

LuLu's eyes narrowed. "He immediately came after Dana. She said he told her the loan sharks would come after her now, because Violet was the co-signer and now Dana was by default. Except he didn't count on Dana being smarter than that. She's the older sister, and one tough cookie who doesn't cower from his threats."

I nodded. "I witnessed that."

LuLu's mouth tightened. "Which tells me something important. Ozzy expected Violet to still be alive."

I stilled. "You think he didn't plan to kill her."

"I think," LuLu said carefully, "that Ozzy wanted to scare her. Coerce her. Pressure her. But if she died, his problems didn't magically go away. They got worse."

Vex tilted his head. *A man who profits from fear does not profit from a corpse.*

"Ozzy benefits from Violet being alive and terrified," LuLu continued. "Dead Violet gets him nothing but suspicion. He's harassing Dana more than ever now."

I nodded slowly. "Which puts him in the suspect pile for a couple things, but not at the top of Violet's murder."

"Correct," LuLu said. "Now, Percy."

My jaw tightened. "Let me guess. It's worse than I think."

"Oh, much worse." LuLu scrolled again. "Violet's phone records show Percy Johnson didn't just send her a few drunk texts. He sent her dozens."

I felt my stomach twist. "Stalker-level?"

"Absolutely," LuLu said. "Creepy. Possessive. 'You owe me closure.' 'You can't ignore me forever.' 'I know where you'll be.' That sort of thing."

My skin prickled. "At the festival."

"Yes," LuLu said. "And the night before WishFest, Violet texted Dana that Percy had 'crossed a line' and she was thinking about filing a complaint."

"Which would've humiliated him," I said.

"And cut off his access," LuLu added. "Percy thrives on proximity."

"Did he threaten her?" I asked, wondering if he was doing the same to Dana now.

LuLu hesitated. "Not explicitly. But the subtext is…gross. He frames himself as the victim constantly. 'After everything I did for you.' 'You wouldn't even have this life without me.'" She shook her head. "She's the one with money, not him."

Vex's tail snapped. *Entitlement again.*

"And," LuLu continued, "we can't forget Percy tried to force Violet to drink the cocoa he gave her. No one knows for sure if she drank it or not."

I closed my eyes briefly. "So, he had physical proximity."

"Yes," LuLu said. "But again, Percy wants Violet obsessed with him. Not gone."

"Unless he snapped," I said quietly.

LuLu nodded. "Which is always the wild card."

She took another sip of coffee, then set the mug down more carefully. "Now, for Wendy."

I let out a breath. "Please tell me it's not worse."

"It's…different," LuLu said. "Wendy Washington didn't poison anyone."

"Go on."

"She tried to blackmail Thomas Whitaker."

I blinked. "The choir director?"

"The one and only," LuLu confirmed. "My source said Wendy told him she knew about a donation discrepancy from last year's Winter WishFest. Something small but embarrassing enough to cost him his position. His job is something she knows is important to him."

"Was there really a donation discrepancy?"

"No," LuLu said. "But Thomas didn't know that."

"So, she pressured him to give her the lead," I said.

"Yes," LuLu said. "She threatened to 'go public' if Violet wasn't replaced."

"And Thomas?"

"He refused," LuLu said. "He told her Violet had earned that position, and he was a man of his word. That the choir wasn't political."

I grimaced. "Which Wendy did not appreciate."

"She was furious," LuLu said. "Wendy *does* benefit from Violet's death, but I don't think she did it. She loses her rival, sure, but she also becomes the obvious next target for suspicion."

"And she's not subtle enough to pull off poisoning," I said.

LuLu smiled grimly. "Exactly."

I stared into my coffee, the steam curling like unanswered questions. "So, none of Violet's enemies quite fit."

"They fit for conflict," LuLu said, "but not for execution." Silence settled between us for a beat. Then LuLu looked at me. "Your turn."

"Calderis and I went to Elarion."

Her eyes widened slightly, but she remained silent.

"We went to the Elixiria Gardens," I continued.

LuLu leaned in. "You didn't go to the Elders?"

"No," I said. "On purpose."

"Good," she replied immediately, and then frowned. "I don't trust them, especially because Calderis still hasn't told his father I'm his girlfriend. They know I'm under his protection, but they think it's because I'm an ally. I don't understand why he wants to keep our relationship a secret. Maybe he's just not that into me."

"That's not it, I promise. It's just, things with his father are complicated."

"Well, I'm not going to wait around forever for him to go public, but enough about that. What did you find?"

I took a breath and told her everything. About Eryndel. About the inquiry for a refined Cardiac Glycoside. About the words *hinge* and *weaken the foundation*. About his refusal to create death and his warning about brewers beyond the Gardens. About old fissures and smuggler paths that still spiraled upward, paths that could open into places like the Whisperwoods and the outskirts of Wishville if someone knew where to look.

LuLu didn't interrupt once. When I finished, she sat back slowly, her eyes intense and dark. "So, someone in Elarion wanted you gone for sure, then?"

"Yes," I said. "Or wanted the treaty destabilized enough that my absence would matter."

"And they couldn't get the compound from the Gardens," LuLu said, cataloguing facts in her brain. "So, they went illegal."

"Yes."

"And they might have crossed over through old fissures," she added. "Which means they didn't need to be seen entering Wishville."

I nodded. "And they wouldn't show up on Holden's radar as a normal suspect."

LuLu's mouth curved into a thin, determined smile. "Then here's the good news."

I arched a brow. "There's good news?"

"Yes," she said. "If the poisoner came from Elarion, they underestimated one thing."

"What's that?"

She leaned forward, her eyes snappy. "They underestimated how nosy, stubborn, and interconnected a small town can be when it decides something is *wrong*."

I couldn't help the small laugh that escaped me. "That might be the most *Wishville* thing you've ever said."

LuLu reached across the table and squeezed my hand. "You're not alone, Lyra. Not up here or down there. We're going to figure this out."

"We'd better. I might be three-hundred years old, but I'm not immortal. And I fear my time is running out."

CHAPTER
Ten

WINTER WISHFEST HAD a way of making grief look festive if you stood far enough back.

Lanterns glowed along the green like captured stars, strung from bare branches and wooden posts, until the dark itself seemed politely illuminated. Pine garlands wrapped railings and vendor tables, their sharp evergreen scent slicing through the sweeter smells of cocoa, fried dough, and sugared nuts. Carolers clustered near the stage, their scarves bright against the snow and voices rising and falling together as if harmony alone could keep the town upright.

If you squinted, it looked like joy.

I walked the *Ice Sculpture Trail* with my hands buried deep in my coat pockets and back hunched against the cold. The packed snow crunched under my boots, each step muffled by layers of sound. Laughter, music, and the scrape of ice tools still at work farther down the path. My breath fogged in the air and vanished almost instantly, as fleeting as the illusion Wishville was trying to sell itself.

From a distance, I probably looked exactly as I should have.

The Festival Chair smiling when spoken to, nodding at compliments, and pausing at sculptures long enough to look appreciative without lingering like I was searching for something. I even laughed at the right moments, the sound light and automatic.

They wouldn't have noticed how my eyes never stopped moving.

Vex padded at my heels, his black fur dusted with snowflakes that clung stubbornly to his whiskers. His tail flicked with careful disdain, as if winter were a personal affront he was tolerating out of courtesy.

Humans decorate winter the way they decorate danger, he observed quietly in my mind. *They soften it and pretend it is tame, not deadly.*

"I know," I murmured, my lips barely moving as a family swept past, their children clutching cocoa samples with pink-cheeked glee. "I'm not fooled."

Ahead, the ice sculptures rose from the snow like frozen sentinels. A moose carved mid-rear with its antlers branching into intricate crystal lattices. A sleigh pulled by ice horses whose muscles caught lantern light and shattered it into brilliance. A snow owl perched atop a stump, its wings carved so thin they looked fragile enough to melt under a single breath.

People stopped constantly, blocking the trail with their phones lifted, laughter erupting as someone slipped slightly on packed snow or posed dramatically beneath a sculpture. I adjusted my path again and again, letting myself be jostled, apologizing automatically, keeping my posture relaxed even as my pulse ticked faster.

At the center of the trail stood the winter rose arch. A tunnel of translucent petals blushing faintly pink where lantern light struck them. Couples paused beneath it for photos, breathless with cold and romance, and their hands clasped like promises.

It was breathtaking.

It was also crowded enough to hide anything.

The *Hot Cocoa Tasting Trail* ran alongside the sculptures, marked by chalkboard signs shaped like mugs. Vendors ladled samples with names designed to soothe. *Peppermint Swirl. Salted*

Maple Bliss. Midnight Mocha. Gingerbread Cloud. Steam curled into the air, carrying the comforting lie of warmth and sugar.

Every time I saw a cup lifted to someone's lips, my stomach clenched.

Violet Snowe had collapsed beneath lantern light. One moment she was smiling at the crowd, and the next she was crumpling into the snow like a marionette whose strings had been cut. Her lips had turned the wrong color almost immediately. Panic had rippled outward in waves, the festival cheer cracking under the weight of reality.

The cocoa station was the last station on Vendor Row, so we were guessing that was the last thing she consumed because the vendors confirmed she went in order down the row. However, she went down the row pretty quickly because the show was about to start, so any of the items could have been poisoned. The autopsy showed she had a lot in her stomach.

LuLu slipped into step beside me without breaking my stride, her scarf looped twice around her neck with her cheeks flushed from cold and purpose. She carried a notebook like she'd been born with it, which meant no one questioned her presence or her authority.

"Okay," she said quietly with her eyes forward. "Percy update."

My pulse jumped anyway. "Go."

"Percy Johnson is volunteering."

"I know," I said. "He always does. And right now, we can't prove anything except that he handed his ex-girlfriend the cocoa sample that might or might not have been poisoned, so the mayor allowed him to stay on. I don't think he knew about his abusive past either."

"Exactly. Good ole' Douglas Dogooder didn't consider that letting him stay on as a festival volunteer gave him access to all sorts of things."

I glanced sideways at her. "Like what?"

"Supplies. Back tables. Festival gear." She lowered her voice further. "And the town work shed."

My steps stayed even, but something inside me focused. "The public works?"

"Mm-hmm. The storage shed barn behind the green. It has salt bins, extra Styrofoam cups and to-go containers, extension cords, and emergency heaters. Things like that." Her mouth tightened. "Percy's been drifting between booths like he's on supply duty, but he's not actually carrying anything."

"How do you know?"

"I checked the volunteer roster. He's not scheduled. I asked Percy if he was scheduled. He said yes." LuLu's smile didn't reach her eyes. "Confidence of a man who assumes no one checks."

I scanned the crowd again. "Where is he?"

She tipped her chin subtly. "Green beanie. Expensive boots. Left side of the winter rose arch."

I spotted him immediately.

Percy Johnson hovered at the edge of the trail, his posture careful and gaze darting everywhere. He wore his volunteer lanyard like a badge of entitlement. Clean coat. Designer gloves. His hair still perfect despite the cold. He wasn't admiring the sculptures. He was counting.

Counting people? Counting space? Counting time?

Vex's ears angled forward. *That one is pretending he fits in when he does not.*

"I'm going to follow him," I murmured.

LuLu nodded once. "I'll deploy the Wellies."

As if summoned by the word *deploy*, Tilly, Belle, and Dot appeared near the cocoa trail sign.

"I'm telling you," Tilly announced loudly, "the ice sculptures are enchanted."

"You cannot accuse ice of sorcery," Belle protested, already scribbling notes.

"You absolutely can," Dot replied calmly, sipping her tea. "If it deserves it."

LuLu beamed. "Ladies, what's the latest gossip?"

"Enchanted ice thieves," Dot said solemnly.

"There have been thefts of a different kind," Tilly added, lowering her voice only slightly. "Candy canes. Spiced nuts. Decorative bells. Gingerbread ornaments."

I arched an eyebrow. "Those were reported?"

"Complained about," Dot corrected. "Reporting requires forms."

LuLu clapped lightly. "Lyra, why don't you continue along the trail and keep an eye out while the ladies and I…investigate."

"We'll be your distraction," Tilly said proudly.

"What are we distracting this time?" Dot blinked her enormous eyes behind her glasses.

"You from yourself," Belle muttered as she rolled her eyes.

"You are all exceptional distractions," LuLu said fondly.

I didn't argue.

Percy had already started moving again. He slipped off the main path, away from the sculptures and cocoa stands, toward a narrower service trail that curved behind the green. Lanterns thinned. Music softened. The press of bodies eased into brittle quiet.

I followed at a careful distance, letting families and couples drift between us as cover. A child darted across my path and I had to pause, steadying her with a gloved hand and accepting a breathless apology from her mother. By the time I moved again, Percy was nearly at the treeline.

My pulse spiked. I shortened my stride, cut across the snow at an angle, and regained visuals just as Percy crossed the packed ground toward the *town work shed*. The building squatted behind a stand of bare trees, unremarkable and unadorned. Weathered wood. Corrugated metal roof dusted with snow. No lights or decorations.

A place no one noticed unless something went wrong.

Percy glanced over his shoulder once, then unlocked the side door and slipped inside.

I waited, counted to ten, then I followed.

The door creaked softly as I eased it open just enough to slip through, closing it behind me until the latch barely caught. The smell hit me first. Salt, oil, and cold iron. The air felt heavier and denser. Shelving units lined the walls, stacked with bags of sidewalk salt, bins of ice melt, extension cords, traffic cones, and emergency signage. Styrofoam cups sat in plastic crates, identical and unassuming. To-go containers were stacked in piles. A clipboard hung from a nail by the door, blank except for a few hurried checkmarks.

Percy moved fast. Too fast. He knelt by a large salt bin, flipped the lid, rummaged around, and then froze.

Something warm brushed my chest. My pendant.

Percy swore under his breath and slammed the lid shut, the sound echoing in the enclosed space. He shoved something under his coat and then backed away as if the shed itself were cursed, running a hand through his hair. He didn't look triumphant. He looked afraid. He left without checking behind him.

I stayed frozen until the door shut and his footsteps faded. Only then did I move. The salt bin was heavier than it looked. I lifted the lid carefully. Inside, there was a chunk of Styrofoam with some kind of residue on it.

Sweet metal, Vex whispered, sniffing the air.

I always carried plastic gloves and baggies in my coat pocket. Donning the gloves I put the piece in an evidence bag to be tested. What had Percy put under his coat? And what did the piece of Styrofoam belong to…a cup or a to-go container? Was it Violet's sample container? Did she throw it away, and then someone hid the evidence in the shed? Was it Percy or someone else?

"So, Violet was definitely poisoned," I breathed.

But we still don't know which food, or if it was meant for you.

"Correct, but at least now we have some evidence." I turned to leave then froze.

Snow shifted outside.

Vex went rigid. *Someone is there.*

A breath too quiet to belong to wind, and weight shifting deliberately. Whoever it was hadn't followed Percy. They'd waited for me. I moved deeper into shadow, my heart steady, mind alert, and the piece of Styrofoam in my pocket. Because now I understood something important. Percy wasn't the hunter. He was the rabbit, frightened, scrambling, and being used. And whoever was watching the work shed had just made a mistake.

They'd let me find proof.

~

The Snow Globe Gala took over the *Donor Hall* like a storm taking over the sky, suddenly, completely, and with the kind of glitter that made you forget you were standing on ice.

The old community center had been transformed into something that looked like a winter ballroom in a storybook.

White drapery fell from the rafters in swoops like snowbanks, and strings of icicle lights hung in delicate curtains across the ceiling. Pine boughs and silver ribbon wrapped the pillars. Every table wore a centerpiece of frosted branches, cranberries, and tiny glass globes filled with artificial snow that swirled when the bass from the band vibrated through the floor.

Someone had even rigged a machine near the stage that released a slow drift of faux snow into the air every few minutes, so the whole room shimmered as if winter itself had RSVP'd.

It should have felt like magic.

Instead, it felt like pressure.

I stood near the edge of the dance floor in a dark green dress that made me look festive enough to belong here, and I watched Wishville spin around me. People were laughing, their cheeks flushed and hands raised in toasts, with their arms loosening as the band slid from carols into something swingy and familiar. The scent of mulled cider and butter cookies mixed with perfume and polished wood.

Everyone wanted to believe tonight was proof we were still

okay. After Violet's collapse, the whispered rumors, and the anxious looks, this gala wasn't just a fundraiser. It was a performance.

Holden stood beside me in a suit that looked like it had been forced on him by civic duty, his tie slightly crooked as if he'd fought it and lost. He scanned the room, his eyes sweeping exits, hands, and faces, looking for anything out of place. If I was the Festival Chair pretending to be calm, Holden was the police chief pretending this was just a party.

On my other side, Calderis looked like he'd stepped out of a different world, supreme to Wishville, gracing us with his presence. His suit was black, sharply cut, the fabric moving with him like a shadow. He wore no tie, just an open collar that made him look both formal and faintly dangerous.

The overhead lights caught on the high planes of his face and the pale intensity of his eyes. He didn't blend. He never did. But tonight, with the chandeliers and glitter and carefully arranged fantasy of the gala, people interpreted him as the mysterious, devilishly handsome detective who sometimes helped Holden out and dated Lucky LuLu.

LuLu looked radiant in a midnight-blue dress, her hair pinned back with a silver comb shaped like a snowflake. She looked like she belonged on a stage, and the way Calderis angled slightly toward her without realizing it made my stomach twist with something that was part fondness and part alarm. Because if anyone in this room looked closely enough, they'd see what I saw.

They weren't just standing near each other. They were…a part of each other. Connected with their auras slightly glowing, her abilities becoming more evident as they grew stronger. I cleared my throat, and they moved slightly apart.

"Okay," I murmured, keeping my face neutral as a couple twirled past. "We're here for donor lists, schedules, and access."

Holden's jaw flexed. "And to make sure no one drinks anything they didn't pour themselves."

"That too," I agreed.

I had given Holden the evidence bag and he'd had the Styrofoam chunk tested. Just as we'd suspected, it was laced with poison, and the case had changed to a murder investigation. But we still didn't know if the chunk was from a cup or a food container or who hid it there.

Vex, who had been forced by gala etiquette to remain home, service animal or not, couldn't comment. But I could *feel* his absence like a missing stitch. Fenrin, however, had insisted on coming. Not as herself, of course. Somewhere in this room, she was hidden in plain sight, having shapeshifted into something small and forgettable.

A moth. A mouse. A shadow.

I'd told her not to cause chaos.

Fenrin treated that like a personal challenge.

Across the room, the biggest donors stood near the stage like royalty, with Alistair Hawthorne in the front. His suit was tailored enough to make the men around him look rumpled, and the Wellies collectively forget how to regulate their breathing in a synchronized swoon. He was laughing with a cluster of other donors, their flutes of champagne raised and faces tilted toward the photographer as if the camera was a mirror. And tonight, their names would be on every banner, every program, and every thank-you speech.

I watched them for a beat longer than was polite. Then I forced my gaze away and turned back to the table beside me. The donor table. It had been set up near the entrance to the staff corridor, ostensibly for "event administration," but in reality, it was the nerve center of the gala. Clipboards. Seating charts. Donation forms. Volunteer schedules. A binder labeled **SNOW GLOBE GALA: BACKSTAGE ACCESS** in tidy printed letters.

I stepped closer, smiling at the older woman stationed there, who was wearing a moose pin and the exhausted expression of someone who'd been asked where the bathroom was one hundred and sixty-seven times.

"Hi," I said brightly. "Lyra Wells, Festival Chair. I just want to double-check the donor list and the schedule for the entertainment."

"Oh!" The woman's face brightened. "Of course. We're so grateful for everything you've done, dear."

"Happy to," I said, and slid my fingers over the binder.

Holden shifted slightly behind me, his presence a steady wall. Calderis's gaze flicked toward the staff corridor, tracking movement with predatory focus. LuLu leaned in closer, her eyes sparkling like she was at a social event, while her mind, I knew, was working overtime.

I opened the binder. Pages. Columns. Names. Donation tiers. **Platinum Snowfall Donors:** Hawthorne Foundation. Lambros Family Trust. Pike Holdings. **Schedules:** auction preview at seven-thirty, dancers at eight, keynote donation speech at eight-thirty, silent auction close at nine-thirty, raffle drawing at ten.

Then, tucked behind the schedules, was the access log. Who had keys, who had clearance, and who could enter backstage. Volunteer coordinator. Sound tech. Lighting tech. Stage manager. Facilities. And then a line that shouldn't have been there.

Temporary Maintenance Access Approved.

LuLu's fingers brushed my elbow, subtly, as if in question.

I turned the page. A printed maintenance request form was clipped behind it dated three weeks earlier and filed under "facility hazard prevention." The signature at the bottom wasn't Thomas's. It wasn't the usual facilities manager. It was a neat, looping hand that looked like it belonged on a holiday card.

Wendy Washington.

Like a cue summoned by the ink itself, Wendy appeared at the edge of the donor table in a red dress so aggressively festive it bordered on threatening. Her lipstick matched, with her smile sharp enough to cut ribbon.

"Oh, Lyra," she said brightly, and I could hear the performative sweetness in her tone. "I didn't realize you were handling *this.*"

I closed the binder halfway. Not enough to hide what I'd seen, but enough to keep control of it. "Just reviewing the schedule."

Wendy's eyes slid down to the binder, then back up, her smile never slipping. "Good. Because we're running behind on equipment placement. The snow machine is positioned wrong. I told Thomas it needs to be three feet to the left or it'll drift into the catering line and ruin the whipped cream."

A beat passed. Then Thomas himself barreled toward us, sweaty and frazzled, a headset crooked over one ear and a clipboard clutched like a lifeline.

"It is *fine* where it is, Wendy," he snapped, his voice tight. "It's not going to ruin anything."

"It's going to ruin everything," Wendy said, leaning forward like she was about to physically relocate the machine with sheer force of will. "I've run events. You haven't."

Thomas's face went red. "I run the choir and the choir runs the gala—"

"You'll run it into the ground," Wendy cut in smoothly.

I felt Holden's posture shift. Calderis's eyes narrowed. Holden's hand lifted in that calm-but-warning gesture he used on drunk men outside the town bars at midnight.

"Wendy," Holden said, his voice even and authoritative. "Leave Thomas alone. If there's an issue, you bring it to me."

Wendy blinked, as if it genuinely hadn't occurred to her that someone could tell her no. "Chief, I'm just trying to ensure tonight goes smoothly."

"And it will," Holden said. "Without you micromanaging the staff."

Calderis added, low and cool, "If you need something to do, stand still. It will be a new experience."

LuLu coughed into her hand to hide a laugh.

Wendy's eyes flashed as red as her dress. "Excuse me?"

Holden stepped slightly closer, blocking her line to the binder. "Go enjoy the gala."

Thomas exhaled like one of Weylan's balloons deflating, but Wendy wasn't done.

"I need to check the backstage storage," she insisted. "Someone moved the auction display risers—"

Calderis turned his head slightly, his gaze locking on hers with a stillness that made the air feel colder. "Backstage is for staff."

"I'm volunteering," Wendy snapped. "I'm involved."

Holden's voice dropped. "Not tonight."

For a second, Wendy looked like she might argue further. Then the band shifted into a louder song, the crowd cheered at something on the stage, and Wendy realized she'd drawn attention.

She pasted on her smile again. "Fine. But don't say I didn't warn you." She pivoted away, her heels clicking and disappearing into the donor cluster like she hadn't just tried to take over the building.

Thomas dragged a hand through his hair. "Thank you," he muttered to Holden. "She's been like this since Violet died. Like she thinks she's the new queen of the choir. I made her the new lead caroler. You would think that would be enough. If she keeps this up, I'm going to replace her."

Holden gave him a look. "Don't worry about her. Stick to the schedule, keep the backstage locked, and don't let anyone in without the wristband."

Thomas nodded quickly and hurried off, muttering into his headset.

Holden turned back to me. "Now."

LuLu's eyes gleamed. "Backstage."

I closed the binder carefully, but I didn't put it away. I slid it under my arm then LuLu and I slipped toward the staff corridor while Holden and Calderis stayed near the donor table, perfectly positioned to handle the next catastrophe…whatever that may be.

Because rest assured, in Wishville, it would be something.

Eleven

THE STAFF CORRIDOR smelled like dust, electrical heat, and the faint tang of cleaning solution. The music from the donor hall muffled into a thump-thump heartbeat behind us. The fluorescent lights above made everything look less magical and more honest.

LuLu leaned in close. "You saw something."

"A maintenance request," I whispered. "Filed weeks ago. It gave someone temporary access backstage."

LuLu's expression tightened. "Filed by whom?"

I hesitated half a beat. "Wendy."

LuLu let out a slow breath, more controlled than shocked. "Of course it was."

We reached the backstage door which was normally locked. Tonight, it had a laminated sign that read **AUTHORIZED STAFF ONLY** with a cheerful snowman clipart that made it feel like a joke.

I tried the handle.

Unlocked.

LuLu shot me a look. "That's not—"

"I know." My pulse thudded hard. "That's not normal."

We slipped inside.

The backstage area was a maze of curtains, folding chairs,

costume racks, and equipment cases. A stagehand hurried past carrying a coil of cable, barely glancing at us. Someone shouted for gaffer tape. A performer in sequins laughed nervously, practicing a spin with too much energy.

I kept my head down, moving like I belonged with the binder tucked under my arm.

LuLu whispered, "We need the actual request. The original."

We found the facilities bulletin board near the stage manager's table covered in clipped memos, printed schedules, and scribbled notes. And there it was. A maintenance request form with the exact same date.

Requested work: Inspect and restock ice melt bins, replace thermos liners in staff beverage stations, check heater cords, secure storage access for Winter WishFest equipment staging.

Reason: "Prevent hazards, ensure safety compliance."

It was written perfectly. Too perfectly. Like someone had Googled what to say. And the approval signature line? Stamped. No oversight or manager initials or follow-up. Just…granted.

LuLu leaned in, her voice barely audible. "This is how someone got access without anyone questioning it."

My mind raced through it. Weeks ago, before Violet collapsed or anyone was looking for tampering, backstage access meant access to anything in the storage shed. Someone on the inside could easily plant something to be used during the festival and walk away.

"This wasn't a last-minute crime," I whispered. "This was planned." A soft movement brushed my ankle. I looked down. A small gray rat with amber eyes blinked up at me.

Fenrin.

She lifted her tiny head like she was proud of herself.

LuLu's lips twitched. "Oh, honey, please tell me you didn't come as…that."

Fenrin's rat eyes narrowed as if offended, then she scampered forward with silent confidence, slipping under a curtain toward the storage rooms. LuLu and I followed at a distance, careful not to draw attention. The hallway beyond backstage was dimmer and quieter. The air changed to less perfume and more cardboard and cold metal. Fenrin paused at a storage door, nosed it open with alarming competence, and slipped inside.

We hovered at the doorway.

Inside were shelves stacked with silent auction items: baskets wrapped in cellophane, framed prints, a bottle of expensive wine, gift certificates clipped to glittery boards. Or at least...there should have been.

The shelves were half empty.

LuLu's face went still. "Where—"

A squeal ripped through the air, high-pitched and panicked. Then another. Then a chorus of screams.

LuLu's eyes went wide. "Oh no."

Fenrin had vanished from the storage room.

A second later, the dressing room curtain flew open and a dancer stumbled out, her eyes wild, shrieking, "There's a rat!"

Chaos detonated.

Performers screamed, jumping onto chairs. Someone flung a sequined shawl like it was a weapon. A stagehand dropped a box of props that clattered across the floor.

The stage manager shouted, "Someone help, there's a rabid rat back here!"

And before I could move, Wendy's voice sliced through the noise from the corridor like a blade. "What is going on back here?"

Oh, perfect.

How had Holden and Calderis let her slip past them?

In the middle of the screaming, the missing auction items, and the falsified maintenance request, one thing became brutally clear...whoever was doing this didn't just want someone dead. They wanted Winter WishFest to collapse.

And they'd been laying the groundwork for weeks.

～

The Twisted Loaf was already warm when I stepped inside the next morning, the windows fogged from the collision of cold air and fresh bread. Snow clung to boots near the door, melting into dark crescents on the floor. The bell over the entrance chimed softly, a sound so normal I could almost forget about the crisis Wishville was currently in.

Betsy Plum had the ovens going full tilt, and the smell of butter, yeast, and cinnamon wrapped around me like a warm blanket I hadn't realized I'd been craving. Coffee steamed from oversized mugs behind the counter, and a low murmur of voices filled the space. Locals decompressing, replaying last night's chaos in quieter tones now that the rodents, music, and lights were gone.

Wishville always processed things over carbs.

LuLu was already there, perched at our usual corner table with her notebook open and a pen tucked behind her ear. She looked bright-eyed and alert. Holden sat across from her, his jacket draped over the chair back, and both hands wrapped around a mug like it was a necessary anchor. Calderis stood near the window at first, watching the street with his back half-turned to the room, as if old habits refused to loosen their grip just because the danger had technically passed.

I slid into the empty chair beside Holden and blew out an exhausted breath.

"Good morning," LuLu said with a chipper tone.

"Is it good?" I replied.

Betsy appeared almost immediately, as if summoned by shared exhaustion. "Coffee?" she asked, already reaching for a mug.

"Yes," I said. "Please. Strong enough to rewrite reality."

She smiled sympathetically and poured. For a few moments, none of us spoke. The food arrived. The warmth settled. Outside, someone laughed, the sound bright against the snow-muted street. It felt wrong and comforting all at once.

Holden broke the silence. "So. Whoever poisoned Violet didn't just want her dead."

I nodded slowly, my fingers tightening around my mug. "No. They possibly wanted me dead and the festival to fail."

LuLu leaned forward. "Or to be seen failing."

Calderis turned from the window then, his gaze sharp and focused. "Those are not the same thing."

"No," I agreed. "And that's what's bothering me."

The Snow Globe Gala had been chaos. Screaming performers. Missing auction items. Wendy's attempted takeover. A falsified maintenance request that had granted quiet, unquestioned access weeks in advance. It wasn't impulsive or emotional. It was structured.

Planned.

Holden said, "Half the town is still talking about the gala."

"Exactly," I said. "If you wanted to scare people away from Wish-Fest, that would do it. If you wanted donors to panic, volunteers to question whether this was safe, and town leadership to scramble."

LuLu tapped her pen against her notebook. "Or if you wanted to discredit the person in charge."

My stomach tightened. "That's the other option," I said quietly. "Someone didn't want WishFest ruined. They wanted *me* ruined."

Holden's jaw set immediately. "Lyra—"

"I know," I cut in gently. "But think about it. I'm the visible one. Festival Chair. The face people see when something goes wrong. If Violet dies at my event, if donors walk out of the *Snow Globe Gala*, if auction items vanish backstage…that lands on me."

Calderis's eyes darkened. "So, we are in agreement. The attack was personal."

"I believe it *could* be," I said.

LuLu tilted her head. "So, let's walk through this again and see if we missed anything."

I nodded. "Okay. First option: a rebel."

The word settled heavily between us.

"If someone wanted to weaken the treaty," I continued, "undermining WishFest would do it. If I am gone, then WishFest collapses. And if the well can't grant someone's wish, that cracks the foundation."

LuLu scribbled something down. "A rebel wouldn't need the town to know why the festival mattered. Just that it failed."

"And Violet?" Holden asked. "Collateral damage?"

I swallowed. "Possibly." I stared at the tabletop, the grooves worn smooth by years of elbows and coffee cups. "But there's a problem with that theory."

LuLu looked up. "Which is?"

"If this was about breaking the treaty, the method was…messy. Human. Falsified maintenance requests. Poisoned Styrofoam of some sort. Silent auction thefts. Missing cash from vendors." I shook my head. "That doesn't feel like an ideological strike. It feels like someone who knows Wishville. Someone who understands how our systems work."

"Someone local," Holden said.

"Yes."

"And that brings us to option two," LuLu said. "Someone who wants to hurt you."

I didn't like how easily that fit.

"Who would want to ruin you as Festival Chair?" Holden asked.

My mind ran through faces. Names. Old slights. New tensions. "Anyone who feels sidelined. Anyone who thinks they should be in charge. Anyone who thinks I embarrassed them."

Calderis watched my expression shift. "You are thinking of someone."

"I'm thinking of several someones," I said carefully. "But Wendy stands out. She inserted herself into logistics. Filed a maintenance request weeks ago. Tried to access backstage last night under the guise of 'helping.'"

Holden frowned. "She also doesn't strike me as someone who would poison a woman."

"No," I agreed. "She's controlling, not murderous."

LuLu's pen paused. "But she might be useful to someone who is." That thought tracked.

"Someone who needed access," LuLu continued. "Someone who needed paperwork to look legitimate. Someone who knew Wendy would push and push and never question why she was being asked to sign things."

Calderis nodded. "A proxy."

I rubbed my temple. "Which brings us back to motive. Why me? Why WishFest?"

Holden leaned back slightly. "You've changed things."

I looked at him. "I have?"

"You've made the festivals thrive, drawing big crowds," he said. "You've tied them to community instead of just tradition. You've pushed for transparency. You didn't let things slide after Violet collapsed. You didn't let the *Snow Globe Gala* quietly smooth over the chaos." He met my eyes. "That makes enemies."

I swallowed.

"And," LuLu added gently, "you stand in the middle of things other people want to control."

The café door opened, letting in a blast of cold air and a pair of laughing teenagers. Normal life pressed in around us, oblivious to the weight of what we were saying.

"So," I said finally, "either someone wanted WishFest to fail to weaken the treaty...or someone wanted me to fail to regain power."

"And it could be both," Holden said.

"Yes," I admitted. "It could."

Calderis folded his arms. "Then the next question is simple. Who benefits?"

I let that question roll through me. Who benefited from Violet's collapse? From donor panic? From missing auction items? From casting doubt on my leadership? I straightened slightly. "Whoever did this didn't expect us to look past the surface. They counted on chaos and fear and people wanting everything to go back to normal."

LuLu smiled thinly. "Bad luck for them. Normal is not our strong suit."

Holden lifted his mug in a small, resolute gesture. "We'll find them."

I wrapped my hands around my coffee, the heat grounding me. Snow continued to fall, quiet and relentless. WishFest wasn't over yet, and neither was the fight for what it represented.

CHAPTER
Twelve

THE SNOW FORT *Competition* should have been harmless.

It wasn't.

From the rise overlooking the meadow, it looked charming enough. Children were dragging plastic sleds piled with snow blocks, and parents were bundled in scarves and wool hats, shouting encouragement that was only half joking. Triangular flags snapped in the wind, marking off square plots of land like rival kingdoms staking claims. Someone, almost certainly Tilly, had decided medieval battle music was appropriate background ambiance, so war drums and horns blared faintly from a speaker duct-taped to a folding table.

I stepped down into the field, my boots crunching over snow packed hard by dozens of feet, my clipboard tucked under my arm like a talisman. The cold hit immediately, burning my lungs with each breath. The air smelled like pine sap, damp wool, and that faint metallic tang that always came with deep winter, layered over the sweeter scent of cider drifting down from Vendor Row.

Vex perched on my shoulder, his black fur already dusted with snowflakes that melted and refroze into glittering specks. *This is not how fortifications are constructed*, he informed me.

"They're children," I murmured. "Lower your standards."

Civilizations fall this way, he replied solemnly.

Finch stood near the maintenance sled at the edge of the field, a small notepad clipped to his sleeve and his gray beard rimed with frost. He moved with the calm efficiency of someone who had spent his life fixing things that broke honestly, like pipes, generators, and fences, problems that announced themselves clearly and could be solved with patience and the right tools.

"Pack from the base up," he called to a cluster of kids. "Snow needs pressure. Like stone."

They nodded solemnly, then immediately did the opposite.

Elliot Crane moved nothing like Finch. He jogged past me with a crate balanced against his hip, his breath puffing white and boots kicking up powder as he crossed the field. He dropped the crate near the judges' tent harder than necessary, then straightened quickly, scanning the meadow like he'd misplaced something. Or was checking to see who had noticed.

Vex's claws pressed lightly into my coat. *He's a clumsy one.*

"He's still learning," I said.

I drifted closer to the supply sled, crouching as if to tighten a loose strap while my eyes cataloged what was piled there. Shovels. Buckets. Lantern stakes. Rope. Sandbags. Too many sandbags. And the crates themselves were newer than the rest with clean plastic instead of the town's battered green bins, no faded stencil or inventory tag.

"Did we expand the supply list?" I asked lightly, not looking up.

Elliot startled, just a fraction, before recovering. "Figured better safe than sorry."

Finch frowned. "I don't remember approving extras."

Elliot's face reddened. "Thought we talked about it earlier."

Finch rubbed his jaw, clearly replaying the morning in his head. "Maybe." He shrugged. "If it's here, use it." That was Finch. Always practical and go-with-the-flow.

Elliot nodded once and then looked at me. "My mother said thank you for the soup."

I smiled in return. "Tell her she's very welcome." And I would thank the Wellies later, after they finished arguing about whether thyme was emotionally appropriate in general.

The horn blasted, loud and brassy, and chaos surged forward. Teams rushed their plots, shovels biting into snow, buckets filling and dumping in frantic rhythm. Snow flew. Laughter spiked. Someone toppled backward and came up grinning, covered head to toe in powder.

Elliot moved from plot to plot, stopping just long enough to help by lifting a bucket here, adjusting a lantern stake there, and offering advice. It wasn't long ago he had been one of the kids in the competition.

I followed at a distance, observing them. They worked well on their own, but not so much as a team. "Finch," I called, raising my voice over the din. "Who's tracking supply distribution?"

Finch gestured vaguely. "Everyone takes what they need. That's the point."

I nodded. "Of course." It was also the flaw.

A sharp voice cut through the noise. "Hey, who took our lantern?"

Heads turned. A volunteer stood near the western edge of the field, staring at an empty hook, her cheeks flushed from cold and irritation. "It was there two minutes ago," she insisted.

Finch straightened. "Lanterns don't sprout wings."

Only Whispen cats do, I thought. I scanned the snow. Footprints layered over footprints, scuffed lines crossing until nothing looked distinct anymore. Perfect cover.

"I'll grab another," Finch said.

"No," I said quickly. "Let's log it."

Both men looked at me.

"It's just a lantern," Elliot said, scratching his stubbled chin.

"It's just data," I replied evenly. "And data matters."

The men nodded.

Vex purred softly. *She's tightening the net.*

I wrote on my clipboard about the missing lantern and the time when the horn sounded and the distraction peaked. Because someone was mapping the festival, and mapping meant intent.

A sudden collapse of laughter erupted as a fort wall crumbled, snow spraying everywhere. Elliot ducked behind the structure, and I followed.

"Elliot," I called. "Can you help me for a second?"

He popped up. "Sure. What's up?"

"Inventory," I said. "Walk me through what came from the shed."

"All the usuals," he said. "Plus donations."

"From whom?"

He shrugged. "Didn't catch a name."

"When?"

"Early. Before sunrise."

Cold slid deeper into my bones. "Funny," I said mildly. "Finch unlocked the shed at seven."

Elliot opened his mouth, then closed it.

Snow drifted between us, soft and deceptively quiet.

Finch's voice carried from across the field. "Everything good?"

"Yes," I said. "For now."

Elliot shrugged. "I should get back."

"Of course," I said, stepping aside.

As he jogged away, Vex leaned toward my ear. *Desperation smells sharper than fear.*

I watched Elliot vanish back into the chaos, then lifted my gaze to the meadow—the forts rising unevenly, the laughter, the illusion of harmless fun. Someone was learning how to create a distraction.

And I was beginning to think that someone wasn't acting alone.

∾

The sledding hill roared like a living thing.

Children shrieked as sleds launched downhill, plastic runners skimming over packed snow. Whistles pierced the air. Cowbells rang. Volunteers shouted times and lane numbers with exaggerated seriousness. At the base of the hill, the hot cocoa stand steamed like a beacon, the scent of chocolate, sugar, and marshmallows cutting sharply through the cold.

Timed runs meant structure.

Structure meant predictability.

Predictability meant opportunity.

I stood near the starting gate, my clipboard in hand and boots planted firmly as Ozzy Snowe argued loudly with a volunteer in a neon vest.

"I was here first," he snapped. "I just stepped out."

"You stepped out during your heat," the volunteer replied flatly. "That forfeits your run."

Ozzy scoffed. "That's ridiculous."

I raised an eyebrow. "Rules don't pause for impatience, Ozzy."

He turned, flashing a grin that didn't reach his eyes. "Lyra Wells. Have a heart. Back me up."

"I am backing the rules." Forget my heart. My head was onto him.

His smile slipped. "Figures." He stalked off toward the cross-country ski loop, his boots crunching hard as he muttered under his breath.

Edward stood nearby, a notebook open as he tallied donation envelopes from the cocoa stand. I stepped up beside him and peeked over his shoulder. His handwriting was precise. Careful. Every line measured. Every movement deliberate.

"Busy station," I said.

"Always," he responded pleasantly. "People are generous when they're warm."

"Or distracted," I said.

He chuckled. "Same thing."

A sled shot past us, spraying snow. Edward shifted, blocking me from the blast.

"Thanks." I moved.

"No problem." He moved with me.

"Do you ski?" I asked casually.

He blinked. "No, why?"

"Ozzy apparently does," I said, nodding toward the tree-lined loop where skiers disappeared and reemerged at staggered intervals. "That's his fourth lap today."

Edward's pen paused. "Keeping warm I presume."

"Or moving between stations," I replied. The loop conveniently circled around the festival grounds, passing all of the stations.

Ozzy returned moments later, his cheeks flushed and eyes wide with something more than cold. "Edward!" he called. "Did you log my donation yet?"

Edward smiled tightly. "You haven't donated."

Ozzy laughed. "Details."

They stared at each other, sharing tension. Different men with the same hunger for success, I suspected. Edward was a go-getter, driven and greedy from what the mayor said, but the mayor was desperate for help. Ozzy was also driven and greedy to win by gambling. Neither had reached a level of success to satisfy them, it seemed.

Another whistle blew. A sled launched. The crowd surged forward, laughter and shouting swelling as people pressed closer to watch. And in that moment of chaos, Edward reached for the cash tin.

I stepped in smoothly. "Careful."

His hand froze.

"That's already been counted," I added.

"Of course," he said, withdrawing it. "Just securing it. Well, I'm off to the next station." He gave me a nod as he walked away.

Vex's tail flicked. *Greed wears politeness like perfume.*

I watched Ozzy strap on his skis again and disappear into the trees in the same direction. The ski loop curved out of view. Movement. Loops. Gaps. Patterns. I made another note about sled times and flow. It was intricate choreography.

And someone had memorized the steps.

The cross-country ski loop didn't look dangerous.

That made it worse.

It wound away from the main festival grounds in a slow, deliberate arc, vanishing into the trees where the lights thinned and the sound of the crowd faded into something quieter and more brittle. Lanterns hung at intervals along the path, their glow muted by falling snow, each pool of light surrounded by shadows that felt deeper by contrast.

I stood at the trailhead with my clipboard hugged to my chest, watching skiers strap on boots and adjust poles with the particular seriousness of people who believed winter sports were a moral test. Breath fogged the air. Snow whispered underfoot.

Vex shifted on my shoulder, his tail flicking uneasily. *This path is wrong.*

"It's just longer," I murmured.

No, he said. *It's isolated.*

That was true.

The ski loop had been designed as a scenic route—quiet, meditative, a place to escape the noise of WishFest while still technically participating and passing the vendor stations at various points. It was also the one activity that pulled people completely out of sight for long stretches of time.

Which meant it was perfect.

I scanned the check-in table where volunteers recorded names and times. Two teenagers in WishFest hats stamped hands and waved skiers forward, laughing as they tried to keep ink from freezing. The clipboard on the table already held a neat list of names, times logged carefully in columns.

Ozzy Snowe had finished yet another loop. He stood off to one side, stretching his legs with exaggerated vigor. He glanced at his watch, then at the path, then back toward the festival grounds like he was calculating something.

Edward lingered near the table, ostensibly helping tally donations collected along the route, small tins stationed at rest points "for the winter outreach fund." The same fund that didn't officially exist, but someone thought it was a good idea after all and started one. At least that was how he explained it when I asked. For now, I chose to observe, but it still seemed odd.

Patterns stacked on patterns.

I stepped closer to the table. "How many tins are on the loop?"

The volunteer blinked. "Three, I think."

"I count four," I said quietly.

She frowned. "Do you?"

I nodded. "One at the trailhead, one at the overlook, one by the frozen creek…and one at the turnaround."

Her face paled slightly. "I didn't put one at the turnaround."

Edward cleared his throat. "Someone must've moved it for convenience."

"For whose convenience?" I asked.

He smiled, smooth as ever. "The skiers."

Vex's claws flexed. *Lies echo differently out here.*

Ozzy glanced over, his eyes narrowing. "You starting my heat or what?"

I looked at him. "You're eager, for someone who has already competed in several heats all day long."

He shrugged. "Cold makes me restless."

Or nervous. I waved him forward. "Go."

Ozzy pushed off, his skis slicing clean lines into the snow as he disappeared into the trees again.

I waited.

Edward checked his watch.

I frowned. "You tracking time for everyone?"

"Just keeping things orderly," he said.

"Order doesn't require anticipation," I replied.

The next skier went. Then another. Each one swallowed by the trees, lantern light flickering briefly before vanishing. The loop felt longer every time I watched someone disappear.

I took a breath and stepped onto the trail.

"Lyra," the volunteer said quickly. "You don't have skis."

"I'm walking it," I said. "Someone should. Don't worry, I'll stay off the trail."

Edward's smile flickered. "It's a long loop."

"I know."

Vex pressed closer to my neck as I moved forward, my boots crunching softly over packed snow. The lantern light thinned quickly, shadows stretching long between the trees. The air felt colder here.

Behind me, the festival continued with faint music and distant laughter, but out here, everything felt exposed.

This is not a good idea, Vex said.

"It's necessary."

Necessary gets people hurt.

I didn't answer.

Halfway to the first overlook, I saw the tin. It sat off the path, half-buried in snow where it hadn't been earlier. The lid was ajar. I crouched, my heart thudding, and lifted it.

Empty.

Footprints surrounded it. No skis. I straightened slowly, scanning the trees.

"Hello?" I called. My voice sounded wrong out here. Too loud. Too thin.

A sound came back. Not a voice, but movement. A scrape. A shift. I turned. Ozzy emerged from the trees, his breath heaving and his cheeks flushed deeper than exertion alone could explain.

"You okay?" he asked too quickly.

"I should be asking you that," I said.

He gestured vaguely. "Loop's longer than I remembered."

"Funny," I said. "You've done it five times today."

His jaw tightened. "You following me now?"

"I'm following the money," I replied.

He laughed harshly. "You think I'm stealing from my own town?"

"Your cousin's town," I clarified. "I think you're desperate. And desperation makes people careless."

His gaze flicked to the lantern behind me and the shadows beyond it. "I'm not the only one out here," he said, looking uneasy.

Chills peppered my arms. "Who else?"

He hesitated just long enough. "I saw someone ahead of me. I didn't recognize them."

I narrowed my eyes, not sure I could believe a word he said. "On skis?"

"No," he said. "Walking."

Vex went utterly still. *For some reason I believe him.*

"Which direction?" I asked.

Ozzy pointed, deeper into the loop. A gust of wind stirred the branches, snow shaking loose in a soft hiss. We both jumped. The lantern light flickered, and I took a step back instinctively.

"Go," I told Ozzy. "Back to the trailhead. Now."

He hesitated. "What about you?"

"I'll follow."

He didn't argue for once, which told me he was more spooked than I realized. He pushed off, his skis carving fast lines back the way he'd come.

I stood alone for a beat, my breath loud in my ears.

This theft seems bigger somehow, Vex said quietly.

"I know." I turned back toward the path and froze.

Footprints crossed it. Not ski tracks. Boots. Fresh. They led off the trail, into the trees, away from the lantern light. Someone had been close. Close enough to watch me. A branch snapped somewhere to my left. I backed up slowly, my heart hammering and eyes scanning the darkness.

"Not today," I whispered.

I turned and walked fast, my boots crunching too loudly, refusing to run. The festival lights appeared ahead like a promise, growing brighter with every step. By the time I reached the trail-head, Ozzy was gone. But why did I feel like the person watching me had nothing to do with Ozzy?

The volunteer looked up anxiously. "Everything okay?"

I forced a smile. "Fine." But my hands were shaking. Because this wasn't just about money anymore. I knew it in my gut. That person in the woods had been after *me*.

CHAPTER
Thirteen

THE WISHING LOUNGE always made it easier to pretend Wishville was exactly what it sold itself as. Warm, safe, and twinkly. A little enchanted at the edges, like the town's charm could be nailed into place the way the artfully crooked shingles were nailed onto the bar's roof. Deliberate and whimsical, even though everyone knew crooked things leaked if you weren't careful.

Holden held the door for me, one hand settling at the small of my back as we stepped inside, and for a moment, the cold snapped off like a switch. Heat wrapped around us. The air smelled like spiced whiskey and rosemary fries, with a bite of citrus from someone's cocktail and the faint sweetness of cinnamon drifting from the bar.

I loved our date nights.

A low thrum of folk music played over the speakers, something with a steady drumbeat and a voice that sounded like pine smoke. Twinkling lights were strung across the ceiling in lazy loops, giving everything the soft illusion of being dipped in starlight. Patched leather booths lined the walls, worn and comfortable, like they'd absorbed a thousand small-town confessions and never repeated a word.

"Okay," Holden said under his breath as we walked in, his eyes sweeping instinctively over the room. "This is actually nice."

I smiled softly, thinking, *And necessary.* We had made a promise to make time for date nights and to prioritize each other. "I told you, best bar food in town and second-best fries."

"Second?" He arched an eyebrow.

"The Wishbone Café's wedges are sacred," I said. "Willa would personally banish me if I said otherwise."

Holden's mouth tipped up as the hostess led us to a booth tucked into a corner that felt private without being isolated. We slid in across from each other. He shrugged off his coat, then reached across the table and took my hand.

His thumb brushed my knuckles. "You okay?"

I inhaled slowly. Even the air here was different, warmer, softer, and layered with comfort. It would've been easy to let it lull me into believing the day hadn't happened.

"I'm here," I said honestly. "That's the best I can promise right now."

He didn't push. Holden just held my hand, steady like a dock post in rough water, staring tenderly at me with his stormy gray eyes.

The waitress came by, cheerful and efficient, and Holden ordered a whiskey flight like a man with refined tastes instead of the guy who still preferred diner coffee and straightforward beer. I appreciated his effort, but I liked the straightforward guy just fine. I ordered something citrusy and pink because I wanted something fun and festive to take my mind off my worries.

When we were alone again, with just the folk music, the soft clink of glassware, and the low murmur of other conversations, I let my shoulders drop a fraction. It felt like the world had narrowed to patched leather and starlight.

Holden watched me for a beat longer, then said quietly, "Talk to me, Lyra."

I took a sip. The cocktail tasted like grapefruit, wintergreen, and false calm, but I knew there was always calm before the storm. *"The Snow Fort Competition,"* I started, knowing I couldn't escape my worries, so I might as well talk through them with the person who could help me best.

He exhaled like he'd been waiting for the inevitable. "Something happened."

"Supplies went missing, and not in a way that made sense." I kept my voice low, aware of how words carried in small spaces. "A lantern disappeared off the hook."

Holden's gaze sharpened. "Stolen?"

"Maybe. Or it was moved. But the timing seemed wrong." I traced the rim of my glass with one finger, grounding myself in something physical. "Elliot was acting strange."

Holden leaned in slightly. "Strange how?"

"He was moving too fast and eager. Like he was trying to stay one step ahead of something." I paused, choosing my words carefully. "There were new crates by the supply shed with clean plastic and no town tags. He said they were donations dropped off before sunrise."

Holden's jaw tightened. "Before Finch unlocked the shed."

I nodded once.

Holden didn't swear out loud, but I saw it in the flex of his jaw. "That means the crates weren't checked or logged. Anything could have been stored in them."

"Like more poison. And someone could have lied about what was in them," I said softly. "Finch isn't the type to notice someone lying to him unless it hits him in the face."

Holden's hand tightened around mine. "What about the tins you mentioned earlier? On the ski loop."

I felt a chill creep up my spine despite the warmth in the booth. "The cross-country loop had a cash tin on the curve instead of the rest stop like the others. And when I checked it, the lid was ajar and it was empty. Someone had dragged it off the path slightly, like they didn't want it seen until after the race ended."

Holden's eyes narrowed as if he could read my mind. "And you felt watched."

I nodded again, slower this time. "There were boot prints, not ski boots, crossing the trail and heading into the trees."

Holden's posture shifted in a way I recognized when he moved from boyfriend on a date to Chief of Police. His shoulders squared. "You should tell Doug about this since it involves official WishFest business."

"I did." My voice caught a little, and I hated that it did. "I reported everything from Elliot and the missing supplies to the tin and the boot prints. Doug promised he'd look into it."

Holden's expression didn't soften. "Doug's overwhelmed."

"I know," I said quickly. "I don't want to blow things out of proportion and cause unnecessary public panic." I looked down at our joined hands. "I've been on edge since Violet…" I could feel my voice get smaller. "Holden, what if the poison really was meant for me. I mean, am I imagining things?"

Holden's thumb brushed my knuckles again, slow and steady. "You're not imagining anything."

The waitress brought our food then. Rosemary fries piled high in a basket, burgers that smelled like garlic and char, and Holden's whiskey flight arranged neatly on a wooden tray. For a few minutes we did what we were here to do: eat, taste, and laugh lightly when Holden made a face at the smokey whiskey. But even in those small moments, my mind kept looping back to lantern hooks and boot prints and Elliot's too-bright smile.

When Holden reached for my fries, I slapped his hand out of instinct.

He grinned. "Still alive in there?"

"Don't test me when it comes to my food," I said teasingly, and for a heartbeat, it felt almost normal.

Almost.

By the time we paid and stepped outside, the wind hit us hard, stripping the warmth off our skin. Snow drifted in thin, lazy spirals beneath the streetlights. Downtown Wishville glowed with the festival décor of garlands, lanterns, and twinkle lights wrapped around lampposts like the town had dressed itself up to prove it deserved happiness. They were slightly battered by the weather, but still holding on.

Holden pulled his coat tighter and glanced around automatically.

The Wishing Lounge sat on the edge of downtown, close enough to the central square that you could hear faint distant music, but far enough that the alleyways felt quieter, narrower, and edged with shadow.

We had barely reached the sidewalk when I saw movement.

A man stepped out of the alley between the restaurant and *Wishville Wheels*, Sparks's mechanic shop. The man's shoulders were hunched, and his face half hidden beneath a knit hat. It was Percy Johnson.

I frowned.

Holden saw him at the same time. His hand dropped instinctively to where his holster would be if he were on duty. He wasn't, but Holden didn't need a badge to be a threat.

Percy froze for a fraction of a second, then lifted his hands slightly in mock innocence.

"Evening," he said, his voice too casual.

And then I saw the other movement...the shadow sliding away in the opposite direction.

A hooded figure walking fast with their head down, disappearing toward the darker stretch near the side street.

My pulse kicked hard.

Holden stepped forward. "Percy."

Percy's eyes glanced at me, then away. "Chief."

"I'm not on duty," Holden said. "But you are still you."

Percy huffed out a laugh. "That's poetic."

I stepped closer, my breath fogging as I sent a pointed glance toward where the hooded figure had been. "Who was that?"

Percy blinked as if he genuinely didn't understand the question. "Who was what?"

"The person in the hood," I said, keeping my voice steady.

"Walking away. You came out of the alley, and they came out the other side."

Percy glanced over his shoulder like he was seeing the street for the first time. "I didn't see anyone."

Holden's eyes narrowed. "Funny. We did."

Percy's jaw flexed. "I was just checking something."

"What?" I asked.

He shrugged. "Thought I heard a noise. Someone messing around back there. You know how small towns are. Kids. Vandals."

The excuse landed like a stone. Too generic and too easy.

Holden took another step, close enough that Percy's bravado faltered just a notch. "You don't work here, Percy. You don't have a reason to be behind Sparks's shop."

Percy lifted his chin. "Maybe I do."

"And maybe you don't," I said. "But I'm done with maybes. Violet is dead. She was poisoned, Percy. What did you take from the work shed? What kind of Styrofoam was in the salt bin?"

Something flashed across Percy's face like anger, guilt, or something else. It was gone so quickly I couldn't name it. "I didn't see any Styrofoam. Just trash. I don't know anything about poison, and I didn't kill her," he snapped.

Holden didn't react outwardly, but I felt the shift in the air. "We didn't say you did."

Percy's nostrils flared. "You're thinking it."

"I'm thinking you're where you shouldn't be," Holden said. "Again."

Percy looked past us toward the glow of downtown like he wanted to walk away and couldn't decide if it would make him look guilty. "I'm leaving," he muttered.

"You didn't answer Lyra's question about the person in the alley," Holden said.

Percy's eyes cut back to mine. "I don't know who that was."

I held his stare. "Then why were you back there?"

He swallowed hard, then forced a shrug. "I told you, I thought

I heard something. Nothing was there. End of story. Are we done now?"

No, but I nodded once anyway.

Holden stared at him for another long beat, then stepped back slightly. "Go," he said. "And stay away from dark alleys and work sheds. They're not safe."

Percy didn't need to be told twice. He shoved his hands into his pockets and walked off, his boots crunching hard like he wanted the sound to prove he wasn't sneaking around. The moment he disappeared around the corner, the mechanic shop door swung open. Sparks stepped out, wiping his hands with a rag, his fingertips sizzling and breath steaming in the cold.

His eyes shot between us, assessing. "So, Percy's back again, I see."

Holden's mouth tightened. "Back again?"

Sparks snorted. "Several times. Always comes out of that alley like he's looking for something…or waiting for someone."

My stomach sank. "Why didn't you tell us?"

Sparks lifted a shoulder. "Didn't know if it was worth your time. Everyone's crawling out of the woodwork during WishFest. But yeah, this one doesn't sit right."

Holden's gaze hardened. "Any info is worth my time."

Sparks nodded, then his eyes shifted to me. "You okay, Lyra?"

I forced a smile that probably looked more like a grimace. "I'm fine."

He didn't look convinced. "I'll keep watch. Cameras are pointed at the alley anyway. And I can have Weylan watch from above."

A thin sliver of relief slipped through me. Weylan in the sky meant a wider view. Less shadow.

Holden nodded once. "Do it."

Sparks jerked his chin. "You got it." He retreated back into the shop, the door closing with a solid thunk that sounded like a promise.

Holden turned to me, and the hardness in his eyes softened slightly. "You ready to go home?"

I looked down the street where the hooded figure had vanished. "Yeah," I admitted. "This has been one long day."

Holden's hand found mine again, warm even through our gloves. "I won't let anything happen to you, Lyra."

I squeezed his fingers, appreciating the gesture, but I wasn't naïve. A human was no match for the kind of threat I suspected I was up against as a half-blood. As we walked away from the glow of *The Wishing Lounge*, the folk music faded behind us. I couldn't shake the feeling that the festival lights weren't keeping the darkness out.

They were just making it easier for the darkness to choose where to settle.

The next morning, the night crowd had gone but the festival itself hadn't slept. It had simply shifted. Lanterns still glowed softly in the pale morning light, their flames smaller now, steadier. Snow creaked underfoot with that particular brittle sound it made when the temperature dropped just a few degrees more.

I stood at the edge of the green with LuLu beside me, Vex perched on my shoulder like a living shadow, and Fenrin weaving between our legs in her ginger cat form, with her tail high and amber eyes curious. Steam rose from our mugs as we walked, our breath fogging the air.

"This is the calm before everyone realizes something's still wrong," LuLu said lightly, blowing on her coffee.

I snorted. "You say that like it's not every morning in Wishville."

She smiled, but her eyes were clear and focused.

We headed first toward the *Candle-Making Workshop*, tucked beneath a canvas awning strung with evergreen garlands. Long tables were lined with jars of wax, trays of herbs, and small bowls of essential oils—pine, clove, orange peel, and cedar. The air smelled warm and comforting, making me think of kitchens and safety and hands wrapped around mugs.

A volunteer waved cheerfully. "Morning, Lyra! Everything survived the night."

"So far," I said. "Any issues?"

She shook her head. "Just one spilled batch. And Belle tried to convince someone to stir counterclockwise for better energy."

Behind her, the Wellies clustered with Tilly adjusting a scarf that didn't need adjusting, Dot carefully labeling jars with exact precision, and Belle sniffing the air dramatically.

"Counterclockwise disrupts intention," Belle said firmly. "I don't make the rules."

Dot pushed her glasses up. "Actually, you do. You made them up last night."

Tilly leaned toward me conspiratorially. "My spleen journal told us to experiment."

"With chaos?" I asked.

"Always," Tilly said brightly.

Vex purred. *I support their methodology.*

Across the table, Dana Snowe stood quietly, her hands wrapped around a candle jar she hadn't poured yet. Her eyes looked tired, red-rimmed and shadowed, but her posture was composed. Controlled. Grief pressed tightly beneath a smooth surface.

I hesitated, then stepped closer. "Dana. I'm glad you came out this morning."

She offered a small smile. "Violet loved the candle workshop. Said it smelled like Granny's house."

"I'm sorry," I said softly.

She nodded once. "Me too."

Fenrin brushed against Dana's boots, then circled back to LuLu, her tail swaying in support.

We moved on to the *Frost Charms Station*, where delicate glass vials hung from twine, catching the light like trapped snowflakes.

Inside each vial were tiny silver charms, bits of quartz, and etched slips of paper where participants wrote intentions like protection, clarity, and warmth.

A volunteer beamed. "We've had a lot of people asking for protection charms."

LuLu's pen paused mid-note. "Any reason?" she asked gently.

The volunteer shrugged. "Just…a murderer on the loose and all the stealing going on lately. People don't feel safe."

"Our police chief is doing his best to change that, and we're here to ease your minds in any way we can."

She thanked us, and we moved on.

At the far edge of the green, the *Knit-Along Circle* glowed around a low bonfire. Yarn baskets sat open, with steam rising from hands as needles clicked rhythmically. The fire crackled softly, the scent of burning birch cutting through the cold.

The Wellies had migrated here, naturally. Dot was correcting someone's stitch tension. Belle was dramatically recounting Violet's last performance to a captive audience. Tilly was attempting to knit with her gloves still on.

"This is impossible," she declared. "Winter is hostile to art."

"Take off the gloves," Dot said.

"And risk exposure?" Tilly gasped.

Dana sat on one of the benches nearby, her hands wrapped around a mug, staring into the fire like she was reading something there.

LuLu stopped walking.

I felt it before I saw it…the way the air around her shifted, like pressure was dropping. Her breath hitched. Her eyes unfocused.

"Lu," I said quietly.

She didn't respond. Her grip tightened on her mug, and her knuckles whitened. Vex went rigid on my shoulder. Fenrin froze mid-step.

Oh no, Vex murmured. *It's happening.*

LuLu swayed slightly, her eyes turning glassy and lips parting like she was about to speak but couldn't find the words. The world seemed to narrow around her as if the crackle of the fire was too loud, the knit needles too sharp, and the smell of smoke suddenly overwhelming.

"LuLu?" Tilly asked. "You okay, honey?"

LuLu gasped. The mug slipped from her hands, shattering on the packed snow.

Everyone turned.

She blinked hard, her breath coming fast, then she pressed a hand to her chest. "I…sorry, I'm fine. Just dizzy."

I stepped in immediately and put one arm around her, trying to think of what to say. "You need fresh air."

"I *am* in fresh air," she muttered weakly.

"Oh, right."

Dana stood abruptly. "Do you need to sit?"

LuLu shook her head. "No. I'm…" She swallowed. "I'm okay." Her eyes met mine.

And I knew. "Give us a minute," I said gently to the group. "Too much excitement before coffee."

The Wellies nodded in unison, instantly solemn.

"Psychic spill," Dot whispered knowingly.

"Rude of the universe," Belle added with a shake of her head.

Tilly crossed herself with her needles, then hesitated and crossed herself again just in case.

Dana lingered a second longer, worry flickering across her face. "If you need anything, give me a holler."

"I will," I said. "Thank you."

She nodded and returned to the bench.

I guided LuLu a few steps away, behind the candle tent where the wind was blocked and the sounds dulled. She leaned into me, breathing shakily.

"What did you see?" I murmured.

She swallowed hard. "Two ominous shadows."

My stomach dropped. "Two?"

"Two hooded figures," she whispered. "Separate. Moving

differently. One was…angry, focused, and personal. Like it was circling something precious."

"And the other?"

LuLu's hands trembled. "The other was methodical, counting, and timing. It didn't care who got hurt as long as the system worked. It's the two hooded figures we're looking for. They definitely don't know about each other and only cross paths because the festival put them in the same place."

"So that confirms they aren't connected. Could you tell who these people are?" I asked.

She shrugged faintly. "I'm not sure. That was all I saw."

Vex shifted closer. *Two separate predators. One feast.*

I set my jaw. "It was hard enough trying to find one hooded figure, but two feels nearly impossible, especially when they aren't connected."

LuLu squeezed my hand. "We'll find them, but Lyra, I don't know if this is related… someone is watching you in both visions."

My heart thudded hard. I straightened, forcing my shoulders back as the sounds of WishFest swelled again around us, bringing me back to reality. The click of needles, the laughter, the hiss of candles being poured were what I focused on. I had to keep this festival running.

"Then we keep going," I said quietly. "Same plan as always, just more on guard."

LuLu managed a shaky smile. "Act normal?"

"Exactly," I said. "Give them an opportunity to come to me. They have no idea what I'm capable of." We stepped back into the glow of the festival, where the Wellies immediately resumed their antics and the fire crackled like nothing beneath it had changed.

But I knew better now.

CHAPTER
Fourteen

WISHVILLE'S COLD WAS FAMILIAR. Woodsmoke, pine, and frost that bit at your knuckles and made your breath plume. Elarion's cold was older. It pressed in like a living thing, layered with magic and memory, scented with mineral-rich water and luminous moss. The air hummed faintly, a vibration I felt in my bones.

We didn't arrive dressed as ourselves out of respect for Elarion. Holden, Calderis, and I wore our ceremonial robes, the fabric heavier than everyday wear, woven with sigils that caught the bioluminescent light and reflected it back in muted silver.

Holden's robe was deep slate blue, structured and precise, the insignia of The Covenant Three stitched at the shoulder. It still seemed strange on him, still new, but definitely earned. Calderis's was darker, nearly black, edged in pale metal that marked him unmistakably as Chief Enforcer. Mine flowed in layered whites and silvers, the Guardian's mantle settling against my shoulders like a familiar weight.

LuLu stood beside us, her hands folded nervously at her waist. She looked magnificent in Serena's robe, with her long dark hair swirling around her shoulders like silk under water. My mother was smaller than me, slightly shorter and more narrow through the shoulders. The robe was still long on LuLu, but a far better fit than mine would have been. The fabric shimmered softly, old magic woven into every strand, responding to her presence with a faint glow like moonlight on water.

LuLu looked…right. Not just a human trying to fit in, but a special human with a psychic gift who had been chosen.

"You don't have to do this," I said softly, though it was far too late for that.

LuLu lifted her chin, her eyes shining with nerves and resolve. "I do. Calderis didn't just choose me. I chose him, knowing who he is and where he came from. If he's going to tell them about us, then I'm not hiding. I will be right there by his side."

"As you should be." I smiled and squeezed her hand.

Fenrin, who had insisted on coming, shifted into her ginger cat form before we crossed and now prowled the edge of the stone platform like she owned Elarion outright. Vex perched on my shoulder, perfectly content, his tail swaying lazily.

Calderis appeared beside us without ceremony, as he always did, one moment shadow and the next solid. His silver hair hung long and loose, alive with movement as his clear-glass eyes swept over us.

"You are sure?" I asked him quietly.

His jaw flexed. "I have delayed long enough."

Holden adjusted the fall of his robe, clearly uncomfortable but determined. "Just so we're clear, if your father tries to incinerate me with his eyes, I'm standing behind you."

LuLu snorted despite herself.

Calderis arched a brow at Holden, then his gaze fixed on LuLu. For a heartbeat, something softer flickered there—pride, maybe, or gratitude. "We will go to my home and host dinner properly."

Holden muttered, "Onward, Chief. Let's get this over with."

Elarion unfolded around us as we moved. Crystalline structures rose like frozen music, with bioluminescent vines curling along stone archways and water channels winding through the city like veins of light. People noticed us. Heads turned. Whispers followed.

And they noticed LuLu most of all.

Calderis's home sat at the edge of a quieter district, carved into a rise of silver-veined stone. The door recognized his blood, opening with a soft pulse of light beneath his palm. Inside, the air was warm and fragrant with cedar smoke and crushed herbs. Calderis moved with precise efficiency, hanging his cloak, then smoothing the front of his robe like he was preparing for battle rather than dinner.

"You're nervous," LuLu said gently.

"I am not," he replied instantly.

"Your body says otherwise," she said. "It's doing that tense thing again."

"It's not," he said.

"It is," Holden and I said together.

Calderis exhaled through his nose and turned toward the kitchen space without another word. Dinner preparation felt surreal. He cooked with the same careful focus he brought to enforcement. Thin cuts of venison-like meat, marinated in herbs that smelled of rosemary and smoke, cooked over a pale blue heat that never flamed. I chopped luminous root vegetables that stained my fingertips faintly silver. LuLu arranged jeweled fruit on a platter with hands that trembled just enough to notice. Holden set the table because I told him to, muttering about Dweller plates being "aggressively ceremonial."

When everything was ready, Calderis stood still for a moment, breathing as if centering himself. "I will call them," he said.

The crystal embedded in the wall pulsed once.

The knock came almost immediately, short and formal.

Vaerion entered first. Calderis's father was tall and lean, his ceremonial leather dark and severe, silver stitching marking his rank and lineage. His storm-glass eyes swept the room, taking in Holden's robe, mine, and then...LuLu.

His gaze stopped and then hardened.

Elanith followed, elegant and composed, her silver hair braided down her back. Her eyes softened briefly when they met mine, then slid to LuLu and widened as they registered the robe. Serena's robe. My mother had been her friend. Her gaze turned sad for a moment before she brushed it off and smiled faintly with a nod.

Lumira entered last, younger than Calderis, her silver-blue hair loose around her shoulders and moving as if in a dance. Her eyes widened slightly when she saw LuLu, then warmed with immediate understanding.

"Brother," she said with glee. "Thank you for inviting us. It's been too long since we've had a family dinner."

Vaerion said nothing.

Calderis bowed his head towards her, and then we all sat. He stood behind LuLu's chair and pulled it out for her, a deliberate, unmistakable gesture. His mother's eyes warmed, but Vaerion watched like the act itself was a provocation.

"I have chosen," Calderis said without preamble.

Silence dropped hard.

LuLu's hand trembled, and Calderis covered it on the table protectively.

Elanith's voice was calm, and her smile overly tight. "Chosen what, my son?"

"Chosen her," Calderis said. "LuLu is my life partner."

Vaerion's eyes narrowed. "A human?"

LuLu lifted her chin. "Yes, but not just any human. I have talents of my own."

Lumira's lips curved faintly. "I like her."

Vaerion rose abruptly, anger rolling off him. "This is not permitted. You are Chief Enforcer. Covenant. Bound by duty—"

"I am bound by truth," Calderis cut in.

"You bring a human into our world, jeopardizing the treaty," Vaerion snapped, his eyes glaring at the robe. "And in *her* robe."

Elanith sucked in a breath but said nothing.

"The treaty is not in jeopardy. She has been a help, and you know it. As for the robe, it was loaned to LuLu by *Serena's* daughter," Calderis said, his voice dangerously quiet.

"Do not speak her name. She is dead to us," Vaerion growled.

"She is still my mother," I said quietly but firmly.

Holden shifted to a ready position. I reached beneath the table and stilled him.

LuLu's voice trembled but held. "I didn't ask for this dinner to hurt anyone. I simply wanted to get to know you. To know Calderis's world."

Vaerion laughed once, sharp and bitter. "You have no right. You don't belong here and never will."

Calderis surged to his feet. "Enough."

Vaerion rose and faced him fully now. "You disgrace our bloodline."

"Do not speak of disgrace," Calderis said.

Lumira stood too. "Father—"

"Silence," Vaerion roared. "This will not stand."

"This is *my* life," Calderis said firmly. "Only I will choose how I live it."

"Then choose wisely, for there is no turning back." Vaerion stared at him for a long, searing moment...then turned and strode out.

The door closed hard.

Elanith remained frozen for a breath, her eyes shining with restrained grief. She rose, smoothing her robes. "Give him time," she whispered, more to Calderis than anyone. Then she followed Vaerion out, her footsteps quick and controlled.

The house fell silent.

Lumira stayed. She poured herself a glass of water, unshaken, then looked at LuLu with clear, steady eyes. "You're brave. That will suit you well here."

LuLu swallowed. "I don't feel brave."

"Good," Lumira replied. "Brave people rarely do." She turned to Calderis. "He will come around."

"When?" Calderis asked.

"When he realizes duty without love is just obedience," Lumira said softly. "And you were never built for obedience."

Calderis closed his eyes.

I exhaled slowly, the weight of ceremony pressing down on all of us. Outside, Elarion hummed on, ancient and watching. And nothing—absolutely nothing—would be the same again.

The quiet after Vaerion stormed out felt wrong in Calderis's house. Not peaceful, just hollow. The air still smelled like roasted herbs and the citrusy sweetness of the jeweled fruit LuLu had arranged with trembling hands. Plates sat half-touched. The pale blue heat source glowed steadily as if nothing had happened, as if Elarion itself refused to acknowledge emotional mess.

Lumira had offered her calm reassurance, *give him time, he'll come around,* but I could still feel the fracture in the room like a hairline crack in glass. Calderis sat too still. LuLu's smile had gone from brave to brittle.

Holden leaned close to me and murmured, "They need space."

I nodded. He was right.

So was the part of me that didn't want to leave them alone in the aftermath of that kind of rejection. But LuLu's fingers had already woven through Calderis's under the table. And Calderis, who never reached for comfort in public, had squeezed her hand tighter.

That was their moment to have.

"I'm going to take Holden to my house," I said quietly, my voice careful. "We'll be nearby if you need us."

Lumira's gaze softened. "Serena's house?"

My chest tightened at the name. I nodded.

Calderis looked up sharply. "You do not need to—"

"Yes," I said gently, cutting him off before he could argue from duty instead of emotion.

LuLu's eyes met mine, grateful and glossy. "Thank you," she whispered.

Lumira said her goodbyes and left first.

Holden stood, smoothing the front of his ceremonial robe awkwardly. Even after several months of being part of this world in secret, he still wore Elarion's symbols like he was afraid they might burn him. "Try not to start a civil war while we're gone," he muttered, attempting humor.

Calderis's mouth twitched. "No promises."

We left quietly, stepping out into Elarion's luminous night. The city looked even more unreal after the tension of dinner. Crystal towers glowed from within, channels of water reflected starlight like liquid glass, and bioluminescent vines curled along bridges.

Holden walked close to me, his posture alert but less tense now, like the anger had drained out of him and left only concern. "You okay?" he asked.

I considered lying. Instead, I blew out a puff of air. "I'm…Elarion-tired."

He huffed softly. "That a thing?"

"It is when this place reminds you of everything you've lost," I said, my voice low. "And everything you're responsible for."

Holden's hand found mine. "Lead the way."

My mother's house sat farther from the central district, tucked along a quieter ridge where the stone was darker and the flora glowed softer, as if even the realm respected the need for privacy there. The path leading to it was lined with pale trees whose leaves shimmered like thin frost. The air smelled like water and moss and something floral I couldn't name.

The house itself was smaller than Calderis's, built into the stone like it had grown there rather than been constructed. The doorway was framed in carved symbols I used to trace with my fingers as a child. The windows were rounded and deep-set, like watchful eyes.

I paused at the threshold.

Vex hopped down from my shoulder and prowled forward,

his tail high as if he'd done this a hundred times. Fenrin, still in her ginger cat form, slipped past him, her nose twitching, then she rubbed against my ankle.

Holden stood beside me, silent.

"It still feels like she'll open the door," I admitted.

Holden's voice was gentle. "Does it ever stop?"

"No," I said. "It just changes shape."

I pressed my palm to the door. It opened with a soft pulse of light, recognizing my blood.

Warmth greeted us immediately, subtle, like the house had been holding onto it for centuries. The air smelled faintly of dried herbs and something citrusy, like my mother had once simmered peel and spice just because she liked the scent.

The main room was tidy like abandoned places always were, with everything exactly where it had been left, untouched by time but heavy with it. A woven rug lay near the hearth with pale patterns forming spirals. Shelves lined the walls with carved bowls and crystals and stacks of bound journals.

Holden's gaze swept the space with a cop's instinct, then softened. "She lived here alone?"

"Not always," I said. "My father was here too for a little while." I swallowed. "Before he had to leave."

Holden's brow furrowed. "Because of the treaty."

"Because of what my mother had to do to keep us alive," I corrected quietly.

I moved toward the hearth, my fingers brushing the stone mantel. The surface was cool, but the touch sparked memories. My mother sitting there with me, braiding my hair, humming a song that sounded like water over rocks. My father's laugh, low and warm. The way he'd lifted me onto his shoulders like I weighed nothing.

Homesickness hit like a sudden drop in temperature.

I turned away quickly, as if movement could shake it off.

Holden followed without pressing. He stopped near a shelf

stacked with journals and ran his fingers along the spines. "You miss it," he said.

"I do," I admitted. "More than I let myself." I sat on the edge of the rug, pulling the robe tighter around me. "Wishville is home now too. But sometimes…sometimes I walk through town, and it feels like I'm wearing someone else's skin. Human festivals. Human gossip. Human problems."

"But you're half human."

"Yes."

"And then you come here and it's…what?" Holden asked.

I hesitated. "It's another part of me that makes sense."

Holden lowered himself beside me, his robe pooling awkwardly on the floor. "I don't miss Boston," he said, surprising me.

I blinked. "You don't?"

He snorted softly. "No. I miss the food sometimes, and the ocean." His mouth tipped up, then faded. "But I don't miss the city. It always felt like…noise."

I studied him. "But you miss your parents."

His jaw tightened. "Yeah."

I waited. Holden didn't talk about his past very often.

"My mom died when I was little," he said quietly. "I don't even remember her voice the way I want to. I remember the smell of her shampoo and this gold bracelet she wore that clicked against the counter when she cooked." He stared at the floor for a beat, like he could see it there. "My dad raised me. He was… steady. Not perfect, but steady."

My chest tightened. I reached for his hand, and he let me take it.

"And then he died because of me," Holden said. The words dropped heavy.

"Holden—"

"It was a guy I put away," he continued, his voice flat like he'd rehearsed saying it without breaking. "Convicted. Sentenced. Everyone said it was a clean case. Justice served." His fingers curled around mine. "He got out on a technicality, then came after my father because he couldn't get to me."

"I'm so sorry." I knew what it was like to lose a parent. First, my father. And now, even though my mother was alive, I still felt as if I'd lost her.

Holden's eyes were dark now, stormy. "He broke into my dad's house. My father fought back. He wasn't supposed to. He was supposed to call the police. But he was stubborn, and he thought he could handle it." Holden's jaw clenched. "He couldn't."

Silence pressed in. I squeezed his hand tighter, feeling the pulse there, steady and alive.

"It eats at me," he admitted. "Every day. Because the job doesn't just take your time, it takes your people. And I keep thinking if I'd done something different, if I'd watched the case closer, if I'd pushed harder, if I'd—"

"You didn't kill your father," I said fiercely.

Holden's throat bobbed. "But my choices put him in the path."

I shook my head, tears pricking hot behind my eyes. "Holden..."

He turned to me, his voice rough. "That's why I'm so determined nothing happens to you, Lyra. Because you're in danger just by existing. And I—" His breath hitched. "I can't lose another person I love."

My chest ached so hard it felt like breaking. "I love you, too," I whispered then leaned in and pressed my forehead to his. "You're not alone. Not anymore."

He closed his eyes, and for a moment, the world narrowed to breath and warmth and the quiet crackle of a fire that wasn't lit. Then Fenrin jumped onto the low table with a soft thump, startling us both. She sniffed a stack of journals, then pawed at the top one with irritating insistence.

"Fen," I murmured. "Not now."

She pawed again, harder.

Vex leaped up beside her, his blue eyes bright. *She wants that one.*

Holden pulled back slightly, clearing his throat like he'd been caught being human. "Is she trying to tell us something?"

Fenrin's tail flicked like a flag snapping in the wind. She pawed the journal again, then looked directly at me with unblinking amber eyes.

I exhaled. "Fine."

I rose and crossed to the table, lifting the journal she'd singled out. The cover was pale leather, worn at the corners, and the stitching along the spine was unmistakably my mother's work. Precise, delicate, and stubbornly beautiful.

My fingers trembled as I opened it. The first page held my mother's handwriting. Slanted, elegant, and slightly cramped, like her mind always ran faster than her pen. I scanned the entry dates. Old. Much older than anything I'd ever seen.

I frowned. How had I missed this one?

"Lyra?" Holden asked softly.

"I'm okay," I lied automatically, then corrected myself. "I've never seen this before, and I've been over every inch of this place. Maybe she came back recently and put it here so I would find it."

Fenrin hopped down, seeming satisfied.

Vex sat upright and rolled his blue eyes.

I flipped through pages. There were notes on seasonal bindings, warnings about cracks in old seals, observations about the way treaties shifted when humans forgot their weight. And then I saw it. A heading written in firm, dark strokes: **THE PALE ACCORD**

My breath stopped. I'd heard the word *accord* in vague references. Elders muttering, ceremonial oaths, and half-spoken warnings...but never this. Never *Pale Accord*. Never as something separate from the treaty we all believed governed the relationship between Elarion and Wishville.

Holden leaned closer. "What is that?"

"I don't know," I whispered.

I read on. My mother's writing grew tighter, angrier, as if the words themselves cost her.

> *The true covenant was never forged to restrain the Guardian, but to preserve balance itself. It named the Well as a shared sanctuary, not dominion. A threshold between worlds, not a leash upon one. The Accord safeguarded the line of Balance-Bearers, never a single heir. No blood was meant to stand alone. The Elders rewrote what they feared. They altered the spoken law, erased the half-blood clause, and entombed the original Accord, sealing the proof within the hidden Accord Hall.*

My stomach dropped so hard I felt dizzy. "Balance-Bearers? It looks like I was never meant to be the only half-blood."

"Wow, so let me get this straight. The current treaty is a lie, and there was an original treaty called *The Pale Accord*? And now it's buried in a place called *The Accord Hall*?" Holden repeated.

I nodded and kept reading, my heart hammering.

> *Vaerion believes in the recited treaty that now stands. He enforces what he was given. But the original Elders…they keep The Pale Accord locked deep. They fear that it will change things for the worse if it is discovered. The very first Elder nearly destroyed both worlds when he kidnapped a human and tried to unnaturally make himself the only half-blood with all the power. It killed them both and the entity emerged, forever looking for the perfect host in Lyra.*

I froze.

Holden's voice was careful. "Does Calderis know this?"

"I don't think so," I said, my voice sounding thin. "I've never heard of it. Calderis has never mentioned it." I looked up, my mind racing. "But my mother knew. She knew the treaty was altered."

Holden's jaw tightened. "And if that's true…"

"It means she was right, and the Elders lied," I whispered.

"About what the Covenant Three are. About what I'm allowed to be. About...everything." Cold spread through me. I closed the journal slowly, my fingers numb.

Holden searched my face. "You need to tell Calderis."

I swallowed hard. "Not yet."

His brow furrowed. "Lyra—"

"No," I said, sharper than I intended. I forced my voice back down. "Not until we have proof. A journal entry isn't enough. Not against Elders or tradition or Vaerion. Especially not now." I glanced toward the door, toward the city beyond. "There's already tension between Calderis and his father. If I throw this at them without certainty, it will look like I'm trying to divide them."

Holden's gaze softened. "You're trying to protect Calderis."

"I'm trying to protect all of us," I corrected. "Because, if *The Pale Accord* exists, it changes the ground we're standing on. But I don't even know where *The Accord Hall* is. I don't know if Vaerion knows about it or if he's been lied to as well." I exhaled shakily. "I need to find it first. I need to see it, hold it, and bring it back."

Holden nodded slowly. "Okay. So, we find it."

I stared down at my mother's journal with my pulse roaring in my ears. Homesickness didn't feel like longing in that moment. It felt like a warning. Because my mother had left this here for a reason. And if she'd been right...then the story I'd been living in was built on a lie older than WishFest itself.

I looked at Holden and lowered my voice. "Promise me you don't tell Calderis yet."

Holden's hand tightened around mine. "I promise I won't say anything until we get proof first."

I nodded once. "Thank you."

He kissed my hand. "I've got you, Wells." Outside, Elarion hummed on, ancient, luminous, and indifferent. But inside my mother's silent house, a hidden truth had finally breathed again.

And it was going to change everything.

Fifteen

THE BELL above *Enchanted Strands* chimed like it was genuinely happy to see us, which was comforting considering the week we'd been having. Holden and I had wanted to give LuLu and Calderis some privacy, so we'd left early. I'd messaged Calderis telling him we weren't coming back, then I'd asked LuLu to meet me here today for some much-needed self-care.

Warm air rolled over me in a wave of blow-dryer heat, vanilla shampoo, and that sharp, clean chemical bite of hair color that always made me think of new beginnings and bad decisions. Everyone thought I had highlights with my burgundy, green, and gold streaks through my brown hair.

They had no clue everything on me was natural and from another realm.

The salon itself was peak Wishville cozy: honey-colored wood floors, plants that somehow stayed alive through Vermont winters, and mirrors framed in twinkle lights because apparently even hair appointments deserved ambiance during WishFest.

LuLu stomped snow off her boots like the snow had personally offended her, then peeled off her coat with the kind of violent efficiency that meant she was not here for small talk. She was here for some much-needed pampering after meeting Calderis's parents in Elarion last night.

I smiled at the receptionist, Kayla, who always wore winged eyeliner sharp enough to cut glass. "Two chairs. Whatever's available. We're here for…emotional maintenance."

Kayla's grin went sly. "Say less. You're in luck. Marcy's got an opening, and she lives for emotional maintenance." She winked.

LuLu muttered, "I do not live for emotional anything at the moment."

"And yet," I said, sliding her a look, "you're here."

"I'm here because if I don't take my mind off my problems, I'm going to commit a felony."

"A good hair scrub will do that," I said brightly.

Vex shifted on my shoulder, his black fur catching the light like someone had dusted him with starlight and regret. *Humans pay to be attacked by hands and scented water,* he observed in my mind. *Fascinating species.*

"Don't judge," I murmured aloud, then realized two stylists had looked up at the same time.

LuLu elbowed me and then smiled wide at them. "She talks to her cat when she's stressed. That's why she needs an emotional support animal."

"I was, um, just thinking with my face," I lied.

Vex's sparkling blue eyes narrowed. *That was not a face thought. That was a snarky sentence.*

The stylists looked at each other with raised brows, shrugged, and then went back to work.

Marcy appeared like she'd been conjured by gossip itself. She was mid-forties, with curly hair in a messy bun, a black smock, and the kind of warm competent smile that could make you confess your deepest secrets before you even sat down.

"Lyra Wells," she said, drawing my name out like it came with footnotes. "And LuLu Morales. You two look like you've been personally victimized by winter."

"We have," LuLu said flatly.

Marcy clapped her hands once. "Okay. Chairs. Capes. Tell me what we're doing. Root touch-up? Trim? Emotional reinvention bangs?"

LuLu froze. "Do not say bangs to me."

Marcy nodded solemnly. "Heard. No bangs. We do not make choices we can't take back."

I slid into the chair next to LuLu, the vinyl cool through my leggings, and let Marcy drape the cape around me. It fluttered down like a theatrical curtain. "Just a wash and trim for me. Nothing dramatic, and definitely no hair dye."

Marcy's gaze studied my face as if she could see the words *murder investigation* written across my forehead. "Honey, you don't get to say 'nothing dramatic' ever again. Not with those eyes."

LuLu made a sound that was somewhere between a laugh and a growl. "Can you shave my head? Like…emotionally?"

"Absolutely," Marcy said. "But only if we're doing it for empowerment and not a one-way ticket to Crazyville."

"Trust me, I just got back from there and have no intention of returning anytime soon." LuLu pointed at her. "I like her."

"Everyone likes Marcy," Kayla called from the desk without looking up. "She knows where the bodies are buried."

Marcy blinked innocently. "Metaphorically."

Vex's tail swished at my feet. *Possibly.*

Marcy guided LuLu toward the sinks first. "You look like you're holding a grudge between your shoulder blades. Come. We're going to rinse that out."

LuLu allowed herself to be steered with the weary resignation of someone who'd tried to be tough all morning and finally hit her limit. She reclined into the black bowl, and Marcy turned on the water.

The first gush hit LuLu's hair, warm and steady. Her eyes fluttered closed. "Oh," she breathed, like she'd been taken out by kindness.

I watched, amused and relieved in equal measure. LuLu

always ran hot. Fast mind, faster mouth, and a reporter's instinct to chase the truth even if it bit. Seeing her melt into a shampoo was like watching a storm cloud decide to be a pillow.

Marcy worked the product in with practiced hands. "So," she said casually, "are we talking about a man or a mother today?"

LuLu's eyes snapped open. "How did you—"

Marcy shrugged. "It's always a man or a mother. Or money. But you two have the kind of exhausted looks that screams *family drama*." Her gaze slid briefly to me. "No offense."

I gave her a thin smile. "None taken. That's…accurate."

LuLu let her head sink back again. "It's Calderis's parents."

"Calderis?" Marcy wrinkled her forehead.

"Sorry, I talk fast." LuLu laughed a little too loudly. "I mean Cal Deris."

Marcy's eyebrows rose, and then she shrugged. "Mmm. Parents. The toughest critics."

LuLu made a small, bitter sound. "It went…bad."

I leaned forward slightly with my hands folded in my lap under the cape. "Tell her."

LuLu's mouth tightened. "His father looked at me like I was a stray cat that wandered into his kitchen and tracked mud on the rugs."

Vex bristled. *Stray cats would never. Stray dogs are another matter entirely.*

LuLu continued, her voice low. "His father didn't yell. He didn't have to. He just…withheld approval like it was a blade. And his mother, well, she tried. She *did* try. But everything she said was filtered through this idea that Cal belongs to them and to his job. Like love is an inconvenience they tolerate if it follows their rules."

Marcy rinsed carefully, unhurried. "And Cal?"

LuLu swallowed. "He was…perfectly Cal. Calm. Controlled. Loyal. Except I could feel him vibrating underneath it all. Like he wanted to fight back, but he was trying not to tear something that can't be repaired."

My chest tightened, thinking of him in those ceremonial robes. How stiff he'd gone the moment his father's disappointment hit the room.

LuLu's voice softened, and that softness almost hurt to hear. "And then Lyra and Holden left us alone there so they could go to her mother's house, and we could have space. I thought it was going to be worse. I thought the moment they were gone, he would shut down, but he didn't."

Marcy scrubbed conditioner into LuLu's hair when someone called her to her office for a phone call. "Sit tight, hon. I'll be right back."

LuLu blinked rapidly, her eyes suddenly shiny. "He was so good, Lyra. He apologized. Not for his parents. He can't control them. But for putting me in that position. He held my hands and told me he was proud of me for not shrinking. He said he'd choose me again even if he had to do it a hundred times."

My throat went tight. "That's Calderis."

LuLu let out a shaky breath. "And then he said…he said he didn't want me to think he'd ever ask me to be less. That he knows I'm not made to fit into their idea of 'acceptable.'"

My voice went gentle. "And that scared you."

LuLu gave a humorless laugh. "It didn't scare me. It made me furious. Because why should love have to be a battle plan?"

I reached over and touched her forearm, warm through the cape. "It doesn't. Not between you two. The rest is just noise."

LuLu turned her head slightly so she could see me upside down. "It didn't feel like noise. It felt like a door closing between me and his family."

"It's not closed," I said. "It's stuck."

Vex added, *Some doors require claws.*

I ignored him. Mostly.

Marcy came back and finished rinsing LuLu's hair then wrapped it in a towel with a brisk tenderness. "Okay. Deep breath. We're going to blow-dry your rage into something sleek and intimidating."

LuLu sat up, towel-turbaned, looking like a furious woodland sprite. "I want it to be intimidating."

"It will be," Marcy promised.

Then she guided my head down to the sink. The water hit my scalp and I exhaled, long and slow, like my body had been waiting days for permission to let go. Marcy's fingers moved through my hair, and for a few seconds I listened to the salon noise of blow dryers, laughter, the snip of scissors, and someone gossiping about the mayor's tie being crooked at *Town Hall*.

Marcy leaned closer and lowered her voice. "Okay. Now your turn. What's between *your* shoulders?"

I opened my eyes and met my own reflection in the mirror across the room. Festival Chair. Guardian. Half-blood. The person who kept being told she was the only one. "Festival stress and Violet's murder." I shrugged. "I always have something to worry about."

"You poor dear. I'll fix you up good." Someone hollered in back with a crisis regarding the cash register. "Hold that thought," she said. "This is the trouble with being the owner of the salon. I'll be right back." She left again.

"I found something," I said quietly to LuLu. "But you can't tell Calderis, okay? At least not yet."

LuLu's chair turned a fraction, her attention sharpening instantly. "Okay."

I swallowed. "In my mother's house. A journal. One I hadn't seen before."

LuLu's brow furrowed. "Serena's?"

I nodded. "Fenrin basically assaulted a stack of journals until I picked the right one."

LuLu's mouth twitched despite herself. "That tracks."

I took a breath, and the words felt heavy even in a salon full of shampoo and normal life. "The journal says the current treaty isn't the original. It's been rewritten."

LuLu's face went still. "Lyra."

"I know." My hands curled in my lap beneath the cape. "She called the original treaty *The Pale Accord*."

LuLu's eyes widened. "That's real? That's not, like, a rebel slogan or something?"

"It's in her handwriting," I said, and my voice dipped lower. "She wrote that the true covenant wasn't made to restrain the Guardian. It was made to preserve balance. That the Well was meant to be shared. A threshold between worlds."

LuLu stared at me like she was trying to rearrange everything she thought she knew into a new shape.

"And," I continued, my pulse thudding, "she wrote something else. That the *Accord* safeguarded the line of…Balance-Bearers. Not a single heir."

LuLu's voice came out as a whisper. "So, you're not supposed to be the only half-blood."

"That's what it says." I swallowed hard. "*No blood was meant to stand alone.*" The salon suddenly felt too bright.

LuLu's hands clenched around her towel. "And the Elders—"

"—*rewrote what they feared*," I finished, because Serena's words had branded themselves into my brain. "They altered the spoken law, erased the half-blood clause, and sealed the proof in a place called *The Accord Hall*."

LuLu leaned forward, her eyes fierce. "Where is it?"

"I don't know," I admitted. "The journal says it's buried. Sealed. Hidden."

LuLu's voice sharpened. "And Vaerion?"

My stomach twisted. "That's the problem. I don't know what he knows. I don't know if he's protecting ignorance or protecting a lie."

LuLu's gaze flicked away, and I could see it—the dinner table, the way Vaerion's silence had cut. "You think he knows."

"I think it's possible," I said carefully. "But I'm not going to accuse him without proof. Not when Calderis is already bleeding from that relationship."

LuLu's throat bobbed. "So, you're not telling Calderis."

"Not yet," I said. "I will. I have to. But only when I can put something solid in his hands. *The Accord Hall. The Pale Accord.* Evidence he can't explain away, evidence his father can't dismiss as rebel propaganda."

LuLu's eyes softened, just a fraction. "That's...smart."

"Also cowardly," I muttered.

Vex's voice slid into my mind like a knife wrapped in velvet. *Strategic. Not cowardly. If you light a match in a room full of old grudges, do not act surprised when it explodes.*

I blew out a breath. "It feels like I'm standing on a fault line," I whispered. "One side is Wishville. Humans. A town that thinks the well is folklore. The other is Elarion. Elders. A world that thinks control is peace. And if the truth comes out...if humans find out about Dwellers...scientists will want to study them. Treasure hunters will tear the mountain open. People will exploit what they don't understand. It's a much different world today than it was back then."

LuLu's jaw tightened. "But keeping the truth buried lets the wrong people keep power."

"Yes," I said, the word tasting like iron. "Exactly."

"Technology," Marcy huffed, shaking her head as she returned and then finished shampooing, rinsing, and wrapping my hair in a towel. "Okay," she said briskly, snapping back into salon brightness. "We're going to dry you, trim you, and send you out looking like you sleep eight hours and don't carry burdens in your purse."

LuLu let out a thin laugh. "Can you do that for my soul, too?"

Marcy winked. "Sweetheart, I'm good, but I'm not magic."

Vex's tail snapped. *Incorrect. She is hair magic. Lesser, but still magic.*

"Marcy, it happened again," someone shouted from up front.

"For the love of Pete. Sorry, ladies. I'll be back in a jiffy." She hustled off, grumbling every step of the way.

LuLu looked at me then, really looked. "Lyra, if what you said is true, then someone went to extreme lengths to keep it hidden."

"I know," I said quietly.

"And your mother wanted you to find it."

"I think she did," I admitted, remembering the pale leather journal cover and the way Fenrin had insisted.

LuLu's voice went low and firm. "Then we don't stop until we find some answers."

"Agreed."

Marcy returned again and finished working her magic in silence, then spun LuLu's chair toward the mirror and fluffed her hair like she was preparing her for battle. "There," she announced. "You look like a woman who could make a man cry with one sentence."

LuLu blinked at her reflection. Then her mouth curved, small but real. "Good."

"And you," Marcy said, turning to me, "we're doing 'soft but unkillable.'"

I snorted. "That's accurate."

"Let me grab my big round blowout brush for this." She turned to the counter.

LuLu leaned closer, her voice dropping for my ears only. "Promise me something."

"What?"

"You won't go looking alone again."

My chest tightened, and I nodded once. "I promise."

Vex added, *And if either of you do, I will bite both your ankles.*

Marcy turned back to us with the biggest brush I'd ever seen as LuLu's eyes narrowed. "Did your cat just threaten us?"

"Wow, you really are stressed, honey. Cats don't talk." Marcy laughed.

I smiled knowingly at LuLu. "Of course not, silly." Her psychic gift was growing stronger if she could read Vex's mind now.

Vex's eyes gleamed in the mirror.

LuLu sighed. "He's definitely going to bite someone."

"Only, if necessary," I said, knowing Vex would have both our backs if it came down to it.

And as Marcy's scissors began their steady snip-snip rhythm and then the blow dryer roared to life, I let myself cling to the smallest, strangest comfort of all...for the first time since Winter WishFest cracked open and everything started bleeding truth, I didn't feel alone in it.

CHAPTER
Sixteen

BY AFTERNOON, WishFest had decided to pretend everything
was fine. The sky was a hopeful blue, sunlight flashing off the
snow like it had something to prove. Music drifted between
booths, the smell of cocoa and fried dough carried on the cold air,
and laughter rang out with just enough force to feel intentional. If
you squinted, Wishville almost felt like itself again. No tunnels,
no bodies, and no truths clawing their way up through the ice.

Almost.

I tucked my clipboard under my arm and headed toward the
Ice Block Hauling Competition, my boots crunching over packed
snow. The event had been a WishFest staple for decades, which
meant people loved it and no one questioned whether dragging
hundred-pound blocks of ice through a cheering crowd was a bad
idea.

Teams clustered at the starting line, ropes looped around
massive ice blocks carved from the frozen lake. The ice glowed
pale blue in the sunlight, slick and deceptively elegant. Finch
stood near the rope markers, his hat pulled low, already in the
middle of a debate with a volunteer.

"That rope needs to be six feet back," he said. "Six. Not 'about
six.'"

"It was closer last year," the volunteer protested.

"And last year someone nearly lost a kneecap," Finch shot back. "We learn or we suffer."

Maisie Flint from *The General Store* handed out gloves at a folding table, clucking at anyone who tried to compete bare-handed. "You'll thank me when you still have fingers," she told a teenage boy who looked deeply unconvinced.

Betsy Plum waved at me from beside the hot cider urn. "Lyra! We're ready when you are. I bribed the volunteers with cardamom knots."

"That's not bribery," I said. "That's leadership."

Elliot stood near Finch, holding the timing clipboard. He looked tired but focused, his knit cap pulled low and shoulders squared like he was determined not to let anything go wrong on his watch.

"Everything set?" I asked.

He nodded. "Path's salted. Ropes checked. No running starts this year."

Finch muttered, "I'm still mad about people cheating last year."

Ozzy wandered up with two paper cups of coffee and handed one to Edward, who accepted it with a nod. "Who's hauling first?" Ozzy asked. "I've got money on the high school kids." He didn't seem worried in the least. Now that I thought about it, I hadn't seen the two large men who had been following him when he first arrived in town since then.

Edward smiled faintly. "They have better leverage."

"See?" Ozzy said. "He gets it."

The whistle blew, and the first teams surged forward. Boots slipped. Ropes snapped taut. Someone shouted encouragement that immediately turned into a curse when they lost their footing. The crowd cheered, Betsy rang a cowbell, and Finch covered his eyes at least twice.

By the time the winners were announced—two breathless siblings who collapsed laughing into the snow—I was already moving on.

The *Ice Skate Relay Races* had taken over the frozen pond, cones marking lanes while music blasted from a portable speaker. Clara's friend Hannah knelt to tie skates for a little girl who insisted she was "basically Olympic-adjacent."

Trip Danderly stood near the start line, his wish flashlight in a holster at his waist and sparkly helmet crooked, vibrating with confidence. "I feel fast," he announced.

"You're standing still," Maisie called.

"Mentally fast," Trip clarified.

I scanned the perimeter while Finch followed, frowning at the cones. "Someone nudged these," he said.

"Accidentally?" I asked.

"Probably," he admitted. "Or the wind. Or Trip."

Trip struck a pose. "I deny everything."

Elliot crouched to straighten a cone, methodically and carefully. "All good now."

The relay kicked off in a blur of blades and laughter. One skater wiped out spectacularly, sliding into a snowbank to applause. Trip made it farther than expected before wobbling, windmilling, and going down in dramatic slow motion.

"I meant to do that!" he yelled from the ice.

"Of course you did," I muttered. By the time the final team finished, my cheeks ached from smiling on command. I checked my watch.

Polar Plunge.

Steam rose from the cut in the ice like the lake itself was reconsidering its life choices. Volunteers like Barry Bungalow from the yoga studio, Willa Hartman from *The Wishbone Café*, and two college kids home for winter break handed out towels and tried to look authoritative.

"This is a terrible idea," Finch said, for the sixth time.

"They signed waivers," Barry replied cheerfully.

"Waivers don't stop hypothermia."

Trip reappeared, already stripped down to a bathing suit and a

Wish Sheriff sash, vibrating with enthusiasm. "This is how you cleanse the soul after exercise."

"You could cleanse it with tea," I suggested.

"Or a shot of whiskey," Willa offered.

"Cowardice to both," Trip said boldly...and jumped. The splash echoed across the clearing. A beat passed...then Trip surfaced with a howl. "Yowzah, that's cold!" They hauled him out, wrapped him in blankets, and steered him toward a heater. His skin was already turning an alarming shade of blue. "I'm fine," he insisted, his teeth chattering. "Do I look fine?"

"No," Finch and I said together.

The crowd laughed, tension breaking. Someone handed Trip cocoa. He raised it in a shaky salute. "Five stars. I would do it again."

I lowered my clipboard to make a note...and felt *it*. That prickle at the base of my spine. The one that had nothing to do with cold. I looked around. At the far edge of the clearing, near the treeline where the snow lay untouched and the light thinned, a figure stood apart from the crowd. Hood up. Hands tucked into pockets. Standing still in a way that didn't belong at a festival built on motion and noise.

Watching.

"LuLu," I said quietly.

She followed my gaze and stiffened. "One of the hooded people."

The figure shifted, just slightly, like they'd realized they were being noticed.

I crouched and brushed my fingers against the snow. "Fenrin."

She surfaced as if she'd been waiting in a snowbank, her fox-red fur rippling as she slipped free of the crowd's edge. Her amber eyes locked onto mine.

"Follow," I murmured. "Quietly. Don't engage."

Fenrin's tail flicked once in acknowledgment, and then she was gone, melting into the shadows, her paws barely disturbing the snow as she tracked the hooded figure into the trees.

LuLu set her jaw. "Murder," she said under her breath. "Or money."

"I don't know which one," I said. "But they didn't come to jump in the lake."

Behind us, Finch was still lecturing Trip about hypothermia while Betsy refilled cocoa cups like warmth could fix everything. WishFest kept rolling, blissfully unaware.

Vex appeared at my feet, his eyes alert.

"Notify Weylan and Sparks," I said quietly.

Vex didn't hesitate. He bolted, a black streak cutting between boots and benches, slipping through the crowd with practiced ease. Someone laughed and assumed he was part of the show. I straightened, forcing my expression back into something neutral. I watched the treeline where Fenrin had disappeared. WishFest wasn't just continuing. It was being used. And whatever that hooded figure was tied to—the murder or the money—they weren't done yet.

Not even close.

By evening, WishFest had shifted from cheerful determination into something quieter and more reverent. Lanterns glowed all across the festival grounds, their glass panes fogged from breath and warmth, turning the snow beneath them into pools of gold. Pine boughs bowed under the weight of frost and twinkling lights, and somewhere nearby, a fire cracked softly, sending sparks up like tiny wishes escaping into the dark.

The main stage stood at the center of it all, transformed into a winter altar. Sheer white fabric draped the sides, catching every breeze. Garlands dusted with artificial frost framed the choir risers, and an ice arch rose behind them, carved with delicate stars and snowflakes that glimmered under the lights. Behind the stage, the mountain loomed. Solid. Ancient. And above it...

The northern lights unfurled.

A collective gasp rippled through the crowd as green and violet ribbons stretched across the sky, slow and luminous, like the heavens had decided to lean in close tonight. The aurora pulsed gently, colors deepening and fading in long, breath-like waves.

For a moment, even Wishville forgot how to speak.

"Oh," LuLu whispered, her voice barely there. "That's gorgeous."

Holden tipped his head back, his eyes tracking the lights. "You know half the town's going to insist this is symbolic."

"It *is* symbolic," Calderis said calmly.

LuLu shot him a look. "Of what?"

"Change," he replied. "Revelation. Reckoning."

I sighed. "You could've led with 'pretty.'"

He considered that. "It is also pretty."

We found seats along one of the front benches and sat with blankets draped over our laps and thermoses passed hand to hand. The air smelled like pine sap, cinnamon, and cold metal. Boots crunched softly as people settled in. Willa Hartman moved down the row offering cookies with the quiet urgency of someone who believed desserts were the answer to grief. Maisie Flint handed out hand warmers like rations.

Trip Danderly plopped down two benches ahead of us, wrapped in three scarves and a borrowed parka.

"You alive?" Holden asked.

Trip saluted him with his wish flashlight. "I'm a sheriff like you. Hearty at the core."

The lights dimmed, saving Holden from having to reply.

Thomas stepped onto the stage, followed by the choir in an orderly fashion. He wore a long black coat and carried himself like a man who expected to be obeyed. The choir straightened instantly at the lift of his hands. Their breath fogged the air as they waited, eyes fixed on him.

Then Wendy stepped forward. She sang. The first note cut clean and sharp through the cold, silencing the last murmurs in the crowd. Wendy's voice was a clear soprano, powerful and controlled, each note placed with intention. Not as good as Violet had been, but still pretty. She stood center stage beneath the aurora, a white cape draped over her shoulders with silver thread woven through the fabric so it shimmered faintly when she moved.

Thomas guided the choir behind her, shaping harmony with precise motions, his hands rising and falling like he was conducting the weather itself. The music flowed outward across the grounds.

That was when the snow ballet began.

Dancers emerged from the far side of the festival space, figures in pale blue and white cloaks, their pointe shoes whispering over packed snow. Ribbons trailed from their wrists, catching the lantern light as they spun and leapt, movements loose and fluid, meant to echo winter rather than tame it.

The choreography wasn't rigid. It breathed. It curved. It invited the night to participate.

I felt it in my chest. Something loosened and eased. Near the front, Dana stood with Tasha, who offered her a mini pie. They were around the same age. I was glad Dana had friends in this town. They both were wrapped in dark coats. Dana's face was lifted toward the stage, her expression soft and reverent. For a few minutes, grief loosened its grip on her.

"It's beautiful," she murmured.

Tasha squeezed her hand, her eyes shining as she nodded.

The choir swelled. Wendy's voice rose higher, cutting through the harmony like a blade of light. And then...bracelets clinked, cutting through the moment.

"Positions," someone whispered far too loudly.

I closed my eyes for a moment, marveling over how they could still surprise me.

The Wellies had entered the ballet.

Tilly appeared first, having somehow transformed a white scarf into a makeshift tutu, tinsel pinned into her hair like a questionable crown. Belle followed, her cardigan cinched with a glittery belt, with sheer ribbon tied around her wrists. Dot brought up the rear, draped in a dramatic polka dot shawl and wielding two paper snowflakes like sacred talismans.

They tromped onto the snow just behind the official dancers, their boots crunching loudly.

Holden let out a low groan. "Please tell me they're not—"

"Oh, they are," LuLu whispered, vibrating with delight.

The Wellies began to *interpret* the music.

Tilly attempted a graceful spin and immediately wobbled, her boots sliding. Belle caught her elbow at the last second, turning the near disaster into what almost resembled choreography. Dot advanced solemnly, lifting her paper snowflakes toward the sky like she was summoning winter itself.

Onstage, Wendy held a flawless note, her gaze fixed forward.

Thomas's jaw tightened. His conducting grew frantic.

The crowd noticed. Laughter rippled through the benches, not cruel but warm. Relieved. People leaned closer together, their arms brushing and smiles breaking through the tension that had clung to the town all week.

The Wellies swept their arms dramatically, scarves and shawls trailing. Tilly executed a determined hop she clearly believed was a leap. Belle followed with a stately step that might have been elegant if she weren't wearing snow boots. Dot attempted a pirouette and nearly collided with a swan ice sculpture.

"Core!" Belle hissed.

"I *am* core-ing!" Tilly whispered back.

Near the front, Alistair Hawthorne stood with a cup of mulled cider, watching the stage…until Dot maneuvered directly into his line of sight and executed a slow, deliberate snowflake flourish.

Alistair blinked. Then a slow smile tipped up the corners of his lips.

Dot froze mid-pose, her owlish eyes wide. "He smiled," she blurted in awe.

"At me," Belle insisted.

"That Lord's a leaping," Tilly said. "Or he liked *my* leap."

"You mean your hop," Belle corrected.

"Leaping, hopping, twirling…who cares. It was worth it," Dot said dreamily.

Good Lord, they had microphones pinned onto their costumes.

The music swelled. Wendy lifted her chin, her voice soaring, trying to drown them out. The aurora brightened, green ribbons dancing overhead as if responding to the sound. Thomas brought the choir toward the final cadence. The dancers—official and unofficial—reached their finale. Thomas lowered his hands. Wendy held the final note, then released it into the night.

Silence.

Then applause, thunderous and immediate, as the choir exited the stage. People rose to their feet, clapping mittened hands, cheering. Someone whistled. Trip attempted to whistle and failed heroically.

On the snow, the Wellies lingered as the dancers left, bowing over and over. Dot bowed too deeply and tipped forward. Belle caught her…again. Tilly waved proudly toward Alistair. He lifted his cup in acknowledgment and tipped his hat gallantly.

Calderis watched, looking bewildered. "Is this…courtship or a mating ritual?"

"Yes," I said, "to both."

He frowned. "It appears hazardous."

"Love often is," LuLu said, glancing at him and then looking away.

As the crowd dispersed beneath the aurora, their laughter lingering, I walked near the edge of the stage, letting the night settle back into my bones. That's when I heard raised voices. Low, sharp, and controlled…but vibrating with something just beneath the surface. I slowed without meaning to, drifting closer to the edge of the stage as people passed around me, laughing and chattering, their attention still fixed on the aurora and the applause echoing through the trees.

Wendy's voice cut through the night. "I did everything you asked."

I froze.

Thomas answered just as quietly, his tone tight. "And you're still doing too much."

"You mean I'm still not getting what you implied," Wendy snapped. "You made it sound like this would *lead* somewhere."

"I implied opportunity," Thomas said. "Not control."

"And yet you keep acting like you can give it to me," Wendy hissed. "Like my future depends on you."

I edged closer to the choir tent, careful to keep my steps light, the snow muffling my boots. The canvas shifted slightly in the breeze, shadows flickering inside—two figures standing too close, too rigid.

Thomas exhaled sharply. "You're not entitled to anything beyond the role you were given."

Wendy laughed under her breath, sounding sharp and humorless. "Funny. That's not how you talked before auditions."

Silence fell, thick and dangerous.

Then Thomas said, "Lower your voice. You got what you wanted after Violet died."

I leaned just a fraction closer, and the canvas rustled.

"Did you hear that?" Wendy asked suddenly.

I stopped breathing.

Footsteps shifted inside the tent. A shadow moved closer to the entrance. My mind raced, too late to retreat without crunching snow and too obvious to bolt. I'm the Festival Chair, I reminded myself. I belonged here. I forced my shoulders to relax, straightened, and deliberately scuffed my boot against the snow, making just enough sound to announce my presence without panic.

The tent flap snapped open. Thomas stepped out, his expression already smoothed into something professional and controlled. His gaze flicked to me, sharp and assessing. "Lyra," he said. "Enjoying the concert and ballet?"

"Very much," I replied evenly, lifting my clipboard like it had always been my intention to stand there. "The turnout was incredible. I'm making sure the grounds are clearing safely."

Behind him, Wendy appeared in the tent opening, her smile tight and eyes still bright with something unsettled.

"Everything okay?" I asked, polite and neutral.

Thomas nodded once. "Just post-performance logistics."

"Of course," I said, meeting his eyes without flinching.

For a beat, I thought he might push. Might question why I was standing exactly where I was. Then someone laughed nearby. A lantern swayed, and the night reclaimed its noise.

Thomas inclined his head. "Good evening." He stepped away.

Wendy lingered half a second longer, her gaze sliding over me, measuring, suspicious, and calculating. Then she turned and followed him into the darkness.

I blew out a slow breath, every muscle in my body loosening at once.

Behind me, Holden's voice drifted closer. "There you are. You okay?"

I turned, forcing a small smile. "Fine." But my heart was still racing. Because whatever Wendy and Thomas were tangled in wasn't over. And I had the distinct, unsettling feeling that next time, someone wouldn't walk away so easily.

CHAPTER
Seventeen

MORNING ARRIVED GENTLY, like it didn't want to startle anyone. The snow had softened overnight, the sharp edges of yesterday's footprints blurred into something kinder. The festival grounds smelled warm and sweet already. Maple syrup heating in wide pans, smoke curling from the chestnut roasters where cast-iron drums turned slowly over open flame. The sky was pale and bright, winter-blue stretched thin with promise.

If you didn't know better, you might've thought WishFest was healing.

I followed the sound of laughter toward the *Maple Syrup Snow Candy Station*, where a long table had been set up with fresh snow packed smooth and shallow. Volunteers poured hot amber syrup in looping ribbons, the liquid hissing softly as it hardened into glossy, sticky candy.

Dana stood near the end of the table. She was bundled in a dark coat that looked too heavy for the mild morning, her gloves clenched tight in her hands. Her hair was pulled back neatly, almost severely, as if order were something she could still control. Two local women hovered close. Tasha Frimble with her practical scarf and no-nonsense posture, and her grandmother, Ethel, steady and warm, her presence as grounding as the snow beneath our boots.

"You have to try it," Tasha insisted, pressing a small paper plate into Dana's hands. "Maple syrup cures many things. Not all, but many."

Ethel nodded solemnly. "Especially grief. And shock. And cold feet. My elderly cats Monsieur Buttons and Madame Frizzle don't like when my feet are cold."

Dana smiled faintly, the expression flickering like it wasn't sure it wanted to stay. "Violet loved this," she said quietly. "She used to say it tasted like childhood."

"That sounds like Violet," Ethel said gently. "Always finding poetry in simple things."

Dana's fingers trembled just slightly as she picked up a wooden stick and lifted the hardened syrup from the snow. She took a careful bite, then closed her eyes for a beat. "Oh," she breathed. "That's…still good. Just like I remember."

Ethel beamed like she'd personally invented maple trees.

I hung back for a moment, watching Dana's shoulders loosen just a fraction. Around her, the station buzzed softly with women chatting, kids laughing, and steam rising into the crisp air. *The Chestnut Roasting Station* nearby crackled and popped, the smell nutty and rich, grounding in a way nothing else quite was. This was the version of WishFest Violet would've loved.

Simple. Warm. Familiar.

I stepped closer. "Morning, Dana."

She turned, startled for half a second before her face smoothed. "Lyra, good morning."

"How are you holding up?" I asked, knowing there was no good answer and asking anyway.

"I keep forgetting," she said quietly. "Then I remember. Over and over again."

Ethel reached out and squeezed her arm. "That part takes time."

Dana nodded, but her gaze slid away toward the edge of the

grounds where the trees thickened. The smile she'd been holding slipped. We drifted together toward the chestnut roasters, where a volunteer handed Dana a small paper cone filled with warm, split shells. Dana cradled it like it was something precious.

"I didn't think I'd make it out today," she admitted. "But Violet would've been furious if I missed this."

"She would've dragged you herself," Tasha said firmly. "By the sleeve."

Dana let out a small, surprised laugh. "Yes. She would have."

The women lingered a bit longer, chatting about recipes and past festivals, before one by one they were pulled away—a neighbor calling, a volunteer shift starting, someone needing help with gloves or cups or directions.

Eventually, it was just Dana and me. The noise of the festival continued around us, but there was a small pocket of quiet where we stood.

I hesitated, then asked gently, "Are Ozzy and Percy still giving you a hard time?"

Dana's shoulders stiffened. "Ozzy," she said slowly, "has backed off, if you can believe it."

Relief flickered through me. "That's good."

"Yes," she agreed. "He apologized. Awkwardly. Very awkwardly. He said he was under a lot of stress and took it out on me. But he oddly seems better now for some reason."

I nodded. That tracked. I had a suspicious feeling it had to do with the disappearance of those scary-looking men. Someone or something had made them go away.

"And Percy?" I prompted.

Her grip tightened on the paper cone, chestnuts shifting inside with a soft rattle. "He's still around," she said. "Still watching. Still finding excuses to run into me."

My jaw set. "Has he threatened you like he did Violet?"

Dana hesitated. "Not...directly," she said. "But he doesn't need to. He knows how to look at someone in a way that reminds them what he's capable of."

I felt a cold line settle along my spine. "Have you told Holden?"

She shook her head quickly. "No. I don't want to make things worse. He already has a history—"

"Which makes it *more* important," I interrupted gently. "Dana, Percy has a violent past. You don't have to downplay that to protect anyone."

She nodded. "I know."

I studied her face—the careful composure, the grief that felt real and raw, the way she kept her body angled toward the crowd as if she needed witnesses just in case.

"You're not alone," I said. "If Percy does anything, you come to me. Or Holden. Or LuLu."

Dana nodded. "I will." A beat passed. Then she added softly, "I just want this to be over."

I nodded. "I should get back to my rounds," I said at last.

Dana looked relieved and disappointed all at once. "Thank you for checking on me."

"Of course."

As I turned away, the chestnut roaster flared briefly, a sharp pop echoing through the air. I glanced back once more. Dana flinched over the popping, just slightly, then forced herself to relax. She stood there alone now, chestnuts cooling in her hands and maple candy forgotten on the table behind her. The festival swirled around her with kind voices, warm food, and shared memories.

I made a note on my clipboard to check on her more often and kept walking, the scent of sugar and smoke following me. Dana had lifted her chin and stepped back into the crowd, the perfect image of a grieving sister being supported by a town that wanted to believe this was the worst of it.

I wasn't so sure.

~

Wishville Police Station smelled like burnt coffee and wet animals. I stepped inside and stamped snow from my boots, the echo too loud in the quiet hallway.

Holden's office door was open.

Weylan leaned against the filing cabinet, his arms crossed and jacket still dusted with snow. Sparks sat at Holden's desk, one boot hooked around the chair leg and a tablet balanced in his hands like it was an extension of his body.

Holden looked up as I entered. "You're right on time."

"That's never a good sign," I said, closing the door behind me.

Sparks huffed a quiet laugh. "You and your signs."

"I pay attention to signs. They usually lead me to something important."

Weylan pushed off the cabinet. "Speaking of important...we saw Percy again."

That single sentence tightened something in my chest. "Where?" I asked.

"Not the alley behind my shop," Sparks said. "They moved after you saw them."

"Smart," Holden muttered. "Or paranoid."

"Both," Weylan said. "He's being watched, and he knows it."

I folded my arms. "So where did he go?"

Weylan nodded toward the map pinned to the wall. Wishville and its outskirts marked in colored pins and thin pencil lines. "Old snowmobile access trail. East side. Cuts behind the closed sawmill before looping back toward the river."

I frowned. "That area's barely used."

"Exactly," Sparks said. "No businesses. No lights. Just trees and snow."

"And sightlines," Weylan added. "From above."

I looked at him. "You followed from the air?"

Weylan's mouth twitched. "I was already up...with a balloon this time."

Holden gave him a look. "You can't just say that like it's normal."

Weylan shrugged. "It's normal for me."

Ignoring them, Sparks tapped the tablet, waking the screen. "We've got video."

Holden straightened immediately. "Let's see it."

Sparks turned the tablet so we could all see. The footage was grainy but clear enough. Snow drifted across the frame, illuminated by a distant security light. The angle was low, ground level, handheld but steady.

Percy stepped into view first. Even through the screen, his body language was unmistakable. Shoulders hunched. Head down. Hands jammed deep in his coat pockets. He paused, scanning the treeline like he expected the forest itself to accuse him.

"He's nervous," I said quietly.

"Or angry," Holden replied.

"Those aren't mutually exclusive," I said.

A second figure emerged from the shadows. Hood up. Face hidden. Movements economical and controlled. They didn't hesitate or fidget. They stopped a few feet from Percy, close enough to talk but not close enough to touch.

The hooded figure lifted one hand.

Percy flinched.

"That tells me a lot," Sparks muttered.

"Show me the handoff," Holden said.

Sparks scrubbed forward. The hooded figure reached inside their coat and pulled out a small package. Not big. Roughly shoebox-sized. Wrapped dark, edges squared, no markings visible.

Percy hesitated. Then he took it. The moment their hands touched, Percy jerked back like he'd been burned. The hooded figure leaned in, just slightly.

"No audio," Sparks said. "I was close enough to zoom in, but the wind was too loud."

"But body language counts," I said. "That wasn't friendly."

"No," Holden agreed. "That was transactional."

I swallowed. "So, Percy's still meeting the hooded figure, but for what?"

"That is the question," Sparks said. "And they changed locations once the alley got compromised."

Holden's jaw tightened. "Meaning they know we're watching."

"Or they assume," Sparks said. "Which is just as dangerous."

I stared at the paused frame…the moment Percy took the package. "Can we tell what it is?"

Sparks shook his head. "It's too wrapped. Could be the missing cashbox tin. Could be something else."

Something else.

My mind jumped immediately to Dana's tight smile. Her careful words. Percy's lingering presence. The way fear had crept into her voice when she talked about him. "Dana seemed afraid of him, and we know he was threatening Violet. Do you think he's threatening Dana?"

Holden didn't answer right away. "He might be, but why? Violet's gone."

Weylan folded his arms again. "Whatever it is, Percy didn't like receiving it."

"No," I said. "But he took it anyway."

Holden leaned back in his chair and scrubbed a hand over his face. "Percy's either being paid…or being controlled."

"And either way," I said, "he's not acting alone."

Sparks nodded. "There's something else." He scrubbed back again and slowed the footage. The hooded figure turned away after the exchange, disappearing into the trees. Percy stood there alone for a long beat, with the package tucked under his arm. Then…he looked up.

Straight at the camera. Not directly, not like he saw it, but like he felt watched. His expression hardened. "That," Sparks said, "is not the face of a man relieved to have money."

"No," Holden said softly. "That's the face of someone trapped."

A chill crawled up my spine. "Can we follow the hooded figure?" I asked.

Weylan shook his head. "Not without exposing myself. They vanished into dense cover."

"And Percy?" I asked.

"He went straight home," Sparks said. "No stops. No detours."

Holden clenched his jaw. "He's scared."

"Or desperate," I said.

"Or both," Weylan said.

I looked between them. "If Percy's being used, he's going to crack."

"Yes," Holden said. "But that doesn't mean he won't hurt someone before he does."

My thoughts went back to Dana standing stiff, clutching chestnuts like a lifeline.

"I'm worried about Dana," I said.

Holden's gaze sharpened. "I'll send her protection."

"But she won't want it," I said.

"We won't ask," Holden replied. "I'll have her watched secretly."

Sparks locked the tablet. "I'll keep cameras moving around town. Different angles. Different times."

"And I'll stay airborne," Weylan said. "Quietly."

Holden nodded once. "Good."

I thought of the frozen frame of Percy holding the package. Whatever he'd just accepted...it wasn't freedom. And whoever was under that hood was orchestrating something. I turned toward the door, unease coiling tight in my chest. WishFest glittered outside with lanterns, music, and laughter. Inside the station, the truth was taking shape. And Percy Johnson was standing right in the middle of it.

Not as the mastermind.

But as a man one bad decision away from becoming the next disaster.

CHAPTER

Eighteen

THE SNOWFLAKE STAMP *Passport Trail* was a charming, family-friendly scavenger hunt through downtown. Collect a stamp at each participating booth, fill your little booklet, redeem it for a prize at the WishFest tent. In practice, it was a slow-moving herd of mittens and ambition, punctuated by parents bribing children with cocoa and grown adults taking the stamping far too personally.

I slipped through the crowd with my clipboard and a half-drunk coffee, checking that the stamp stations had ink, the volunteers weren't freezing, and no one had decided to turn the "passport trail" into an excuse to climb on anything.

Vex rode on my shoulder like a tiny, judgmental scarf. *Your species enjoys being marked with symbols like livestock.*

"It's a souvenir," I muttered.

So is a scar.

I ignored him and waved at Maisie Flint, who was running the stamp station outside *The General Store* with the intensity of someone managing a federal election.

"Stamp booklets open," she barked at a man who tried to stamp the cover. "Open. I'm not branding your principles."

"I'm new," the man protested.

193

"Then learn fast," Maisie snapped.

I smiled and made a note: **Maisie is one argument away from starting her own government.** That's when I saw him. Alistair Hawthorne stood near the snowflake stamp table like he belonged in a magazine spread titled, **Winter Philanthropy: How to Look Effortlessly Wealthy in a Small Town.** His coat was tailored so well it made everyone around him look like they'd dressed in the dark. He held a passport booklet delicately between two fingers, as if it might stain him with earnestness.

And beside him stood...Tilly Nettlesblossom.

She wore a dramatic white cape that looked suspiciously like a repurposed curtain, pinned at the throat with a glittering brooch shaped like a pinecone. Her cheeks were rosy with cold and determination. She was explaining something with grand hand gestures, nearly taking out a nearby child with her scarf.

"I told you," Tilly was saying, her voice pitched just loud enough to carry, "the stamp trail is not merely an activity. It is a *journey*. A narrative arc. A pilgrimage of joy." She fluttered her extra-long, glitter covered, fake eyelashes that looked more like sparkly centipedes.

Alistair's mouth curved. "A pilgrimage."

"Yes," Tilly said solemnly. "And I personally believe we are meant to complete it together."

Vex's claws flexed lightly against my shoulder. *Is she courting him with stationery?*

"Apparently," I whispered.

Tilly thrust the booklet at Alistair like she was presenting a contract. "Now, when you receive the snowflake stamp from Betsy's booth, you must hold the booklet with confidence. No trembling. The snowflake can sense weakness."

Alistair looked down at the empty squares with his thick eyebrows arched high. "Can it?"

"Absolutely," Tilly said. "It's Vermont. You have to be hearty to live here. Everything senses weakness."

I tried to keep walking like I hadn't heard that.

Alistair's gaze slid to me, amused. "Festival Chair."

"Mr. Hawthorne," I said politely. "Enjoying the passport trail?"

"Immensely," he replied, with dry sincerity. "I'm being coached."

Tilly beamed. "He's a quick learner."

He winked at her, making her blush.

I glanced at the booklet. It already had three stamps. "Oh," I said. "You're moving fast."

"Efficiency," Alistair said, nodding. "Time is a resource, you know."

Tilly leaned closer to him, lowering her voice in a dramatic purr. "And so is romance."

Alistair blinked once, then laughed softly. "So I'm learning."

I kept my expression neutral through sheer practice. "Well. Good luck with your pilgrimage."

As I moved on, checking in at other stations along the way, I felt Vex's silent commentary like a presence at my temple. *If he survives this, he deserves a medal.* It took a while to get through my morning rounds.

Next up, *The Soup Crawl* began at noon, which meant downtown smelled like simmering comfort and competitive seasoning. Participating businesses had set up soup stations in front of their doors, ladling out small samples into biodegradable cups, while crowds moved between them like migrating birds.

When I arrived, I checked in with Betsy at *The Twisted Loaf,* where a giant pot of creamy roasted garlic and potato soup steamed under a canopy.

"You look like you've been ambushed," Betsy said, as she handed a cup to a woman in earmuffs.

"Just witnessing courtship," I murmured.

Betsy's eyes lit. "Oh no. Not the Wellies again."

"It's...very much again."

"Where?" she asked eagerly, her eyes sparkling with delight.

I nodded down the line and shook my head.

Alistair was there too. My jaw unhinged. *This* time, he wasn't with Tilly. He was with Belle Crimp. Belle had upgraded for the occasion, wearing a long wool coat in a rich cream color, red lipstick that meant business, and a scarf draped over her shoulders like she was starring in a movie about a woman who definitely had secrets. She held her soup cup with both hands, angled just so, as if steam could be seductive.

"I told you," Belle was saying, her voice low and rich, "this soup has undertones of longing."

Alistair lifted his spoon. "Longing?"

"Yes," Belle said firmly. "And restraint. It's a soup that wants something it cannot have."

Alistair tasted it with exaggerated seriousness. "I do sense restraint."

Belle's gaze narrowed, pleased. "You have a refined palate."

Vex sighed audibly.

"Don't," I warned.

I didn't say anything, he replied with pure innocence. *I merely exhaled in despair.*

I could relate as I stepped closer, holding my clipboard like a shield. "Mr. Hawthorne. I see you're making the rounds." *In more ways than one,* I thought. "Enjoying the *Soup Crawl?*"

"Immensely," he said again, as if he had a programmed playlist of replies. "I'm being educated."

Belle smiled like she'd won a prize. "He appreciates nuance."

"I appreciate soup," Alistair corrected gently.

Belle didn't flinch. "Soup is nuance."

I bit the inside of my cheek to keep from laughing.

Betsy had followed me and whispered, "He's stopping at all the events today, isn't he?"

"Apparently he gets around," I responded just as quietly.

Betsy's grin turned wicked. "He's about to be the most fed man in Vermont."

Alistair's gaze flicked to the next booth. "Where to now?"

Belle hooked her arm through his without permission. "Next stop, the butternut squash bisque. It's practically foreplay."

Alistair's brows rose. "You don't say?"

"I do," Belle assured him with a giggle.

I watched them glide away, Belle leaving a trail of perfume and confidence behind her.

Vex's eyes narrowed. *I am beginning to understand why your town requires law enforcement.*

"I can think of a few ladies who might benefit from being locked up." I sighed and kept making my afternoon rounds. After several more stops, I glanced at my watch. It was now late afternoon.

Next up, *The Whiskey and Chocolate Tasting* had taken over the heated tent near the main stage. I stepped inside and the air was warm and heavy with sweetness—dark chocolate, caramel, bourbon, spice. Fairy lights were strung across the ceiling, giving the whole place a decadent glow, like WishFest had briefly decided to become upscale.

Holden would hate it, saying it's too crowded and too loud, with too many people trying to talk over each other while holding tiny glasses like they were on a date with their own taste buds. LuLu would love it, but she was off covering something else. I was here because being the Festival Chair meant I had to make sure the tent didn't devolve into a tipsy stampede.

Speaking of stampedes, I spotted Alistair again.

He stood at the tasting table with a small whiskey glass in hand and a chocolate square balanced on a napkin like it was precious. Women were scrambling to get the closest spot to him, but beside him stood Dottie Quench.

Dot wore a dramatic black shawl that made her look like a widow in a Victorian novel, except for the black polka dots. Her expression was pure ambition. She held a tasting card and a pen and was explaining the pairing notes as if she'd invented whiskey.

"This," Dot said, pointing at the label, "has a smoky finish.

But not the kind that lingers. The kind that *haunts*." Her lips fluttered, drawing attention to her deep purple lipstick. She must have used lip plumper...or she was having an allergic reaction.

I blinked.

Alistair swirled his glass. "Haunts?"

"Yes," Dot whispered, drawing the s out. "Like a handsome regret."

Vex let out a noise in my head that I could only describe as a mental gag. *She is describing liquor as if it has unresolved emotional trauma.*

"It might," I whispered back, at a loss for words, adding helplessly, "we don't know its past."

Dot popped a chocolate into her mouth, then nodded with deep approval. "Mmm. Bitter...like truth."

Alistair tasted his chocolate and murmured, "Like the truth."

Dot's eyes lit up behind her enormous round glasses. "You understand."

Alistair glanced at her with amusement. "I'm learning."

I approached, my clipboard ready and voice polite. "Mr. Hawthorne."

He turned, smiling wide. "Festival Chair. Enjoying the day as much as I am? You seem to be everywhere?"

"Trying to. I'm working," I said. "Being everywhere is my job."

"Mine, too. I'm supporting the local economy," he replied, lifting his glass slightly.

Dot nodded vigorously. "He's being extremely generous."

Generous was an understatement. I'd watched him buy passport booklets for three families who'd forgotten theirs, donate to the soup crawl charity jar at every booth, and tip the teenage volunteer at the cocoa station like he was a waiter at a five-star restaurant.

I looked at him. "The town appreciates your support."

"I like to experience things fully," he said.

Dot leaned closer and stage-whispered, "He likes to experience *us*."

Alistair's brows rose. "Ah yes, you lovely ladies are giving me quite the experience, I must say."

Dot held up her tasting card. "And we're not done yet. I have notes on how best to take your experience with me to the next level. If you'd like."

Alistair smiled. "I suspect you do."

I couldn't help it. I laughed once, a short burst that surprised me.

Dot's head snapped toward me as if she'd forgotten I was there. "Lyra?" She blinked.

"Sorry," I said. "It's just...you're all acting like this is some sort of—"

"Competition?" Dot supplied.

"Yes. Like a reality dating show, and he's the prize."

Dot's eyes narrowed. "It is...and he definitely is. Just wait until you get to our age. Things aren't so easy when gravity grabs hold of you."

"But you're best friends," I said.

"Which makes it all the more exciting, my dear." She winked.

Vex's tail flicked against my collarbone. *I am begging you to remind them they are adults.*

"They won't listen," I whispered back.

Alistair sipped his whiskey and looked genuinely entertained. "If it helps, I'm not being pursued against my will."

Dot blinked. "So, you're—"

"Enjoying myself," he said smoothly.

Dot straightened as if she'd been knighted. "Good." Then she turned to the volunteer behind the table and said, loudly, "We'll take two more tasting flights."

Alistair murmured, "Dot, you're a little devil in disguise. Who knew?"

"Oh, hush, you're making me blush," Dot said, her eyes glittering. "This is courtship, after all."

I rubbed my forehead. "I'm going to pretend I didn't hear that."

You did hear it, Vex said smugly in my mind. *And now you must live with it forever.*

I scanned the tent. People were laughing, glasses were clinking, others were nibbling chocolate like it was a serious responsibility. Everything looked normal. Fun and safe on the surface, but there still were watchers around.

I could feel them.

"Are you okay?" Alistair asked.

I blinked. "Yes. Why?"

"You look like you're solving a puzzle," he said.

"Trying to. This murder and these thefts have me stumped, I admit."

"Well, I for one, hope Detectives Thorn and Deris figure things out soon. I wouldn't want anything bad to happen to my girls." He winked at Dot.

Dot leaned into Alistair, lowering her voice to something syrupy. "My hero."

Alistair laughed again, soft and real. "It's my pleasure to take care of you lovely ladies."

Across the tent, a volunteer called for help with the line, and I took the escape gratefully.

As I moved away, Vex murmured in my head, *If the Wellies succeed in wooing this man, the laws of nature will collapse.*

"Don't underestimate them," I whispered.

I am not underestimating them. I am praying for the stability of the universe.

I smiled despite myself and continued my rounds, the scent of whiskey and chocolate clinging to my coat. WishFest glittered on. And somewhere in the midst of it, between stamps, soup, and sugar, people kept choosing joy, even while the truth prowled at the edges...

Waiting for the right moment to bite.

By the time the *Hot Toddy Speakeasy* opened, WishFest had slipped into its evening skin. Calderis, LuLu, and Holden had joined me. The public lanterns dimmed, replaced with softer pools of amber light tucked beneath awnings and strung low through the trees. The entrance to the speakeasy was intentionally ridiculous—down a narrow alley behind the old brick storefronts, past a chalkboard that read **PASSWORD REQUIRED** in looping script.

Trip Danderly stood at the chalkboard wearing suspenders and a fedora he absolutely did not earn. "Password?" he asked, folding his arms and blocking the entrance as we approached.

"Don't play games with me, Trip," I warned.

He leaned closer, looking both ways before whispering, "Maple."

I stared at him with an arched brow.

He grinned. "It's always maple."

LuLu laughed. "We are the least secretive secret society in history."

Holden just shook his head and ushered us through the door.

Inside, the space had been transformed into a Prohibition-era fantasy. Strings of warm lights zigzagged across the ceiling beams. Tables were draped in deep red cloth. Mismatched glassware glittered on trays. A small jazz trio in the corner played something slow and smoky, the trumpet curling around the room like a ribbon of sound. The air smelled like cinnamon, clove, citrus peel, and whiskey.

Mayor Doug Delaney stood near the makeshift bar, his coat off and tie loosened, looking like a man trying very hard to appear relaxed. He held a steaming mug and nodded gravely at anyone who made eye contact, as if personally approving the concept of warmth.

"Festival Chair," he said when he saw me. "Chief."

"Mayor," Holden replied.

"Hi, Doug." I smiled.

Doug leaned closer. "Turnout's good."

"It is," I said, scanning the room automatically. Vendors were tucked into corners and locals clustered around tables with laughter rising and falling in waves. Even Ethel had made an appearance, perched upright with a hot toddy and the posture of someone who refused to be cold on principle.

Calderis stood slightly apart from the bar, watching the room with that unreadable stillness he wore like armor. He didn't drink the toddy. He didn't need to. His gaze tracked movement instead—doors, exits, hands exchanging glasses.

LuLu accepted her mug and inhaled deeply. "Okay, this is dangerous."

"It's cinnamon," I said.

"It's confidence," she corrected.

Vex was draped across my shoulders like a decadent accessory, with his tail curled loosely. His nose twitched. *The humans are willingly consuming heat. Fascinating.*

"It's called comfort," I muttered.

It smells like poor decisions, he replied.

Holden stepped closer to me, his voice low. "We need to talk." The shift in his tone cut through the music.

"What happened?" I asked quietly.

He glanced toward Doug, who was now speaking with one of the vendors near the bar. "Another report came in."

My stomach tightened. "Missing cash?"

"Yes."

"How much?"

"Enough."

That was not the answer I wanted. "From where?" I asked.

"Two vendors. The candied nuts booth and the handmade ornament stand. End-of-day counts didn't match. Short by a few hundred each."

LuLu's smile faded. "That's not a miscount."

"No," Holden said. "It's not."

Calderis stepped closer, his eyes narrowing. "The pattern continues."

Doug excused himself from the vendor and approached us, looking older than he had an hour ago. "I hate to bring this up tonight, but we can't ignore it."

"Has anyone seen anything?" I asked.

Doug shook his head. "Nothing concrete. A few volunteers mentioned someone moving quickly through the crowd before closing. They had their hood up."

"A hooded figure?" LuLu asked, her eyes darting to me.

Doug nodded grimly. "Same description as before."

Holden's jaw tightened. "We need to increase visible presence."

"And spook whoever it is?" I asked.

"Well, flushing them out hasn't worked," he said.

The jazz trio slid into a faster rhythm, their laughter swelling at the bar. Someone clinked a glass and called for another round. The room felt warm and festive. Too warm for the words we were speaking.

Calderis leaned slightly toward me. "This one is bold."

"Or desperate," I said.

Doug rubbed a hand over his face. "Maybe it's a group of people. All I know is they seem to be one step ahead of us all the time."

"That's an interesting theory," Holden replied.

LuLu lowered her voice. "There are literally so many possibilities."

"Yet nothing we can confirm," Holden said.

"Alistair's here," I murmured, scanning the room. Sure enough, he stood near the far table, elegant as ever, holding court with a small cluster of locals. The Wellies orbited nearby—tonight all three together, though each angled subtly toward him like synchronized satellites.

"Of course he is," LuLu muttered.

"And thank goodness for people like him." Doug followed my gaze. "He's donated generously this week."

"Ozzy seems to be less tense. He's even been seen placing bets," Holden said thoughtfully.

A burst of laughter erupted from the corner as Dot attempted to demonstrate how to properly garnish a hot toddy with "emotional authority." Belle corrected her wrist angle. Tilly declared the lemon peel symbolic.

The scene would've been charming if not for the knot tightening in my chest. More money gone. Same description. Same timing. I stepped away from the group, drifting toward the edge of the room where the light dimmed and the music softened. I pretended to examine the drink menu chalkboard while my mind spun.

Vex shifted slightly, his body going still. *You feel it.*

I glanced at him and nodded. A subtle prickle along my skin. The sense that the warmth of the room didn't reach everywhere. That somewhere beyond the glow of lanterns and the swirl of music, something colder stood. I turned my head slowly. Across the room, near the entrance—half-shadowed just beyond the brightest pool of light—someone stood very still.

Their hood was up.

Their face was obscured.

They were watching...*me.*

My breath caught. They weren't close enough to hear us or close enough to touch, but they were close enough to see, and measure, and wait.

"Holden," I said quietly, still staring at the hooded figure, when I felt his presence behind me.

Holden followed my gaze, tension snapping into place instantly.

The hooded figure shifted, then turned, and slipped back through the door into the dark alley beyond.

Holden was moving before I finished exhaling, pushing through the crowd, Doug calling after him. Calderis followed with silent speed. LuLu reached for my arm, steadying me as the room tilted between music and motion, but I didn't give chase. I stood there for one long second, my heart pounding, knowing with certainty.

This wasn't random or careless. Whoever it was had wanted me to see them.

And as the cold from the open door crept into the warm speakeasy air, I felt it settle into my bones. The certainty that the game had shifted, and I was no longer just observing it. I was being watched and toyed with.

I was the target.

Nineteen

WE DID NOT TELL HOLDEN.

We absolutely did not tell Calderis.

The weight of that decision pressed against my ribs as LuLu and I stood beside the well just after midnight, frost tracing delicate white veins across the ancient stone rim while the last lanterns of WishFest flickered low in the distance. The town was settling into that exhausted quiet that follows celebration, when laughter lingers in the air like a memory, but the world itself has gone still.

"You're certain we can't wait?" LuLu asked softly, her breath curling into the cold air between us.

I kept my palm against the well's surface and let its familiar pulse steady me before answering. "If *The Pale Accord* exists," I said at last, "then every hour we delay is another hour the lie stands unchallenged."

LuLu studied me for a moment, the seriousness in her expression reflecting back the same fire burning in my chest. "And if we're wrong?"

"Then we go home and pretend we were out walking," I replied, though neither of us believed it would be that simple.

I held LuLu's hand and closed my eyes, whispering the

ancient incantation that would allow the shift to take us. The world folded in on itself like breath being drawn inward. Sound thinned. Gravity tilted. Cold air gave way to something denser and charged, and when I opened my eyes again, Elarion stood before us in all its impossible, luminous splendor.

There were no stars here, only a living sky with currents of light that shimmered and drifted like thought made visible. Crystalline towers rose in the distance, faceted and glowing faintly from within, while bioluminescent vines climbed ancient stonework in slow spirals, their leaves pulsing silver-blue in rhythmic patterns that felt eerily like heartbeats.

Waterfalls cascaded from unseen heights into pools that gleamed like molten pearls, sending mist through the air that tasted faintly of minerals and magic. The air in Elarion did not simply move…it thrummed. It carried memory and pressed against the skin as though aware of who walked beneath it.

LuLu exhaled quietly beside me. "Every time," she murmured, "I forget how alive this place feels."

Alive was the right word. Elarion did not rest the way Wishville did. Even in its quieter stretches, something beneath the surface stirred like roots shifting in luminous soil, and crystal veins humming faintly in the deep.

We avoided the main avenues instinctively, keeping to narrower paths that wound toward the Woodswhisper—the mirror image of the Whisperwoods in Wishville—where the glow dimmed and the world felt older, less curated by the Elders' careful architecture. The trees here grew upside down from the ceiling, tall and slender, their bark laced with faint lines of light that pulsed so subtly they were easy to miss unless you were listening.

When I'd studied my mother's journal closer, I'd discovered two pages stuck together. When I pulled them apart, there was a passage that had described *The Accord Hall* as resting "where the earth remembers what the sky denies," and those words had not left me since I'd read them. Which meant not beneath the towers or beneath the Council chambers.

Somewhere deeper…but above, not below, between realms.

We reached a clearing ringed by ancient crystal-barked trees, their trunks descending from the ceiling like silent sentinels around a patch of luminous stone above us that glowed more softly than the pathways near the city center. We were walking on what looked like clouds, as if the world were upside down. I reached and pressed my bare palm against the branches, feeling the cool smoothness of Elarion's crystals beneath my skin.

Then I reached within.

Seismic Sense is not an explosion. It is not force or fracture or spectacle. It is listening. The world under my hand unfolded slowly, like a map etched in weight and pressure instead of ink. I felt the braided roots of the ancient trees above, the shallow caverns shaped by long-dry waterways, the subtle shifts of crystalline growth winding through bedrock like veins of light. I allowed my awareness to sink further, past the familiar patterns, past the surface echo of living systems.

Deeper. Higher. The pressure increased gradually, building behind my temples as the tree grew denser and older. And then… there it was. Not natural, irregular, or wild. A vast, deliberate stillness carved from bedrock, symmetrical in a way the earth does not shape on its own. A chamber so large it felt like an absence in the world's spine.

My breath faltered.

"Lyra?" LuLu whispered, sensing the shift in me.

"I found something," I said, though my voice felt distant in my own ears.

I expanded my awareness carefully around the space, tracing its boundaries. The chamber was circular and immense, supported by columns thick as forest trunks. At its center rose a raised dais, and faint impressions along the inner walls suggested inscriptions or sigils carved deep into the stone.

The Accord Hall.

Not rumor or metaphor, but real.

"How far?" LuLu asked.

"Farther than anyone would casually stumble upon," I replied. "It's anchored high, between realms, near the core strata."

The stone above us felt compacted and reinforced, layered intentionally rather than naturally compressed. Whoever sealed this chamber had not merely concealed it, they had fortified it.

"Find an entrance," LuLu urged.

I shifted my focus outward, tracing fault lines, searching for seams or fractures that might hint at a hidden passage. There were none. No carved tunnel or weakness or spiral staircase winding up into forgotten heights.

The seal was complete.

I drew my hand back slowly and summoned Lumen Wells. The glow gathered between my palms gradually, not as flame but as memory condensed into light, gold and luminous, edged with something older than ceremony. It cast soft reflections against the surrounding crystal trees, reflecting light like a kaleidoscope, and for a moment the forest seemed to lean inward like a prism as if aware of what I was doing.

Carefully, I directed the glow upward into the stone above our heads. At first there was only resistance, as if the earth were reluctant to respond. Then, faintly, the ground shimmered. A ghostly impression flared beneath the surface above, the circular hall illuminated from within. Columns rose like ancient ribs, and sigils glowed faintly along the walls in patterns too intricate to read from this distance. The image lasted only seconds before it flickered and collapsed back into darkness, swallowed whole by the weight of stone below it.

The Lumen guttered out, and I swayed as the effort to hold it caught up with me.

LuLu steadied me with both hands. "You're not allowed to martyr yourself for architecture," she muttered.

"I'm fine," I insisted, though the throb behind my eyes suggested otherwise.

And then the crystal forest shifted. Not magically. Physically. Footsteps moved along the upper ridge path, measured and deliberate, accompanied by the faint metallic whisper of armor.

Guards. At this hour? My pulse spiked.

I pressed my palm to the tree, searching outward, mapping their positions relative to ours. Two figures, disciplined in their movement, sweeping the perimeter. Had they felt the flare of my Lumen Wells?

"Extinguish everything," I whispered.

We retreated into the shadows, white mist swirling around our feet, our cloaks blending with the dimmer light of the wood. I guided us between thicker trunks, careful with every placement of my boots. The guards paused above us, their voices low and unreadable, and for a breathless moment I was certain we had been discovered. But the footsteps resumed and slowly faded into the distance.

Only then did I exhale fully.

The chamber above remained unmoved, patient beneath its layered seal. I pressed my palm once more to the tree and let myself feel the binding woven into the stone above us. It was not brute force that held *The Accord Hall* shut—it was intricate, ancient magic layered carefully over time. Lines of power interlaced so seamlessly they felt like part of the bedrock itself.

"This isn't something we can break open," I said quietly.

LuLu nodded. "It's not meant to be forced."

No, it wasn't. The seal felt less like a wall and more like a gate waiting for a specific key, not curiosity or strength, but something else entirely. But where was the door?

"We found it," LuLu said after a moment.

"We found where it sleeps," I corrected.

And that, in its own way, was a beginning.

～

We were halfway back toward the well portal, out of the Woodswhisper where the world was right-side up once more, when LuLu's steps changed. It was subtle at first, the kind of shift you only notice when you've walked beside someone long enough to recognize the cadence of their breath and the way their shoulders settle when they feel safe.

Her hand tightened around the edge of her cloak, not for warmth, but like she suddenly needed something solid to hold onto. Her gaze snapped to the left, toward a narrow ribbon of trees where the bioluminescent glow dimmed into deeper shadow.

"Lyra," she murmured, her voice barely moving the air. "Stop."

I froze instantly, every muscle going still while the luminous forest continued its slow pulse around us. A waterfall whispered somewhere in the distance. Crystal leaves shimmered faintly as they caught the current of wind.

"What is it?" I whispered.

LuLu didn't answer right away, because she didn't need to. The energy in her face had shifted into that tight, listening concentration that always made the hair at the back of my neck rise. Her eyes weren't looking at the scenery anymore.

They were tracking something invisible.

"I feel…" she began, then swallowed, as if whatever she felt tasted wrong. "I feel attention."

My stomach tightened. "Like more patrols?" I asked, keeping my voice low.

"No," she said, and the certainty in that single word chilled me more than any Elarion night ever could. "Like *intent*."

My gaze swept the path ahead. The stone glowed underfoot, but beyond the safe geometry of the walkway, the path deepened into a tangle of older growth and shadows. The quiet here didn't feel peaceful the way it had earlier. It felt held. Waiting.

"We shouldn't be here," LuLu breathed.

I shifted closer to her without making it obvious, my fingers brushing the edge of my cloak as if I were merely adjusting it, though, in truth, I was grounding myself. I could feel the well's magic still humming faintly under my skin from the Lumen I'd used, and the aftertaste of that power made me wary. Sometimes, when you pulled too hard, the world pulled back.

"Do you think it's Vaerion?" I whispered.

LuLu's mouth tightened. "I think someone is tracking me."

The implication snapped into place with unsettling clarity. Calderis's father had already made his disapproval painfully obvious. If he'd decided LuLu was more than a nuisance, if he'd decided she was a threat, it wouldn't be a stretch for him to send enforcers. Not to confront us outright or make a scene.

To remind her she didn't belong.

LuLu's head turned again, sharper this time. Her pupils seemed to dilate, the way they did right before a vision, except this wasn't a vision. This was instinct amplified by psychic sensitivity, the kind of sixth sense that always felt like a gift until it didn't.

"They're close," she said, barely audible. "To the right. Moving."

I followed her gaze. At first, I saw nothing but the soft glow of vines and the faintly lit curves of stone. Then I noticed what didn't fit. The slight pause in the forest's natural rhythm, the way one cluster of leaves stopped shimmering as if something blocked the light. A silhouette.

Not quite in view, but not quite hidden either.

My pulse began to pound, slow and heavy. "Run?" I whispered.

LuLu's lips parted, then she shook her head. "They'll catch us."

"They'll catch us if we do nothing."

My Seismic Sense unfurled once more without me meaning it to, instinctively mapping the ground beneath us and to either side. I hadn't wanted to draw attention to us by using my powers, but it was too late. I felt two sets of footsteps, light and deliberate, moving along the higher ridge line. Another set, lower, closer, sliding parallel to our path.

Three…at least. "Not just one," I murmured.

LuLu's shoulders stiffened. "I knew it."

She pivoted suddenly, not toward the well but off the path, slipping into the darker growth like a fox darting into brush. I followed without hesitation, my heart hammering as the world changed from open walkway to uneven ground laced with roots and stone. The glow dimmed instantly, the light here more scattered and less predictable.

LuLu moved fast, her cloak held close to keep it from snagging.

I matched her, my senses stretched thin, listening for anything that didn't belong.

A twig snapped behind us. Too crisp. Too intentional.

LuLu stopped so abruptly I nearly collided with her. She turned her head, her eyes narrowing, and then she moved toward it, like whatever she sensed had lit a fuse in her.

"LuLu," I hissed, grabbing her sleeve. "Don't—"

"I can feel him," she whispered, her breath trembling. "He's watching. He's *thinking* at me. I'm not going to let them get away with this."

"You are no match for Dwellers," I insisted. "Don't let your anger cloud your judgement."

Before I could stop her, she yanked free and took off through the trees. For a heartbeat, panic flared sharp and useless, because chasing a watcher into the forest was exactly how people disappeared in legends.

Then I ran after her.

The ground dipped into a narrow ravine where the stone darkened and the air cooled, damp with hidden water. Bioluminescent moss clung to the rock walls, casting faint green light that made everything look unreal and underwater.

LuLu skidded to a stop at the ravine's edge, her eyes locked on the opposite side. A figure stood there. Hooded and cloaked, their face obscured, and deathly still. As if they'd been waiting for her to notice.

My blood turned cold.

He—because something about the build read masculine—tilted his head slightly, and I felt the pressure of his attention like a physical thing.

LuLu's voice came out tight. "Who are you?"

The figure didn't answer. He lifted one hand, slow, almost casual, and the air around him seemed to shift as if he were signaling someone else.

That was all it took to push me over the edge.

My fear hardened into anger. "No," I whispered, and the word came out like a vow.

Heat rose under my skin, not wild, but controlled power I'd learned to shape with intention instead of instinct. I planted my feet and summoned my Magma Ward. It wasn't magma itself but the concept of heat and protection, pulled from the same deep place my Seismic Sense reached when it listened to stone.

The air in front of me warmed rapidly, a shimmer forming like heat over asphalt. I lifted my hands, and the moisture in the air condensed and then evaporated in a hiss. The ground at my feet darkened. Obsidian surged upward in thin, sharp shards—black glass born of heat and pressure—spiking from the stone like defensive teeth.

LuLu sucked in a breath. "Lyra—"

"Get behind me," I said.

The hooded figure didn't move, but the shadows around him shifted again, and suddenly there were two more shapes at the ridge above, barely visible against the dark. Three. My stomach dropped. They weren't random guards. They were Vaerion's men...or someone with access to that kind of discipline.

I narrowed my focus. The obsidian shards rose higher, trembling slightly with the force of my control. I snapped my wrist. The shards shot forward in a sharp arc, slicing through the air with a sound like brittle ice cracking.

The hooded figure moved at last, stepping sideways with unnerving ease, and the shards shattered against the ravine wall in a spray of glittering black fragments. But it did what I needed it to do. It made him react. It made him reveal his speed, agility, and training. I was right. The figure wasn't a curious passerby or lost traveler or enforcer.

It was a watcher after all.

The two figures above began to descend.

LuLu grabbed my arm. "Lyra, you were right. I let my stupid anger get the best of me, but this is nuts. I don't actually want to die. We have to go."

"I know." I drew a breath and pushed my palms outward.

Magma Ward expanded as a barrier of dense, heated air that bent light slightly, turning the space between us and them into a shimmering wall. It wasn't visible as a solid object, but it distorted the world behind it, making the attackers' shapes waver.

Heat rolled across the ravine like a sudden summer gust.

The hooded figure hesitated. He tested the barrier with a step forward, and the shimmer intensified, forcing him back as if the air itself had weight.

LuLu stared at it. "That's insane...and totally awesome."

"It's temporary," I warned, my voice strained. "We need distance."

We ran.

We climbed out of the ravine on the left side, scrambling over stone slick with moss, breath burning in our throats. I kept the barrier behind us as long as I could, feeding it just enough power to hold while we moved, but each second drained me more. My head pounded. The edges of my vision brightened too sharply.

LuLu glanced back once, and her face went pale. "They're still coming."

Of course they were.

We burst into a more open stretch of forest where the glow returned faintly, and I felt the well's direction like a magnetic pull in my bones. The path ahead curved toward the portal point, and relief flared a little too early and hopeful.

A shadow moved ahead.

Another figure.

LuLu stumbled, then caught herself, her eyes wide. "No… there's someone in front of us too."

Four. They'd tried to funnel us.

My throat tightened. I lifted my hands again, forcing myself to breathe through the pain behind my eyes. The ground responded with a low, angry hum. Obsidian surged again, but this time I didn't send it forward.

I spread it.

A fan of black glass erupted into a wide scatter across the path, turning the ground into a field of jagged threat, forcing the figure ahead to stop short. At the same time, I pushed heat outward in a second barrier, not as strong as the first, but enough to distort the space and buy us seconds.

Seconds were everything.

LuLu grabbed my hand. "Now!"

We veered hard left, slipping between trees, following the invisible pull of the well. Behind us, I heard the faint crackle of obsidian splintering, and the hiss of my heat barrier collapsing in waves. My power was fraying. My vision blurred briefly, and I clenched my jaw against the dizziness.

"Lyra," LuLu panted, panic creeping into her voice. "You're—"

"I'm fine," I lied again, because lying was easier than admitting I could feel the edge of my strength approaching fast. The portal point finally came into view. A stone arch, subtle glow, and the air shimmering faintly where worlds overlapped. Relief surged so hard it almost knocked me off balance.

We sprinted toward it.

Behind us, footsteps pounded closer.

LuLu didn't look back this time. She didn't need to. She could feel them.

I threw one last burst of Magma Ward behind us, not a wall but a flare of heated air that blasted outward like a silent shockwave, sending loose stones and glowing leaves spiraling. It bought us exactly one breath.

We crossed the threshold, and the world folded. Elarion's glow vanished. Wishville's cold slammed into my lungs like a slap. We stumbled onto the snow beside the well, our breath ragged and hearts hammering. For a moment, all I could do was bend forward, my palms on my knees, fighting the tremor in my arms as my power settled back into silence.

LuLu straightened first, her eyes wide and face pale. "That wasn't a patrol," she whispered. "I don't think they're Vaerion's men. I think they're part of something else."

"No," I agreed, swallowing hard. "That was a message…but from whom?"

We stood there in the quiet of late-night Wishville, the festival lights out, the well's stone cold beneath my fingertips. Somewhere in Elarion, someone had watched us search for *The Accord Hall.*

And they had decided we were getting too close.

CHAPTER
Twenty

MORNING at my house usually meant one of two things: chaos in the kitchen, or silence so peaceful it felt like a miracle.

This morning was neither.

The kettle hissed softly on the stove, sending up a ribbon of steam that fogged the window above the sink, and the smell of toasted bread and cinnamon rolled through the room in warm waves that had no right to feel comforting after the night LuLu and I had just survived.

Outside, fresh snow glittered on the porch rail, bright enough to make you squint, and the whole world looked deceptively clean. Inside, I sat at the table with LuLu, a plate of toast between us and two mugs of tea growing cold, while my body did that delayed reaction thing where it pretended it was fine until it suddenly wasn't.

My arms still felt faintly heavy, like the magic I'd used in Elarion was lingering in my muscles as a dull ache, and every time I blinked, I had the uneasy sense that I'd left something unfinished behind my eyes. LuLu was doing a spectacular job of pretending she wasn't shaken. She'd tied her hair up into a tight ponytail and was slicing an apple with more force than necessary, as if the fruit had personally offended her.

Fenrin lay near the hearth in fox form, curled in a tight red coil with one ear swiveling toward every sound in the house, her tail twitching occasionally like she was counting threats. Vex sat on the windowsill, his tail wrapped neatly around his paws, watching snow fall with the thoughtful expression of a creature who considered reality an ongoing inconvenience.

"You're not eating," LuLu said without looking up.

"I am," I lied, lifting my toast and taking a bite that tasted like sawdust.

LuLu's knife paused. "You're doing the thing where you chew like it's a chore."

"It *is* a chore," I muttered. "Everything is a chore today."

Before she could respond, a knock hit the front door. Not a polite little tap. A decisive, authority-laced knock that made the air in the room tighten. Fenrin's head lifted instantly. Vex's ears angled forward. LuLu's knife froze mid-slice.

I stared toward the hallway. "Please tell me that's Betsy with sympathy muffins."

LuLu's eyes narrowed. "If it is, then Betsy's angry. I can feel that person's aura, and it's not good."

The knock came again…harder.

I pushed back my chair and crossed the kitchen, my socks sliding slightly on the wood floor because I'd forgotten to put slippers on. My hand hovered on the doorknob for half a beat before I opened it.

Holden stood on my porch, his shoulders squared, bearded jaw set, and gray eyes stormy. And beside him…Calderis. He looked like he'd stepped out of a myth and into my morning without bothering to ask permission. His pale hair was damp from snow, his cloak dusted with white, his piercing blue gaze fixed on me with a stillness that made my stomach tighten.

They weren't just here together.

They were aligned.

That was the most alarming part.

"You have got to be kidding me," I muttered.

Holden's gaze flicked past me into the house like he was taking inventory. "We need to talk."

Calderis didn't waste breath on a warm-up, adding, "Now."

I stepped back and let them in because refusing would only prolong the inevitable. The cold rushed in with them, curling around my ankles, and Fenrin rose smoothly from the hearth, positioning herself at LuLu's feet like an armed bodyguard in fur form. Vex remained on the windowsill, looking entirely unimpressed, yet his eyes never left me.

Holden shut the door behind them, his movements controlled in the way they always were when he was angry and trying to maintain control. Calderis scanned the room once, his eyes landing on LuLu, then on me, with a brief pause that suggested he was noting every variable.

"You went to Elarion," he said.

It wasn't a question.

LuLu set her knife down carefully. "Good morning to you too."

Calderis ignored that. "Two women in disguise were seen near the Woodswhisper late last night."

I held my expression neutral, which took effort because my entire body wanted to flinch.

"Word travels fast," I said lightly.

Calderis's gaze sharpened. "Not fast. *Precisely.*"

Holden stepped closer, crossing his arms. "Weylan got word from Elarion and relayed it to Calderis. Calderis relayed it to me. And now we're here."

LuLu leaned back in her chair, her eyebrow lifting. "Look at you two. Teamwork. Should I take a picture?"

Holden didn't smile.

Calderis didn't blink.

Vex, however, lifted his head and spoke out loud, his voice crisp and entirely too composed for a creature who had once knocked a candle off my table out of boredom.

"If you do take a picture, please ensure my left side is featured. It is my better side."

Holden glared.

Calderis's jaw bulged.

LuLu's mouth twitched.

I closed my eyes. "Vex."

He twitched his tail. "What? Tension is bad for digestion. I am helping."

Calderis's gaze shifted to Vex with a hard look that intimidated the strongest of men. Vex merely yawned. Calderis's focus snapped back to me immediately, like he refused to be derailed. "Why," he said, each syllable clipped and dangerous, "were you in Elarion without telling me?" The fury in his voice wasn't loud. It didn't need to be. It was the kind that lived in restraint.

I swallowed. My fingers curled lightly around the edge of the counter as if wood could ground me. "I went looking for my mother," I said. "And last time I checked, Elarion is my home, too."

LuLu's eyes shot to me sharply, but she didn't interrupt.

Calderis's expression didn't soften, but something in his gaze shifted, a brief flicker of emotion buried under duty. "The unrest with the rebels is escalating. It's dangerous there now for everyone. You should have told me."

"I couldn't," I said quietly. "Not without raising questions."

Holden's eyes narrowed. "You went looking for her in the middle of everything that's going on? I deserved to know, too, or don't I matter anymore?"

"Of course you matter to me," I said softly. "I needed answers. That's all."

"Answers are not worth your life," Holden snapped, and the anger in his voice was about more than my well-being. He sounded hurt.

I met his gaze. "I didn't plan to get chased."

"What?" He gaped at me. "No one said anything about getting

chased, but you just proved my point," he said tightly. "You never plan…period."

LuLu pushed back from the table, unable to hold still anymore. "It sure is dangerous," she said, her voice sharpening like a blade. "Especially when someone sends enforcers after us." She watched him closely, and I knew she was testing to see what he knew.

Calderis's head turned toward her so fast it was almost startling. "Enforcers are loyal to me."

LuLu laughed once, short and humorless. "That is the most optimistic thing you've ever said."

Calderis's jaw tightened. "My father is a lot of things, but I don't think he would actually go behind my back and order an attack."

"You actually believe that?" LuLu demanded.

Calderis's eyes flashed. "I trust the structure of command."

"Not everyone is loyal like you." LuLu leaned forward, slapping her palms on the table. "I trust what I felt. Those men weren't patrolling. They were hunting. They weren't curious. They were coordinated. That wasn't random."

Holden shifted his weight, his gaze moving between them like he was watching a storm form. "Serena is the leader of the rebels. I don't think she would order an attack on either of you."

LuLu's eyes filled with anger now. "All I know is whoever it was cornered us in the woods like they knew exactly where to funnel us."

Calderis's face looked as if he'd just thought of something and then it went rigid, the muscles along his jaw tightening as if he were trying to contain something bigger than anger. "Lyra, did you use your magic in the Woodswhisper?"

"Of course I did," I said. "To save us."

"I mean before the attack," he said carefully.

Shoot. I remembered my initial Seismic Sense and Lumin Wells. "Yes," I said quietly.

"And you didn't think," he said slowly, his voice low and

deadly, "that perhaps if it were the Elders' guards, they would respond to an unauthorized flare of magic near restricted ground?"

LuLu's laugh sharpened. "Unauthorized flare? You mean Lyra breathed too loudly and the forest decided she needed to be punished? She is the Guardian of both realms. She should have the right to go wherever she wants and use whatever powers she wishes."

I held up a hand, trying to keep the conversation from igniting into something we couldn't take back. "We were careful."

Holden's eyes cut to me. "But you obviously weren't if you were attacked."

I stared at him.

"You went without telling anyone," he said. "You went into an unfamiliar terrain with a political enemy watching from the shadows. That isn't careful, Lyra. That's reckless."

The worst part was that he wasn't wrong, and I'd put LuLu in jeopardy.

LuLu's voice softened just a fraction. "We didn't go looking for trouble."

"I know," Holden said, and his frustration looked almost like fear. "But you found it anyway. You two always seem to."

Calderis drew a slow breath, then looked at me with something almost like betrayal. "You could have been killed." His gaze settled on LuLu. "Both of you."

"We weren't," I said, instantly regretting how small and defensive it sounded.

Calderis's eyes narrowed. "That is not reassuring."

Fenrin's tail snapped against the floor, thumping once, as if she'd grown tired of the humans arguing and wanted to remind everyone she had teeth and wasn't above using them if they didn't feed her soon.

Vex hopped down from the windowsill with a graceful thud and padded across the table, weaving between the plates like he owned the place. He sat directly between Holden and Calderis like a referee. Then he spoke out loud again, perfectly calm.

"If you are finished measuring whose anger is the most heroic, the two females are still alive, which seems relevant. Also, the toast is becoming cold, which is tragic."

LuLu blinked.

Holden frowned.

Calderis looked like he might strangle the cat and then remembered he was a dignified Dweller and decided not to.

I couldn't help it. A laugh burst out of me, half-relief and half-exhaustion.

Holden's shoulders loosened a fraction, like the absurdity had cut through the edge of his rage.

LuLu exhaled, rubbing her forehead. "The cat's right."

Calderis looked at Vex, then at me, and something in his face shifted from fury into forced control. "A truce," he said stiffly. "For now."

Holden nodded. "For now."

LuLu crossed her arms. "But we're not done talking about Vaerion."

Calderis's gaze locked onto hers. "I will speak with him."

"You'll do more than speak," LuLu said.

Calderis didn't answer immediately, but the silence held a promise.

I let out a slow breath and forced my tone into something lighter than my nerves. "Okay," I said. "Truce. Breakfast. Then we figure out our next steps like adults."

Vex swished his tail. "An ambitious plan. I like it."

Fenrin yawned widely, showing teeth in the most pointedly indifferent way possible.

Holden stepped back toward the door, still tense but no longer radiating heat. "We are not leaving you unguarded anymore," he said.

Calderis nodded once. "Agreed."

"Good luck with that." Vex made a sound suspiciously like a snort.

I stared at my sassy cat. "You can go back to not talking again anytime now."

LuLu lifted her mug in mock salute. "To the apocalypse of our lives. I might need something stronger in this mug."

Holden's mouth twitched with almost a smile. "Eat, Lyra."

Calderis's gaze pinned me. "And no more excursions."

I opened my mouth to protest, then closed it again because I didn't actually have a defense that wasn't stubbornness dressed up as courage. "Fine," I said. For now. Because *The Accord Hall* still slept above binding magic and stone.

And someone had already noticed we were almost strong enough to wake it. We just couldn't get inside.

By midmorning, WishFest had returned to its carefully constructed illusion of joy.

Snow still clung to garlands draped across lampposts, children darted between adults with mittened hands sticky from maple candy, and the marching band's brassy rendition of *Winterlight Waltz* echoed across the festival clearing with determined cheer.

If anyone sensed the tension simmering beneath the surface of town politics and personal betrayals, they were doing a masterful job of pretending otherwise.

The Snow Queen Coronation Ceremony marked the official end of the parade, and as Festival Chair, I stood near the stage with a clipboard I wasn't actually reading, scanning the crowd out of habit more than necessity.

Holden stood off to the side in his police chief's jacket, his arms folded but eyes alert, tracking movement. Calderis lingered a few feet behind him, his dark coat standing out against the pale snow, drawing curious glances from tourists who didn't quite know what to make of him. LuLu hovered by my side, pretending to adjust ribbon arrangements while very obviously eavesdropping on three women arguing about whether the snowflake sashes were crooked.

Thomas stood at the podium in a tailored winter coat, his voice warm and controlled as he introduced the final segment of the ceremony. "And now," he said, smiling toward the crowd, "we crown this year's Snow Queen, celebrating the spirit of community, tradition, and dedication that makes WishFest what it is. Congratulations Tasha Frimble."

Polite applause rippled outward as the crown was placed upon her head.

Wendy stood at the edge of the stage in a cream-colored coat with faux-fur trim, her hair perfectly styled, and her expression composed but edged with something brittle. She looked radiant in the way people do when they are trying very hard not to look rattled.

If anyone hadn't known about the tension simmering between her and Thomas, they would have thought nothing of it. Until the ceremony ended. The crowd was about to disperse after glittering under the winter sun when a sharp voice cut cleanly through the applause.

"Before anyone else celebrates, I have something to say." The sound landed like a stone dropped in a frozen pond.

Heads turned.

Thomas froze at the podium.

At the base of the stage, his wife stood rigid, her wool coat unbuttoned despite the cold, and her cheeks flushed not from weather but fury. She held her phone in one hand, her knuckles white around it.

The crowd's polite chatter dissolved into murmurs.

"Patricia," Thomas began, attempting a practiced smile. "Now isn't the—"

"Oh, it's exactly the time," she snapped.

The microphone on the stand caught her voice clearly enough

without her needing to shout. The entire clearing seemed to lean forward.

"I will not stand here while you pretend to be the moral center of this festival," she said, her voice shaking but unrelenting. "Not after what I've seen."

Thomas's posture shifted subtly to less polished and more defensive. "Let's talk about this privately," he said through clenched teeth.

She laughed once, sharply. "We've been talking privately for years."

A ripple moved through the crowd.

Wendy's face looked smug.

Patricia lifted her phone. "You cheated on me. In the choir tent on opening night."

Gasps broke across the square like a gust of wind.

Thomas stepped down from the podium. "That's absurd."

"Oh?" Patricia's thumb moved across her screen. "Then explain this." She tapped, and the audio blasted from the phone's speaker, tinny but unmistakable. Fabric rustling. A low laugh.

Thomas's voice. Wendy's. Close, intimate, and undeniable.

The clearing went silent except for the recording.

Then Patricia cast the video onto the projection screen behind the stage for all to see, and the image shifted. The camera angle turned slightly crooked, clearly filmed from somewhere hidden. Wendy's coat lay draped over a folding chair. Thomas stood too close. His hand brushed her waist. The timestamp glowed in the corner of the screen.

Opening night. Five thirty-two p.m.

My stomach dropped. Because five thirty-two p.m. was right before the choir show, and Violet had been at the hot cocoa station right before she hit the stage. Holden stepped closer to me, his eyes narrowing.

LuLu whispered, "Is that—?"

"Yes," I breathed.

Patricia disconnected her phone from the projection screen, her hands trembling now with something closer to grief than fury. "I'm filing for divorce," she said, her voice no longer raised but somehow carrying farther. "I have proof, and I'm done pretending."

Thomas's composure cracked at last. "You don't understand—"

"Oh, I understand perfectly," she said. "And so does she." Her gaze cut to Wendy.

The crowd followed.

Wendy stood utterly still, her expression tight but not surprised...which told me everything.

"She filmed it," Patricia said bitterly. "She filmed the whole thing. Just in case he didn't give her what she wanted."

The square erupted into whispers.

Wendy finally stepped forward. "I didn't plan to use it," she said, her voice steady but cold. "Not unless I had to. You should have made my position permanent."

Thomas stared at her, horror flickering across his face. "You recorded us?"

"You promised," Wendy snapped, her composure fracturing. "You promised I'd get the lead caroler role for good, but I overheard you talking about replacing me. Nothing I do is ever good enough for you."

"And you thought blackmail was the answer?" he shot back.

Holden exhaled slowly beside me. "Lyra," he murmured. "The time."

"I saw it," I said quietly.

Five thirty-two p.m.

Violet had been alive and well at the cocoa station around then. Willa had claimed she'd spoken to her. Thomas and Wendy had been tangled in their own scandal across the grounds.

They couldn't have poisoned her.

Patricia's voice cut back through the noise. "You humiliated me in my own town," she said to Thomas. "So, I'm returning the favor." She turned and walked away before he could stop her.

Silence lingered in her wake.

Thomas stood on the stage, no longer dignified, just exposed. Wendy's back straightened, but her gaze darted briefly toward me. Not pleading or defensive. Almost…calculating. The crowd began to splinter, conversations exploding in every direction.

"Can you believe—"

"In the choir tent—"

"She filmed them?"

"That's when Violet was—"

Exactly. I turned to Holden. "Well, that rules them out."

He nodded once. "On the murder, anyway."

Calderis stepped closer, his gaze sweeping the dispersing crowd. "Human entanglements are…dramatic."

"That's one word for it," LuLu muttered, then added, "Someone has me beat for a change."

Thomas finally looked at me, his face pale and authority gone. "I had nothing to do with Violet's death," he said hoarsely.

"I know," I replied evenly. And I did. The proof had just shouted it in front of half the town.

Wendy caught my eye next, something unreadable flashing there. If she'd filmed that to secure her role, she'd been willing to weaponize humiliation. Which meant she was capable of manipulation. But murder? No. At least not that night.

As Tasha, the newly crowned Snow Queen, stood awkwardly on stage, clutching her crown, unsure whether she was supposed to smile or not, the festival music restarted hesitantly, like someone pressing *play* on normalcy. WishFest would survive this. It always did. But as Thomas descended the steps and Wendy turned away from the crowd, I couldn't shake the feeling that clearing their names only made the circle smaller.

One less theory.

One less pair of suspects.

And somewhere in Wishville, the real poisoner was watching the town implode over infidelity and thinking, Good, let them look there instead.

Twenty-One

BY SUNDAY AFTERNOON, the festival had begun to feel like a stage set that someone kept rearranging while pretending the script hadn't changed. The music still played. The vendors still smiled. The scent of cinnamon, roasted nuts, and woodsmoke still drifted through the crisp winter air like nothing in the world could possibly be wrong.

But Holden and I both knew better.

We stood just off the main festival lane near the command tent, steam rising from our coffee cups into the sunny sky, watching volunteers haul in folding tables while children tugged parents toward the last round of snow games. The world looked orderly, yet it felt anything but.

"We need to look harder," Holden said quietly beside me, his voice low enough not to carry. There was no anger in his tone now. No frustration. Just focus.

I nodded once, my breath visible between us. "We're running out of suspects, and the festival is almost over. Any outsiders will leave soon."

As if the universe had decided we'd earned the next move, Finch came barreling across the snow toward us, his scarf flying behind him like a distressed banner. "Chief!" he called, nearly slipping before catching himself. "Lyra!"

Holden straightened instantly. "What happened?"

"*The Snow Maze* vendor just got hit," Finch said, bent over and gasping. "Cash gone. I saw someone bolt out the side corridor. Hood up. Dark coat."

My pulse spiked immediately.

Holden didn't hesitate. "Which way?"

Finch pointed toward the towering white walls of *The Snow Maze* near the far edge of the grounds, where laughter usually echoed harmlessly between sculpted corridors.

"Block it off," Holden ordered. "No one else gets in."

We were already moving before Finch nodded.

The Snow Maze loomed ahead of us, its packed walls rising well over our heads, glinting faintly under the weak winter sun. From the outside it looked whimsical, almost charming, but I'd walked enough twisting corridors inside it to know how easily someone could vanish if they knew the turns.

We plunged through the entrance. The temperature dropped immediately, the high walls cutting wind and sound so that the world narrowed into crunching footsteps and distant muffled voices. The snow underfoot was churned with tracks from children's boots, volunteer tread, random loops and backtracks, but one set stood out sharply.

Deep. Fresh. Running.

"There," I breathed, pointing.

Holden followed the trail without breaking stride, his boots pounding through the corridor as we rounded the first turn. Ahead of us, a shadow flickered across a cross passage.

"Stop!" Holden barked.

The figure didn't even glance back.

Holden sprinted harder.

The maze swallowed sound in strange ways, bouncing it off curved snow walls so that the direction blurred and movement felt closer than it was. I let my awareness dip just slightly, not enough to draw attention or to flare magic, but enough to feel the vibration of heavy footfalls through compacted snow.

"He's cutting left," I said. "Toward the service exit."

Holden adjusted course instantly. We rounded another corner just as the hooded figure skidded into a narrow side corridor that most visitors wouldn't even notice. He was fast, but not practiced. His movements were frantic rather than controlled. He reached a thinner section of wall near the back perimeter, an emergency breakthrough designed for safety.

He tried to climb. His boots slipped on packed ice. Holden hit him low and hard, tackling him before he could get enough leverage to pull himself over. They crashed into the snow together in a burst of white powder and scrambling limbs. I reached them just as the hood fell back.

Elliot.

For half a second, the image didn't register...then it did. "Elliot?" I said, disbelief flattening my voice.

He froze under Holden's weight, breathing hard, his cheeks flushed bright red against the cold. "I didn't hurt anyone," he blurted immediately, panic cracking through the words. "I swear."

"Then why are you running?" Holden demanded, pinning his wrists behind his back.

Elliot's gaze darted toward me, then toward the maze exit behind us, calculating and desperate.

Finch stumbled into the corridor a moment later, nearly colliding with the wall before catching himself. When he saw Elliot in the snow, something in him visibly broke. "No," Finch said softly, almost to himself. "Not you."

Elliot swallowed, shame flooding his face. "I needed it," he said, his voice shaking now that the chase was over. "I needed the money."

"For what?" Holden asked, his voice filled with frustration.

Elliot's jaw tightened, then trembled. "My mom's treatment," he said finally. "The bills keep coming. Insurance only covers so much. The rest doesn't care if you're trying your best."

The air shifted. For a moment, anger drained away, replaced with something heavier and more complicated.

"That's not the way," I said quietly.

Elliot laughed once, brittle and humorless. "Easy for you to say."

"It isn't," I replied, stepping closer so he could see I meant it. "But this hurts everyone."

Finch shook his head slowly, devastation written across his features. "You could've come to me," he said. "To the town. We would've helped."

Elliot looked away. "They told me that too," he muttered.

"They?" Holden pressed.

Silence stretched.

Snow drifted down softly from the top of the maze wall, catching in Elliot's hair.

"You didn't do this alone," Holden continued, his voice steady but unyielding. "There were too many distractions. Too many clean grabs. It was all too coordinated."

Elliot's shoulders slumped. "They promised I wouldn't take the fall," he whispered.

"Who?" Holden demanded.

Elliot closed his eyes briefly, then opened them with a look that said he'd already decided he was done protecting anyone else. "Edward," he said. "He's the one on the inside. He helps the mayor with deposits. He knows how to adjust totals. Knows where to shave without anyone noticing."

My heart sank. "And Ozzy?" I asked, guessing he was connected.

Elliot nodded miserably. "Ozzy did the grabs," he said. "Quick hands. Knows how to disappear in a crowd. He'd hand it off and be gone before anyone realized."

"And you?" Holden asked.

"I set the distractions," Elliot admitted. "Loose wiring. 'Malfunctioning' lights. I'd cause a scene somewhere else, so the focus shifted."

The generator crisis.

Every small disruption that had seemed like bad luck.

"They said it was harmless," Elliot continued. "Just taking back what the town wasted."

"Who said that?" I pressed.

Elliot hesitated just a fraction too long.

Holden leaned in slightly. "Tell us."

"They both did," he said quickly. "Edward said the books were already crooked. Ozzy said the festival money never really helped people who needed it."

"And when it almost fell apart?" Holden asked.

Elliot's laugh was hollow. "They turned on me." Snow clung to his lashes as he shook his head. "When we almost got caught near the cocoa stand, Ozzy shoved the cash box at me and ran. Edward vanished. They just left me standing there with no choice but to run."

My stomach tightened. "You were the scapegoat," I said quietly.

He didn't deny it.

Holden stood and pulled Elliot up with him. "Where are they now?" he asked.

Elliot hesitated again.

"Right now," Holden added. "Tell me and this will go easier for you."

Elliot's breath hitched. *"The Snowshoe Race,"* he said. "Through the woods. They're volunteering at checkpoints. Easy place to slip off trail. That was the original plan for all of us."

Of course. The racecourse cut deep into forested paths beyond the main grounds, winding through trees thick enough to hide anything. Holden's jaw tightened. Behind us, faint festival music floated through the maze entrance, cheerful and oblivious.

I looked at Finch.

He stood there, his shoulders squared but eyes hollow. "I'll handle him," Finch said quietly, nodding toward Elliot.

Holden didn't argue. "Thanks. I'll send my officers to take him in." Then Holden met my gaze. "Let's go," he said.

And together, we left the maze at a run. Because if Edward and Ozzy thought Elliot would carry their guilt alone...they were about to learn just how fast the snow could turn under their feet.

The forest swallowed the festival noise. The moment Holden and I crossed the final string of lanterns marking the edge of *The Snowshoe Race*, the air shifted from sweet and celebratory to cold and unfiltered, heavy with pine and packed snow and the quiet that only deep woods can hold. The sound of music and chatter from WishFest faded behind us, dissolving into distance until all that remained was the crunch of our boots and the harsh rhythm of our breathing.

The trail wound forward in narrow curves, ribboned markers tied to low branches fluttering faintly in the thin winter light. Snow lay thick and pristine beyond the packed path, untouched except where stray footprints veered off and vanished between trees.

"Weylan," Holden said into his radio as we ran, his voice clipped but controlled. "Status?"

Static answered first, then a voice faint but steady said, "Calderis and LuLu are ahead of you. They appear to have located your suspects."

"Located how?" Holden asked without breaking stride.

A pause hung heavy over the line. "Let's just say they're... contained."

I shot Holden a look.

He didn't slow down.

We rounded a bend where the trail dipped and rose into a

natural clearing ringed by tall, frost-dusted pines. The air felt strangely still there, like the forest itself had paused mid-breath.

And in the center of that clearing stood Ozzy and Edward.

Ozzy's hands were raised, his fingers splayed wide in surrender, his face flushed and mottled from cold and fear. Edward stood beside him, his back hunched. Neither of them looked like criminals in some cinematic sense. They looked like men who had reached the end of their lies and discovered there was nowhere else to run.

LuLu stood slightly behind them, her posture deceptively relaxed but her eyes alert and calculating. Calderis flanked them with an almost unnerving stillness, his dark coat stark against the white landscape and his presence heavy enough to alter the air itself.

Fenrin sat near LuLu's boots in fox form, her tail curled neatly around her paws, her amber eyes never blinking.

Holden slowed to a controlled stop. "Talk."

No preamble. No softness. Edward broke first.

"It was Alistair," he said, the name coming out like something he'd been choking on.

For a moment, I felt my brain resist the shape of it. Alistair Hawthorne, with his polished manners and carefully tailored suits, who drifted from booth to booth like a benevolent benefactor. Alistair, who had spent half the festival surrounded by delighted laughter and admiration.

And yet...the most visible people often made the best shadows.

Holden's gaze hardened. "You're sure."

Edward laughed hollowly, his breath fogging in the cold. "He told us it was ethical. Said the town mismanaged funds. Said he was just redistributing."

Ozzy jumped in, panic making him sloppy. "He's not rich. It's an act. He finds lonely women. Older women with savings and not enough attention. He makes them feel adored, then he drains them."

The words landed heavy and ugly as I thought of my beloved Wellies.

"He got the thugs off my back," Ozzy continued, his voice cracking. "I owed money. Bad money. He made one call and they disappeared. Like magic. Then he told me what I owed him."

"A cut," Holden said flatly.

Ozzy nodded.

"And Edward?" I asked.

Edward's shoulders sagged further. "Alistair knew I was greedy. He watched me. Listened to my complaints about being underpaid. About responsibility without reward. So he pushed for me to handle deposits in the mayor's office. Called me trustworthy."

Holden's jaw tightened. "You adjusted the books."

"Yes," Edward said. "I tried to make the vendor totals match the lighter boxes, but when the vendors noticed discrepancies, I made it seem like small clerical errors."

"And Elliot caused the distractions," Holden pressed.

Edward swallowed. "Yes. We all knew he was desperate. I feel bad about that one. We never should have ditched him, but survival of the fittest, you know?"

"No, I don't," Holden said between his teeth. "I would never *ditch* anyone."

Snow drifted lazily among us, quiet and indifferent. Holden radioed for units, his tone efficient and unyielding. Within minutes, officers emerged through the trees, breathless and tense, cuffs ready.

As Ozzy and Edward were taken into custody, Ozzy looked back once, panic bleeding into regret. "He'll ruin you," he muttered.

"He will try." Calderis's expression didn't change. "I welcome the challenge."

Once the clearing emptied, Holden turned to us. "Let's find Alistair. And when we do...he's mine."

We didn't need to debate where. Alistair would be somewhere public. Somewhere admired. Somewhere central.

We found him at the highest clearing overlooking the festival grounds, where snow sparkled under bright winter light and the view made everything look picturesque and orderly. It was the kind of place tourists photographed and locals claimed proudly.

And there he stood.

Alistair Hawthorne, holding court. Tilly stood close to him, her eyes wide with admiration. Belle flanked him with poised elegance. Dot hovered nearby, watchful and precise. Alistair laughed at something Tilly said, lifting his cup of cider with casual charm. Then he saw us. His smile didn't falter. It shifted.

"Quite the welcoming committee," he said lightly, setting down his cup.

"Step away from them," Holden ordered.

Alistair tilted his head. "From whom?"

Before we could close the distance, he moved with alarming smoothness, sliding an arm around Tilly's shoulders and pulling her in front of him. His other hand rose and a gun appeared, dark against white snow. The clearing went silent, and Tilly inhaled sharply.

Holden froze, as if calculating angles.

Calderis's presence sharpened into something dangerous and ancient.

LuLu tensed in a ready position from her jujitsu classes.

My magic surged instinctively, heat flaring under my skin, but there was no safe direction to send it with Tilly trapped in front of him and the whole town watching.

"Let's remain civilized," Alistair said calmly.

Belle's mouth fell open.

Dot's eyes narrowed to slits.

Tilly's expression hardened.

Suddenly, Belle dropped her handbag with surgical precision and pivoted sharply, striking upward beneath Alistair's wrist with surprising strength, snapping his gun arm wide.

Dot lunged low at the same instant, hooking behind his knee and driving her shoulder into his hip with a force that had no business coming from someone who regularly discussed book club plot holes and the aches and pains of the over fifty club.

"Cardigan Crushers' flank maneuver!" Dot barked like a WWE tag team.

Alistair stumbled.

Tilly broke free. And instead of shaking…she straightened, her eyes blazing with indignation. Then she launched herself forward with the full weight of righteous fury and sparkly boots, driving into his chest and taking him down flat into the snow.

They hit hard.

Snow erupted around them.

"Took you long enough!" Tilly declared, planting a knee on his shoulder.

Belle adjusted her scarf. "We were building suspense."

Dot planted her own knee near his ribs. "Coordination matters."

Holden lunged in, wrenching the gun from Alistair's hand and snapping cuffs onto his wrists in one clean motion.

Alistair stared up in stunned disbelief. "You ridiculous women," he hissed.

Tilly gasped theatrically. "Ridiculous? You're the ridiculous one to think you can make fools out of us."

Belle lifted her chin. "We prefer formidable. And we take care of our own if you haven't noticed."

Dot adjusted her glasses. "We do Pilates. And you're *no* James Bond, darling. Besides, no one messes with my besties. Only *we're* allowed to do that."

"Twice a week Pilates," Belle added.

"With soup cans," Tilly said proudly.

"And grandchildren," Dot nodded solemnly. "Advanced resistance training."

Vex, perched like a dark marble statue on a nearby snowbank, flicked his tail and spoke with crisp approval. *The Cardigan*

Crushers have demonstrated superior tactical capability. I concede my earlier skepticism.

LuLu laughed outright, her gift definitely growing stronger.

Holden's mouth twitched over what the women said, having no clue about Vex's addition.

Alistair was hauled upright, his polish gone and arrogance fractured. "You have no idea what you've disrupted," he spat.

Tilly brushed snow from her coat calmly. "Your dating schedule?"

Belle sighed. "Oh dear. I'll have to cancel Tuesday."

Dot nodded. "Rescheduling Pilates."

They linked arms, triumphantly.

"The Cardigan Crushers killed it," Tilly declared.

"Trademark pending," Belle added.

"Accepting sponsorships," Dot finished.

As officers escorted Alistair downhill in cuffs, the winter sun caught in the snow and scattered light across the clearing like applause. And for the first time all weekend, I felt the tension in my chest ease. Because while we had chased shadows and unraveled schemes, it had taken three underestimated women in festive knitwear to bring the mastermind down in broad daylight.

And Wishville, at last, felt like it could breathe again.

CHAPTER
Twenty-Two

LATER THAT NIGHT, Wishville wore its calm like a costume. The festival lights still draped the square in soft halos, and the fountain kept whispering as if it hadn't witnessed an entire week of secrets slithering through town like eels under ice, but the crowds had thinned into small knots of stragglers and late-hour wanderers.

Tourists clutched paper cones of fried dough, and locals lingered in pairs as if they didn't want to go home and sit alone with the stories they'd been forced to believe. The air smelled of espresso and sugar and wet stone, and every so often a gust would carry the sharper bite of woodsmoke from the bonfires still burning up on the festival grounds.

Holden's apartment was on the fourth floor of the old brick building that faced the square. The one with the slate mansard roof and wrought-iron balconies. When the elevator doors parted, a carpet runner in a herringbone pattern led down the quiet hall to his place, muffling footsteps and giving the whole floor the kind of hush that felt like you were trespassing even when you belonged there.

Inside, the industrial bones consisting of brick wall, exposed beams, and metal window casements were softened by choices that were purely Holden. A dark leather sofa anchored the living room, scattered with throw pillows in salt-and-pepper wool. A low walnut coffee table held a single coaster, placed so neatly it looked like he'd measured it. A pair of framed black-and-white photos, one of a snowy patrol car half-buried in a Boston drift, and one of a Boylston Street finish line, hung above a shelf of carefully battered paperbacks arranged by the color of their spines.

A system that made no logical sense and yet somehow suited him perfectly.

The kitchen ran along the far wall in matte black cabinets, an orderly rank of glassware, and a set of cast-iron pans that looked as if they'd seen more omelets than he would ever admit. There was a cutting board scarred with the quiet evidence of a man who cooked when he needed his hands to do something other than clench.

Beyond the windows, the square shimmered in full Winter WishFest glory. Strings of festival lights arched from lamppost to lamppost, casting a warm amber glow across snow-dusted brick and dark ribbons of asphalt. Paper lanterns in frosted blues and silvers swayed gently above the walkways, and evergreen garlands wrapped with white ribbon framed storefronts in a way that felt celebratory rather than sentimental.

At the center, the fountain stood transformed into an ice sculpture of itself, its water frozen mid-arc in a dramatic crystalline spray, lit from below so it glowed like captured starlight. The entire square looked like it had stepped into its own winter fairytale, alive and humming beneath the cold.

Somewhere in the apartment, hidden, because Holden never did anything loudly, jazz hummed from a speaker, the brush of a snare and a tenor sax letting the late hour breathe between notes. For the first time in what felt like forever, the world wasn't demanding anything from me.

Exhausted, and no words necessary, I smiled as I joined Holden on the couch. The leather creaked softly when he shifted, and I'd tucked myself against him like I could borrow his steadiness. His arm rested around my waist, warm and solid, his fingers idly tracing the seam of my sweater in small, absentminded circles. I had kicked my boots off near the door, and now tucked my feet under his thigh. Every part of me wanted to sink into the simple luxury of not having to speak.

"Your shoulders are up around your ears," Holden murmured, his voice low with more observation than teasing.

I let out a breath that sounded like a laugh. "They live there now."

He hummed, then brushed his knuckles down my arm slowly, the gesture soft enough to feel almost cautious. "You don't know how to stop."

I tilted my head back to look at him, and in the warm lamplight his face looked less like the town's gruff police chief and more like a tired man who had learned how to carry responsibility the hard way. His eyes were a darker gray than usual, shadowed at the edges with exhaustion, and the texture of his beard made him look rougher, more human.

"You sound like you're accusing me," I said quietly.

His mouth twitched. "I'm accusing you of being stubborn."

"That's not new."

"No," he agreed. "But you're also carrying things you don't have to carry alone."

The words hit too close. I still had a hard time relying on anyone other than myself. I swallowed, my gaze glancing toward the square beyond his windows where the festival lights made everything look peaceful. I didn't want to think about my own peril, so I focused on my other worries.

"Violet," I said, and the name tasted like cold metal. "She's still…everywhere."

Holden's arm tightened around me, not suffocating, just anchoring. "We'll get whoever did it."

I wanted to believe we already had. We'd exposed Alistair's theft ring, hauled the accomplices into custody, and watched the town's gossip machine pivot on a dime. But the murder had lingered like a shadow that refused to detach from the person it belonged to.

"I can feel it," I whispered. "That it's close. The truth. It's right there. I keep reaching for it but grabbing air."

Holden's thumb brushed my cheek, his touch warm. "Then we keep reaching." He dipped his head down and pressed his lips to mine. For a handful of minutes, we let the jazz fill the space between us and enjoyed being in each other's arms.

Then Holden's phone buzzed on the coffee table.

The vibration seemed loud in the quiet, jarring enough that my nerves jumped as we pulled apart. Holden's gaze snapped to the screen, and I watched the shift happen in real time: softness draining away from his face and focus sliding into place like a weapon being assembled.

"Thorn," he answered, his voice clipped.

I sat up automatically, dread tightening in my chest.

Holden listened, his eyes narrowing as the voice on the other end spoke. His free hand lifted to rub his bearded jaw, an old tell of his when he was trying to keep his anger controlled.

"Slow down," he said. "Where are you right now?"

A pause filled the space. His gaze cut to me, and my stomach dropped.

"Percy," he said, his voice lowering. "You're positive."

Another pause hung in the air, longer this time.

Holden's jaw flexed. "Do not intervene. You hear me? Do not go inside. You did good, now keep your distance." He ended the call and stared at the phone for a beat like he wished he could snap it in half.

"What?" I asked, already rising.

"One of my informants has been tailing Percy Johnson," Holden said, moving fast now, standing and grabbing his jacket from the back of a chair. "Percy met with known drug dealers. My source confirmed it."

My blood chilled instantly. "And?" My voice came out tight.

Holden slid his phone into his pocket, his keys already in his hand. "Percy went to Dana Snowe's house right after. Looked around before he went inside like he didn't want anyone to see him."

A wave of nausea rolled through me so hard I had to grip the edge of the coffee table. "No," I whispered, and the word wasn't denial so much as a plea to a universe that had already proven it didn't care.

Holden's eyes met mine, and we didn't need to say what we were both thinking: Violet had been poisoned. Dana had been the town's grief-stricken sister, fragile and trembling, the tragic survivor. If Percy was inside her house now…

"He's going to kill her," I said, my voice breaking on the last word.

Holden was already strapping on his holster, his movements brisk and practiced. "We don't know that."

"You don't meet with drug dealers at night and then sneak into someone's house to borrow sugar," I snapped, grabbing my boots.

Holden's gaze flashed with something like agreement, and he didn't waste breath arguing. "Get your coat."

We left his apartment so quickly the jazz was still playing when the door shut behind us, the square still glowing as if nothing had changed. Outside, the cold hit my face like a slap. The festival lights looked beautiful and wrong, twinkling over streets that had suddenly become dangerous again.

Holden drove like the town was an obstacle course. Snowbanks blurred past. The tires hissed on packed snow, and my hands stayed clenched in my lap because if I gave them freedom they might start shaking.

"You should call for backup," I said.

"Already did," Holden replied. "Patrol is staged. We're first because we're closest."

The drive took less than ten minutes and still felt like my heart aged ten years. He killed the headlights two houses down from

Dana's place, and the darkness that followed felt thick and intimate.

Dana's house sat quiet under a dusting of snow, her porch light glowing and curtains drawn. A wreath hung slightly crooked on the door, the kind Violet would have straightened without thinking because she'd cared about small things.

My throat tightened.

Holden touched my wrist lightly. "Stay close," he murmured.

We moved through the yard, keeping low, our boots crunching softly. Every sound felt amplified—our breath, the faint creak of branches, the distant hush of the square. At the side window, Holden lifted a hand, signaling me to stop. We peered through the glass.

Inside the kitchen, Dana stood near the island, her hair pulled back, her face flushed. I didn't see anyone else. She must have sent her staff home. Percy stood across from her, his shoulders tense and hands moving sharply as he spoke. Even through the window I could feel the aggression rolling off him, that old dangerous side people had whispered about in town.

They were arguing hard and fast, their heads too close.

Dana pointed toward the counter, her mouth moving in a rapid stream. Percy's hand snapped out and grabbed something small…something that fit in his palm. Dana lunged, but Percy yanked back. They wrestled, their bodies colliding and hands grappling around the object like it was the only thing that mattered.

Holden's grip tightened around my wrist. "Now," he said.

We didn't bother knocking. Holden shoved the door open with authority that made the hinges groan, and we rushed into the kitchen like winter storming inside.

"Police!" Holden barked.

Dana screamed, stumbling back. Percy spun, his eyes wide, and for a fraction of a second he looked like an animal trapped in a cage. Holden crossed the room in two strides and slammed Percy against the counter, wrenching his arm behind him.

Dana clutched her throat, shaking, tears spilling instantly. "He tried to poison me!" she sobbed. "He tried to poison me just like he did Violet!"

The words stabbed through me.

Percy twisted against Holden's grip. "That's not...ow!" He let out a harsh laugh. "You have it wrong. You have it so wrong."

Holden drove him harder into the counter. "Shut up."

Percy's eyes flashed. "No. I'm done shutting up."

Dana's sobs grew louder.

Holden's voice was tight. "What were you doing here, Percy?"

Percy's breathing was ragged. His gaze darted to Dana, and something ugly twisted across his face. "She made me," he said.

Dana's voice snapped up. "Liar!"

Percy barked a bitter laugh. "You want to call me that now?"

Holden leaned closer, his voice low and lethal. "Talk."

Percy swallowed, then the words burst out like he couldn't hold them back anymore. "She wanted Violet gone. She didn't say it like that, though. She made it sound like a wellness thing. Biohacking. Microdosing. Longevity."

Dana's tears slowed, and she kept shaking her head.

Percy kept going, frantic now. "She said cardiac glycosides in tiny, controlled doses could support circulation. That rich people did it. That no doctor would prescribe the materials. She said she'd pay me big if I used my connections to get it."

My stomach turned, and doubt crept in.

"She told me she was working with some holistic practitioner," Percy continued, his voice cracking with fury at his own gullibility. "She made it sound like another rich-woman trend."

"And when Violet died?" I asked, my voice dangerously quiet.

Percy flinched. "I realized she used it to kill her sister. She put the poison in the sample cup of cocoa and then told me to give it to Violet. I thought she was trying to help me win her back. I had no idea she wanted her dead."

Dana's face tightened, her eyes turning cold.

Percy's eyes stayed locked on her. "I confronted her after

Violet collapsed. I knew it had to be her. She told me she'd blame it on me because I'm the one with the violent past. I'm the one everyone already suspects. She fished the poisoned cup out of the trash after Violet threw it away and planted it in the storage shed to set me up. I found the cup before you guys did, but I didn't realize a chunk was missing. I knew it wouldn't matter anyway. No one would believe me over her."

Holden's gaze flicked to me, grimly.

Percy's voice dropped, raw. "I didn't even know Violet had cut her off. Didn't know Violet controlled the money. I didn't know Violet took away her allowance because Dana couldn't stop spending."

Dana took a slow breath…then she smiled. Her tears dried as if they'd never existed. "Finally," she said softly, and the word was all ice. "Pretending I'm sad my sister is gone was so exhausting."

My blood went cold.

Holden's voice snapped. "Dana—"

Dana's hand moved. A gun rose into view as if she'd been holding it just out of sight this entire time, waiting for the right moment. She aimed it at us with smooth confidence.

Percy went rigid. "Dana, don't."

"Oh, Percy," Dana purred, her voice dripping contempt. "You got soft." She looked at me then, and the expression on her face wasn't grief or fear or even anger.

It was satisfaction.

"My sister was always the favorite," she said, and the sneer stripped the last illusion away. "Granny left Violet in charge of the money, even though I'm older. Violet treated me like a child, like she had the right to decide what I could spend, what I could do, who I could be."

Her finger tightened slightly on the trigger.

"So, I removed her," she said simply, as if describing taking out the trash. "I slipped the poison into the cocoa sample, knowing my greedy sister would hit all the stations. And to ensure she was the one who drank it, I had Percy give it to her. He was so desperate to win her back, he would do anything. I planted the cup in the storage shed for insurance. Now my sister can't control me anymore. The money is all mine."

"And Ozzy?" I demanded, my hands curling, magic stirring under my skin.

Dana's gaze glanced toward the window like she could already see the future. "Ozzy is a loose end. He'll come back once he's out of jail. He'll threaten me again. But I'm not going to be threatened by some cousin who can't control his gambling habit."

Percy's voice was hoarse. "I'm not a murderer," he said, almost pleading. "Dana was always secretive, insisting on talking in person so there would never be a phone or e-mail trail to trace back to her. I thought she wanted the compound for herself. I didn't know she meant—"

Dana's eyes cut to him with disgust. "You were supposed to be useful, but all you are is pathetic."

Holden's voice was dangerously calm. "Put the gun down."

Dana laughed softly. "Sorry, Chief. It's too late for that. Now you're all loose ends as well." The gun jerked, and the shot cracked through the kitchen like thunder.

Time narrowed, and everything moved as if in slow motion.

I reacted with pure instinct. Skycall surged through me. The air pressure shifted as a violent controlled gust snapped sideways, and the bullet's path bent just enough to slam into the wall instead of Holden. Plaster dust exploded.

Dana's face registered shock then she fired again.

I countered and moved the air again, shoving the bullet into a cabinet door that splintered and rattled this time. Holden lunged, but Dana backed away, her rage overriding logic now. She screamed and charged toward me, as if she could tear my power out with her bare hands.

The moment she closed the distance between us, I thrust my hands forward and manipulated the air in the room once more. It hit her like a slammed door. Dana flew backward across the room and crashed into the dining table, chairs skittering, a bowl of pinecones tumbling and scattering across the floor like forgotten ornaments.

I'd knocked her out cold.

As time moved back to a normal pace, Percy stared…stunned. "W-What just happened?" He gaped at me. "W-Who are you?"

"Something you won't remember come morning," I said softly.

Holden crossed the room and pinned Dana as she came to before she could rise, wrenching her arms back, and snapping cuffs on with cold efficiency. Sirens began to rise outside, growing closer. It was over. Holden dragged a groggy Dana upright, holding her firmly. Percy sagged against the counter, shaking.

Holden's gaze burned into Percy. "Who was the hooded figure?"

Percy swallowed hard, already shaking his head. "I don't know."

Holden's voice sharpened. "You met with dealers. You don't know who you met with?"

Percy's eyes widened. "This wasn't my dealers. I swear. They kept threatening me…asking questions about—"

"Nice try, pal, but I'm not buying it."

Neither was I.

"But you don't understand. They—"

"I understand all too well, and you know too much." Holden looked at me.

Percy and Dana had just seen magic in a human kitchen, and that truth couldn't be allowed to survive cleanly. Holden gave me a grim nod. I stepped close, and reached inward for the careful, quiet part of my power.

Memory Seal.

"Wait, what's going on?" Percy's eyes grew huge.

"This won't hurt a bit," I said.

"You can't—" Dana started.

"I can," I said and touched Dana's temple, then Percy's,

smoothing the sharp edges of what they'd witnessed as an amber wave seeped beneath their skin so their minds would not be able to replay these memories with clarity. Bullets would become "near misses." Air shifts would become "luck." My shove would become "she slipped."

When I withdrew, my hands trembled.

"What just happened," Dana asked, blinking.

"Where are we?" Percy looked confused.

The door burst open moments later with officers flooding in, weapons drawn, and voices clipped. Holden handed Dana and Percy over briskly, giving instructions, making it official. Dana was led out, still looking confused. Percy stumbled behind, his face a blank hollow. As they were taken away, the kitchen looked wrecked. There were bullet holes, broken cabinets, and pinecones scattered across the floor like evidence of a party turned rotten.

Holden stepped close, his hand settling at my waist with quiet steadiness. "You okay?"

I swallowed, forcing breath into lungs that felt too tight. "I will be."

I stepped outside into the cold night, festival lights glittering in the distance like nothing had happened. But it had. The murder was solved. The lie had been exposed.

And the truth had finally won.

Twenty-Three

THE DREAM DID NOT BEGIN with images. It began with breath. Not mine. A Dream Whisperer's. It exhaled in a slow, resonant rhythm that seemed to rise from the marrow of the mountain itself, a sound like wind slipping through hollowed bark and over crystalline roots buried deep in soil.

I stood barefoot in the clearing of the Woodswhisper, silver mist curling around my ankles in lazy spirals that shimmered as though they were thinking. Above me, the canopy arched in impossible geometry—branches braided with living light, leaves thin and translucent as glass, each one pulsing faintly, as if the forest were not simply alive but attentive.

Waiting.

The trunk before me rippled.

The seam did not appear all at once—it revealed itself the way truth often does. Slowly and reluctantly, as though testing whether I was prepared to see it. The bark thinned along a vertical line, light gathering beneath its surface until the grain itself seemed to breathe. A narrow spiral hollow formed within the trunk, not carved by tool or time but grown, an interior path that did not feel like a door so much as an invitation.

I stepped closer, compelled by something deeper than curiosity, and placed my palm against the glowing wood. It warmed instantly beneath my touch.

Balance-Bearer.

The word did not echo aloud, and yet it resounded through my bones with the weight of something remembered rather than newly learned. Beneath my feet, the ground shifted in a subtle tremor that rippled outward into unseen depths. I felt and saw the path waiting above and below at once. A climb between layers of oath and stone and silence. A passage not merely through space, but through withheld truth.

Urgency pressed against my ribs.

Purpose.

I woke with that same pressure lodged behind my sternum, my heart pounding so violently it felt as though the bedframe might rattle in protest. The darkness of Holden's bedroom wrapped around me in familiar shadow, moonlight slanting across the ceiling in a thin, silver wash. His arm lay heavy and warm across my waist, his breathing slow and steady beside me, anchoring the world in ordinary reality.

But the urgency remained.

It did not fade with waking. It sharpened.

The Woodswhisper called.

I lay still for several breaths, trying to reason with myself. Trying to insist that dreams did not equal summons, that ancient trees did not send invitations in the middle of the night without consequence. But this had not felt like warning. It had felt like inevitability.

If *The Accord Hall* existed, and my mother's journal left no room for doubt, then it would not reveal itself to a gathering. It would not open beneath the watchful gaze of Calderis or the political caution of his father. It would not respond to strategy, or even to righteous anger.

It would respond to blood.

To a *Balance-Bearer.*

To me…alone.

Carefully, I eased Holden's arm from my waist and slipped from the bed. He stirred faintly, his brow furrowing, but did not wake. For a fleeting moment, I considered leaving a note. A reassurance. A lie that I would be back before sunrise.

I did not.

There are some journeys that cannot be softened by explanation beforehand. They must be taken first and justified later. I dressed in the dim light into dark jeans, a thick wool sweater, boots laced tight, and a coat wrapped close. I slipped out into the square, the cold air biting sharply against my cheeks.

Lanterns still glowed along the pathways, casting silver halos across snow-dusted brick. The frozen fountain shimmered in crystalline stillness, lit from below so that its suspended arcs looked almost alive. Winter WishFest banners fluttered gently overhead, deep blues and frosted whites catching moonlight in quiet defiance of sleep.

Vex appeared at the top of the hill in the festival clearing, his blue eyes bright in the shadows. He'd always sensed my intentions, sometimes even before they fully formed in my mind. I could feel his concern.

You are not going for tea, he observed dryly.

"No," I whispered.

He studied me, his tail flicking once. *Alone?*

"I must."

He let out a long, theatrical sigh. *Then try not to unravel the foundation of two realms without me.*

"I'll do my best." I locked gazes with him. "I promise. Hold down the fort for me while I'm gone?"

I always do. He vanished into the mist almost as quickly as he had appeared.

The well waited at the edge of the clearing, ancient and unassuming. I placed my hand upon its rim and let my magic seep downward into the stone, into root and seam and threshold, as I whispered the incantation and stepped over the edge. The shift between realms was subtle but absolute, like stepping through a breath held too long.

Elarion rose around me in luminous silence.

The realm's nocturnal glow painted everything in soft radiance. Bioluminescent vines trailed along crystalline walkways, towers refracting distant starlight, and the air itself hummed faintly with layered wards and ancient memory. Figures moved in distant arcs, Dwellers gliding across bridges of living crystal like reflections made flesh.

I did not head toward the city.

The forest called.

The Woodswhisper lay at the outer boundary where Elarion's roots thickened and the earth-song deepened. I felt its presence before it came into view, the ground vibrating faintly beneath my boots, and the air growing warmer and denser with something sentient and old. When I entered the clearing, the world around me flipped upside down and clouds swirled around my ankles. The tree that towered before me hung exactly as it had in my dream. Its trunk spiraled and was immense, the bark etched with luminous veins that pulsed in slow rhythm like a heartbeat beneath skin.

"I'm here," I murmured, though the words felt insufficient.

The crystal bark warmed beneath my palm. The seam revealed itself again, not as a sudden fracture but as a thinning. The wood dissolved into light as a narrow interior spiral formed within.

I climbed inside.

The passage was alive. It was not merely wood but something deeper—bone and crystal and root intertwined, warm beneath my hands as I climbed higher. The spiral angled upward and inward simultaneously, twisting in directions that defied spatial logic. My boots braced against natural ridges as I pulled myself higher, my breath steady despite the narrowing space.

The light changed gradually, shifting from forest glow to mineral shimmer. Bark gave way to stone. The air thickened, warmer now, carrying the scent of iron and ancient heat. The spiral ended in a narrow fissure.

I pushed through…and emerged into vastness.

The Accord Hall did not simply exist above Elarion—it felt as though it had been folded into the planet's core itself, a pocket dimension between realms. The chamber stretched in concentric terraces that ascended toward a central dais, columns rising from the floor to an unseen ceiling like pillars grown rather than carved. Golden veins pulsed faintly through dark stone, each one shimmering in quiet response to my presence. The warmth radiating was constant, a reminder that this place had been buried deliberately, sealed away where only the earth itself could witness it.

I moved along the ledge until I found a stair carved into the rock face, spiraling upward in slow, deliberate arcs. With each step, the sigils etched into the surrounding columns brightened faintly, reacting to my ascent.

Balance-Bearer.

The dais waited at the center. A circle of obsidian polished to mirror-dark perfection, surrounded by rings etched like ripples frozen mid-motion. At its heart stood a pedestal, and upon it lay a slab of pale stone. Not white, but pale, like bone. Or ash. Like something once luminous deliberately dulled.

The Pale Accord.

My breath caught as I stepped onto the platform. The golden veins in the surrounding stone brightened in cascading arcs, heat intensifying beneath my boots. I reached out. The slab warmed instantly beneath my palm. The script etched across its surface glowed faintly, and comprehension rose into me not as sound but as certainty.

> *The Well shall stand as a shared threshold and sanctuary,*
> *belonging to neither realm and to both in equal measure. The*
> *Balance-Bearers shall arise in pairs, never singular, that no bloodline*
> *stand alone beneath the burden of both worlds. One wish shall be*

granted each season not as dominion, but as covenant exchange, that peace remain balanced and neither side claim ownership over the other. The Accord shall not be altered save by a Balance-Bearer and witness in full consent.

My knees weakened as the words settled.

Pairs.

Not singular.

No bloodline stand alone.

The Elders had not merely simplified the language. They had rewritten the structure. They had erased balance and named dominion as protection. The chamber responded to my touch, golden veins flaring brighter along the columns, sigils shimmering in acknowledgment. This was not a relic meant to gather dust. It was a covenant waiting for reclamation.

Alone in the deepest chamber between Elarion and Wishville, I stood with the truth buried for generations pressed warm beneath my palm. The hall hummed with something older than either realm's politics.

The Pale Accord had waited for me...and I had finally found it.

The question was, what did I do about it?

The Accord Hall did not echo.

That realization settled into me slowly, like heat seeping through stone. The chamber was vast enough to cradle a cathedral, yet sound here behaved differently. It was absorbed and folded inward, devoured by the mineral hush that wrapped the terraces in solemn restraint. My breath did not bounce back to me. My boots did not send their steps skittering into the dark. So when the temperature shifted behind me and the fine hairs along my arms rose, I knew the change was not environmental.

It was presence.

The golden veins that pulsed through the stone walls flickered. They didn't dim or brighten. They recalibrated as though they were accounting for an additional variable. I did not turn immediately. My hand still rested against *The Pale Accord*, the slab warm beneath my palm, the words of the original covenant echoing through my mind in luminous certainty. The chamber had recognized me. It had answered. But something else had entered its perimeter.

I turned slowly.

He stood at the edge of the dais where shadow met molten light, his form outlined by the gold-thread glow that traced the chamber walls. His hair fell loose around his shoulders, pale gold as if spun from sun that had never touched human sky, and it caught the faint illumination like a blade catches fire. His skin held that luminous Dweller clarity that seemed sculpted rather than grown, and his eyes…his eyes burned with an unwavering molten gold that did not blink or soften.

Recognition struck with the sharpness of remembered fear.

"You," I said, the word tasting of cavern air and mountain stone.

He inclined his head slightly, and the movement was almost courtly. "Balance-Bearer." His voice did not carry loudly, yet it cut through the chamber with quiet authority, settling into the mineral air as if it belonged there.

Memory flashed: the mountain cavern, my mother's power crackling like lightning between us, his hand raised with killing intent until Serena's voice, fierce and commanding, had forced him to stand down.

"You nearly killed me," I said.

His mouth curved faintly, not apologetic or defensive, but satisfied. "And you survived," he replied.

The golden veins in the chamber pulsed once in unison, as though acknowledging the truth in that statement. My magic stirred instinctively, Seismic Sense unfurling beneath my boots in subtle arcs, mapping the density of stone and the flow of heat beneath the dais. *The Accord Hall* responded, but not exclusively to me. There was no rejection of him, no violent recoil.

That unsettled me more than anything.

"You shouldn't be here," I said quietly.

He stepped forward, and the air bent around him with subtle distortion, as if reality were adjusting its posture in deference. "I have been waiting for you," he said.

The words hit with quiet precision.

The dream.

"You were in my sleep," I said slowly, the realization locking into place with a cold click. "You threaded the path. You opened the seam."

His golden gaze held mine steadily. "I possess the Dream Whisper gift. Dream-Threading is an art of patience."

Kael. The name rose unbidden, shaped by whispers from my memory about the rebellion beneath Serena's leadership.

"You lured me," I said.

"I illuminated what already existed," he corrected softly.

Anger flared in my chest, bright and clean. "You manipulated me."

He did not deny it. Instead, he called out the name, "Lokar."

Behind him, movement emerged from shadow. Figures detached from the terraces. Tall, lean forms clad in muted leathers that absorbed light rather than reflected it. Their eyes glowed faintly in the mineral haze.

The man he called Lokar stepped into clearer view with his hood up. Even in this deep chamber, I recognized the stillness in him. The hooded figure glimpsed in Wishville alleys. The one who had lingered just beyond peripheral vision in crowds.

The watcher.

"You've been watching me," I said, keeping my voice steady.

Lokar inclined his head slightly. "Always."

My pulse quickened. "You approached Percy," I said, connecting the dots that now felt painfully obvious. "You tried to make him use the Elarion compound on me after seeing he gave

Dana the human compound. You didn't know Dana was the one who killed Violet."

Lokar's expression did not change. "He lacked resolve."

"He refused," I said.

"He feared consequence," Kael cut in. "He did not possess the necessary appetite."

The image of Percy in Dana's kitchen flashed through me—shaken, furious, flawed but not built for the cruelty Dana carried so easily.

"Because he's not a killer like Dana and you," I said. "You let Violet die."

Kael's gaze sharpened. "We observed human corruption. It was not our design."

I glared at Kael. "You could have had your man stop it."

"I sent Lokar to do a job. Intervention with the human would have revealed too much of our plan. Your distraction with her murder was an added bonus."

Cold fury slid through my veins. "And when Percy wouldn't poison me," I continued, "you waited for an opportunity to lure me away."

"Yes."

The simplicity of it stung.

"You knew I would return to the Woodswhisper," I said.

"The *Accord* calls to your blood," Kael replied.

My heart pounded harder. "You almost had me at the Woodswhisper before," I said, remembering the first time LuLu and I had sensed something wrong. "When we went looking together. We thought you were after her, but really you were after me all along."

"Yes," he said calmly. "But you were not alone. You were cautious. This hall does not open for caution."

The soldiers shifted slightly.

"And tonight?" I pressed.

"You came compelled," he said. "You came believing the call was sacred, just as I planned for."

Heat crept into my palms as Magma Ward stirred beneath my ribs. "Why?" I demanded. "Why orchestrate this?"

Kael's golden eyes burned brighter. "Serena is too restrained," he said. "She speaks of balance while the Elders rewrite history. She negotiates with those who have no intention of yielding power. She allows compassion to soften necessary action."

"She has a heart," I snapped.

He regarded me as one might regard a flaw in a blade. "Exactly." The word hung heavy.

"You want to overthrow her," I said, realization dawning.

"I want decisive leadership." The chamber's golden veins flickered erratically, as though reacting to the force of his ambition.

"You think killing me will do that?" I asked.

"You are her fracture point," Kael said. "If you fall, she will break. The rebellion will splinter. Authority will realign."

"You're going to crush her."

"I am going to remove hesitation."

The soldiers moved then with practiced efficiency. Two seized my arms from behind before my Magma Ward could crest fully into flame. Their grip was iron-hard, and when I drove Seismic Force downward, *The Accord Hall* absorbed the vibration, dispersing it harmlessly through concentric ripples etched into the floor.

The hall would not allow destruction within its core.

Kael's mouth curved faintly at my realization. "You feel it," he said. "This place protects itself."

They hauled me backward, off the dais, away from *The Pale Accord* and toward a narrow passage carved into shadow. The air grew warmer as we descended. Not forest warmth or mineral glow, but something sharper. *Chemical.* The corridor opened into a cavern where copper coils snaked across black stone walls, glass vessels glowed in muted hues, and the scent of crushed botanicals mingled with metallic undertones.

Veinwright Brews.

The lower-level illegal brewers the alchemist Eryndel had warned me about. They made a refined cardiac glycoside that was deadly when he refused to.

Tables carved from obsidian held mortar bowls filled with luminous petals, vials of concentrated extracts, and intricate glass apparatus that pulsed faintly with contained power. The air shimmered with faint vapor, carrying bitter notes that prickled at the back of my throat.

At the center of the chamber stood a low stone basin. Within it, a liquid swirled in slow spirals, glowing faintly in pale gold and sickly green. My lungs tightened before my mind finished processing.

"Wellbreaker's Bloom," I whispered as fear filled me. He must have found out my weakness from my mother.

Kael stepped beside the basin, his pale hair catching the dim light like a halo sharpened into weaponry. "A refined version," he said. "Blended precisely with the plant essence that destabilizes your hybrid physiology."

Foxglove. Oleander. Lily of the valley. Human poison. Dweller-enhanced. The scent alone made my skin prickle with anticipatory nausea.

"It will strip your Dweller half first," Kael continued, his voice almost clinical. "You will feel it withdraw like the tide receding violently from the shore. What remains will be human."

"And death," I said. "I can't survive without my Dweller half."

"Yes."

My heart pounded against my ribs, not from fear alone but from the crushing weight of his certainty.

"Only another half-blood could restore you," he added. "Blood to blood."

The hollow that opened in my chest was vast. "There aren't any," I said.

His gaze did not waver. "No, there aren't."

The chamber's glow seemed to dim slightly under that finality.

"You are Serena's weakness," he said softly. "And she is too soft to survive this."

The soldiers forced me to my knees before the basin. Lokar stepped forward and bound my wrists with mineral-woven restraints that bit cold and tight against my skin, the material humming faintly with warded energy that resisted Dweller manipulation.

The scent of the brew intensified. My magic recoiled instinctively, like a flame shrinking from water.

Kael crouched before me, his golden eyes unwavering. "You should have remained in Wishville," he said quietly. "You were safer pretending the worlds could remain separate."

"And you think killing me will unify them?" I shot back.

He rose smoothly. "I think sacrifice clarifies direction."

The basin pulsed brighter…and the air thickened. And as the first wave of Wellbreaker's Bloom rose toward me in a faint vapor, I understood with brutal clarity that his plan had unfolded precisely as designed.

He had threaded my dreams.

He had watched from the shadows.

He had waited until I came alone.

Now I knelt beneath Elarion's deepest chamber, bound before an illegal brew crafted to dismantle my very nature, while the rebel who sought to unseat my mother stood over me with serene conviction. I should have listened to Holden and Calderis. I should have trusted I didn't have to do everything alone. But it was too late…

The thought of never seeing either of them again was my final undoing.

CHAPTER
Twenty-Four

THE FIRST BREATH felt almost merciful.

That was what made it so insidious.

The vapor of Wellbreaker's Bloom slid into my lungs like cool mountain air, faintly floral, faintly metallic, and deceptively clean. For a suspended heartbeat, I thought perhaps Kael had misjudged the dosage, that perhaps the *Veinwright Brews* had failed him, and perhaps I could still rise and scorch this entire chamber into glass.

Then my magic recoiled. It did not flare in defiance or lash out...it withdrew.

The sensation was not immediate agony, but evacuation. A violent, relentless tide dragging away from shore, stripping sand from beneath my feet, pulling warmth from marrow and leaving behind exposed nerve and hollow ache. My Seismic Sense, which had always lived in the background of my awareness like a steady subterranean hum, fractured into static and then into nothing. The Magma Ward coiled inside my ribs guttered and went dim, as if someone had poured cold ash over a living flame. Even the subtle whisper of Skycall—air shifting obediently at my command— unspooled into silence.

"No," I breathed, but the word fell apart halfway through. There would be no healing myself this time.

The second inhale burned. It scraped down my throat with a bitter edge, blooming in my chest like frost spreading across glass. My pulse began to misfire, skipping beats, hammering erratically against my ribs that suddenly felt too narrow to contain it. The mineral glow of the chamber grew harsher without the Dweller half of me to soften it. My skin prickled. My limbs felt heavy, clumsy, and wrong.

Kael watched with no emotion. He did not gloat. He did not smile. He simply observed as if I were a science experiment. "You feel the severing," he said quietly, as though commenting on a natural phenomenon.

My hands trembled violently now. My fingers tingled and then went numb. I tried to summon Magma Ward on instinct alone, tried to draw from whatever ember remained, but there was nothing to answer me.

I was only human…and dying alone.

My knees buckled. The soldiers holding me loosened their grip because I no longer required restraint. I folded to the obsidian floor, the stone unforgiving against my cheek. It felt colder than it should have. Everything felt colder than it should have.

My heart stuttered violently in response.

Cardiac glycosides. Foxglove. Oleander. Lily of the valley. Violet had died from the human compound. This was its Dweller-enhanced counterpart, precise, amplified, and designed for someone like me. I didn't stand any more of a chance than she had.

The chamber door exploded inward.

Stone did not simply crack, it detonated. Heat surged through the *Veinwright Brews* with the force of a solar flare, blasting copper coils from their moorings and sending glass vessels shattering across the obsidian floor. The scent of crushed botanicals ignited into smoke.

"Kael!" My mother's voice tore through the cavern like thunder splitting a mountain.

Serena entered not as a shadowed revolutionary but as something ancient and incandescent. Her hair streamed behind her like molten silver silk caught in an unseen wind, and her lavender eyes burned with a ferocity that made the golden veins in the stone recoil and brighten in answer. Power radiated from her in controlled waves, bending heat and light into alignment with her fury.

Behind her came her followers. Men and women who had chosen her banner despite the fracture in Elarion's politics, moving with disciplined precision, their weapons humming with restrained force.

For the first time since I had known him, Kael's composure shifted. "Too late," he said.

My mother's gaze found me on the floor, and everything in her expression shattered.

The rebellion dissolved into violence. Her followers collided with Kael's soldiers in a storm of power and stone. Magma struck against golden blades. Seismic fractures rippled outward in controlled arcs that shattered *Veinwright* tables but spared the chamber's structural integrity. Heat barriers flared and splintered in rapid succession, sending obsidian shards skidding across the floor like black rain.

Lokar lunged toward me.

He never reached me.

Serena moved faster than thought. She intercepted him mid-stride, her palm striking his chest with contained force that hurled him backward into a wall of copper tubing. The metal buckled and collapsed around him in a cascade of steam and shattered glass.

Kael met her in the center of the cavern.

Their powers collided with a sound like tectonic plates grinding against each other. Golden dream-thread energy coiled toward Serena's mind, as if seeking entry and influence. She burned it away with visible incandescent clarity, her focus unassailable.

"You would sacrifice your own blood?" she demanded.

"She is your fracture point," Kael countered, pressing forward.

"She is my strength," she roared.

The chamber cracked beneath the weight of their exchange, but Kael had not come to win. He had come to execute. When Serena's followers began to overpower his ranks, and when *Veinwright Brews* tables overturned and illegal compounds spilled into harmless steam, Kael disengaged abruptly, seizing Lokar by the collar and signaling retreat.

"This is not finished," he said, his golden eyes blazing with promise rather than defeat.

Then he vanished into lower tunnels with what remained of his followers, retreat chosen over annihilation.

The cavern fell into fractured silence.

My mother was at my side in an instant. "Lyra," she breathed, cradling my face in hands that were blisteringly warm against my freezing skin.

My vision doubled and swam. My lungs struggled for shallow air. "It's too late," I managed. "He stripped it out of me."

Her fingers tightened. "No," she said fiercely. "It's not too late."

I tried to laugh. It came out thin and broken. "Only a half-blood," I whispered. "And there aren't—"

Her eyes flashed with certainty. "But there is."

The words cut through the fog in my skull, but I was too weak to speak.

She lifted me with impossible gentleness and impossible strength. *The Badlands* passage flared open before us, ancient wards igniting in response to her command. Her followers secured the cavern behind us as she carried me through molten corridors that pulsed faintly with subterranean life.

The air grew hotter the deeper we traveled, thick with sulfur and iron. Underground rivers hissed somewhere below, steam rising in ghostlike curls. *The Badlands* hideout emerged from the volcanic stone, a hidden refuge carved into living rock, shielded by layered wards and lit by low amber flames that flickered in recessed sconces. She laid me on a stone slab etched with sigils I had never seen before, intricate, interwoven, and ancient.

"You're lying," I rasped. "There isn't anyone."

Footsteps approached, measured and steady. I forced my eyes open. The man who stepped into the amber glow was older than the memory I carried, yet unmistakable. His shoulders were broader, his hair streaked with silver, and his face carved by years of endurance. But the line of his jaw, the shape of his eyes…those were unchanged.

"Dad?" I gasped.

Josiah Wells stopped as though struck. "I'm here," he said, and his voice broke.

The world tilted. "You died," I whispered. "The First Elder—"

"He kidnapped your father's ancestor," my mother said quietly, her voice steady despite the storm in her eyes. "He attempted to force the half-blood transformation unnaturally upon himself through ritual blood theft. It failed. It killed her, them both, and only the Entity remains, forever hungry for a half-blood host."

Rage flared faintly in my hollow chest.

"The entity was contained and the treaty formed," she continued. "We were happy for a while, raising you between both worlds, but after the treaty, your father and I had to separate. You stayed with me, but your father and I never stopped meeting in secret. Until your father died of old age, then you and I lived without him until a century ago when I found *The Accord Hall*. I was stunned when I found *The Pale Accord* and learned the treaty I had been fighting to uphold was a lie.

An Enforcer caught me, and we fought, but I knew his weakness and mortally wounded him. When I discovered the woman the first Elder had kidnapped for his unnatural experiment was your father's ancestor, I knew I had to avenge him. I couldn't go on defending a treaty that was a lie. Balance Bearers were supposed to exist and be born naturally the way you were, but I knew I couldn't fight this battle alone."

Josiah stepped closer, kneeling beside the slab. "Your mother brought me back to life," he said.

"I corrected what the Elder corrupted," my mother said. "I went to your father's grave and used the same ritual—balanced properly—with the fallen Enforcer. It worked this time."

"You made him a half-blood," I breathed.

"Yes. It was the only way to resurrect him, and then I destroyed the ritual so no one could ever repeat it again."

The chamber seemed to tilt again. "That's why you ran," I said.

"If either world had discovered him…" she replied, "Humans would have hunted him. Dwellers would have condemned him and punished me. The Elder's loyalists would have finished what they started."

"You let me believe you were gone," I said, and something sharp pushed through my fog.

Josiah's eyes filled. "Every day," he said hoarsely, "I have lived knowing you believed I was dead."

"We couldn't tell you or bring you with us. There was no time, and it was too dangerous. No one knew what I had done. They thought Josiah was dead, and that I had vanished. You were two-hundred years old and safe. Old enough to take my place and keep up appearances until it was time for us to change things through the revolution." Serena's jaw tightened. "We watched you where we could without exposing him."

"I didn't need watching," I whispered. "I needed my parents."

Silence pressed against the volcanic walls.

"You need me now," Josiah said gently.

The sigils beneath me ignited. He placed his palm over my sternum, directly above the faltering rhythm of my heart. His skin was warm, balanced, and steady.

"I'm going to share what I carry," he said. Heat bloomed beneath his hand, a steady infusion of balanced fire. His blood passed from his veins into mine through our touching skin.

Agony erupted first, my body rejecting the reweaving, my nerves screaming as severed strands were forced back together. My heart slammed violently once. Twice. The Dweller half reignited in a blaze of molten gold and crimson. The human half stabilized around it, strengthened.

Magic roared back into my veins—different now. Layered. Deeper. I arched off the slab with a gasp that tore from my lungs, then it settled. Balanced and alive.

Josiah sagged back, breathing hard but conscious.

Serena caught him.

I sat up slowly, *The Badlands* chamber stark and clear around me. "You let me mourn you both," I said again, my voice even more raw. "You let me believe I was alone for one hundred years."

My mother met my gaze without flinching. "If they had known you were not alone," she said quietly, "they would have come for you sooner."

"It didn't stop them," I said.

No one answered that. I was alive. The Wellbreaker's Bloom had failed. But something inside me, something older than magic, had cracked open. They had saved me.

And I did not yet know if that would be enough.

❀

The Badlands never slept.

Even in the quiet moments after violence, after molten power and rebellion and near death, the volcanic heart of Elarion pulsed steadily beneath its carved stone corridors. Heat shimmered along the walls in low amber ribbons. The air tasted faintly of iron and smoke and something mineral-sweet that never quite left your lungs.

I was kneeling now, though only minutes earlier I had been dying on a stone slab etched with ancient sigils. My magic felt different inside me. Not louder or brighter, but deeper.

Balanced.

Layered with a second current that did not feel foreign but did not feel entirely mine either. Josiah's power. My father's. The half-blood life source he had shared with me now resonated quietly beneath my skin like a steady second pulse.

My mother stood across from me, her shoulders squared and hands relaxed at her sides but ready if necessary. My father remained just behind her, silent and present, no longer a secret but not yet part of my world either.

And then the wards flared.

The amber veins along the corridor walls brightened in warning, rippling outward like a signal carried through molten stone. Serena's followers reacted instantly, forming a loose defensive arc at the entrance passage.

I didn't have to guess who it was.

Two shapes tore through the corridor at reckless speed. Vex arrived first, skidding across volcanic stone, his claws scraping in protest. His tail puffed so dramatically he looked twice his size.

You nearly died without me, he declared loudly, affronted beyond reason.

Fenrin slipped in behind him, far more controlled but no less intent in Lion form.

And then *they* came, and I'd never been more happy to see anyone.

Holden burst through the entrance with all the restraint of a man who had abandoned restraint entirely, his short hair still but his beard moving with a will of its own. His boots struck the stone hard, the cold scent of Wishville clinging to his coat in stark contrast to the heat around us. His eyes found me instantly.

Everything in his expression broke.

He crossed the chamber in three strides and dropped to his knees in front of me, his hands cupping my face as if I might dissolve if he didn't hold me in place. "You went alone," he said quietly, but his voice carried fury and fear in equal measure and his eyes filled with moisture.

"I had to," I answered, though even I heard the fragility in it now. I blinked back tears of my own.

His gaze searched mine. "Are you steady?"

"I'm alive...and oddly stronger."

Calderis entered just behind him, his silver hair flowing, posture rigid and gaze sweeping the chamber with Chief Enforcer precision. He took in Serena, his eyes widening when he saw Josiah.

"You took her," he said, his voice calm but edged, and iridescent eyes hard as ice.

Serena met his stare without flinching. "I saved her."

"From *your* people," he growled.

"They are no longer my people." She raised her chin high.

LuLu slipped in next, her breath coming quick and dark hair flying wildly as her eyes blazed like coal on fire. She scanned me from head to toe and then exhaled sharply. "Vex came back frantic, putting Fenrin on alert," she said. "We followed them to *The Badlands*."

I looked down at Vex.

I am your familiar. I feel what you feel, he said, looking pained and exhausted.

"I'm so sorry you had to go through that," I said softly.

You and I are connected, he said solemnly. *Had you died, I would have died happily with you.*

Calderis stepped forward slightly, his attention fixed on Serena and then shifting to Josiah. "You will not keep her here," he said.

My mother's expression softened into something unmistakably maternal. "I will not force her," she said. "Not into rebellion or my alliance or even my war." Her gaze moved to me, steady and searching. "If she stands with me, it will be because she chooses to." The words echoed differently in *The Badlands* than they would have in Wishville.

Here, choice was survival.

My father stepped forward then, the amber light catching in his dark hair, silver glinting at his temples. His presence felt both familiar and unbearably new. "I never meant for you to find out this way," he said softly.

Emotion tightened in my chest, sharper now that I was no longer fighting for breath. "You let me believe you were gone," I said quietly.

He did not defend himself. "I did what I thought would keep you alive," he answered.

"I'm not staying," I said at last, rising to my feet with Holden's help. "At least not now. I need time to think."

My mother nodded once. She didn't plead or command me, she simply accepted the choice as mine to make.

The Badlands opened around us as we moved toward the upper tunnels. Serena's followers stepped aside, their eyes following me with understanding. The heat lessened gradually as we ascended, volcanic glow fading into the cooler bioluminescent shimmer of central Elarion.

I told them of *The Accord Hall* and *The Pale Accord* along the way.

Calderis turned toward the crystalline terraces instead of the well portal. "We should go to see my father," he said quietly, sounding troubled.

There was no argument.

Vaerion's residence rose from the terraces like an architectural declaration of permanence. The mineral walls were polished to a glasslike sheen, veins of controlled light running through them in precise symmetry. Archways curved in disciplined arcs. The sigil of the Elders was etched above the main doors, its lines sharp and unyielding.

Calderis did not wait for a herald.

The doors opened under his hand with a sound that carried farther than intended. Inside, the hearthlight glowed soft and steady, casting pale gold across carved stone.

Elanith rose immediately, alarm flaring in her eyes. "My son?"

Lumira stepped down from the upper balcony, her expression shifting from confusion to concern. "Brother, what's wrong?"

"Where is he?" Calderis demanded.

Vaerion emerged from the inner corridor composed and deliberate, his dark robes falling in precise lines, the Elder mantle clasped at his shoulder. "What compels this intrusion?" he asked evenly.

"*The Pale Accord,*" Calderis said.

The air changed, filling with tension.

Vaerion did not pretend ignorance. "You have seen it," he said.

"No, *I* have," I interjected.

Vaerion's eyes widened a fraction, giving him away.

"You knew," Calderis confirmed, his face revealing his emotions for once.

Elanith's hand rose slowly to her throat.

Lumira looked between them, trying to understand the fracture forming beneath her feet.

"Not at first. I uncovered references after I became Chief Elder," Vaerion said carefully. "Sealed fragments. Mentions in Elder archives. By the time I understood what it had once been, the world beyond ours had changed irreversibly."

"You allowed the altered covenant to stand," Calderis pressed.

"I allowed survival to stand," Vaerion corrected. His gaze landed briefly on Holden. "You believe modern governments would respond with reverence? They would dissect what they fear. They would mine what they cannot replicate. They would place Dweller physiology beneath microscopes and call it progress."

Holden did not argue, because he knew there was truth in that. We all did.

Calderis's hands tightened at his sides. "And so you chose concealment."

"I chose to prevent annihilation."

Silence pressed in around us.

"If the original treaty had endured in another century," Vaerion continued, "perhaps coexistence would have matured gradually. But revelation now would ignite panic and be catastrophic to both our worlds."

Calderis closed his eyes briefly. I knew he understood that, but understanding did not erase betrayal. "Everything I have fought to protect has been shaped by omission."

Elanith stepped forward, tears welling but controlled. "I'm sure your father believed he was protecting our people."

"By teaching me to enforce a covenant he knew was incomplete?" Calderis asked. "I don't want any part of that."

"Where will you go?" his mother asked, a tremble in her voice.

"With me," LuLu said, taking his hand.

Lumira reached for his sleeve. "Brother, please stay. We can determine what comes next together."

"Let him go," Vaerion said quietly.

Elanith turned sharply. "Vaerion—"

"He must define himself outside my shadow," Vaerion said evenly. "If he remains, he will only measure himself against my decisions."

Calderis's throat worked. He looked at me, then at Holden, and finally down at LuLu. "I need time," he said, tightening his hand around hers.

"You'll have it in a safe place with us," Holden replied.

LuLu nodded once. "We're not losing you."

Calderis stepped back from the hearth. From the sigil above the door. From the weight of inherited certainty. "I will return, when I know what I believe, and what I'm willing to fight for."

Lumira dropped her hand.

Elanith whispered his name.

Vaerion did not move. He inclined his head in acknowledgment, not command.

Calderis turned and walked out into the crystalline night of Elarion. The glow of the terraces reflected faintly in his eyes before he disappeared beyond the archway. For the first time since

I had known him, he looked untethered. Stripped of inherited purpose. And as the mineral light shimmered softly against polished stone, I understood something with painful clarity:

The truth had not destroyed us. But it had shifted the ground beneath every one of us.

And none of us would walk the same way again.

Epilogue

WINTER HAD NOT LOOSENED its grip on the hill. Snow still blanketed the path that wound from my front porch down toward town, layered thick where boots had packed it down and then softened again by new flurries that fell as if reluctant to let the season end. My house sat high enough above the square that I couldn't see the banners coming down or the final vendor trucks pulling away, but I could feel the shift in the air all the same. I'd been recuperating after nearly dying, so I hadn't been there to see the festival through, but my staff kept me informed.

WishFest had ended.

The house was warm in contrast, the woodstove burning low and steady, heat curling into the corners of the room and softening the exposed beams overhead. The scent of whiskey, wine, and cedar mingled faintly throughout the room.

Holden sat beside me on the couch, his arm resting along the back cushions. Across from us, LuLu had claimed the oversized chair and tucked her socked feet beneath her, mismatched wool bright against the dark upholstery. Calderis stood near the hearth, as he always did, his posture still impossibly straight even in rest. Vex lay stretched like royalty on the braided rug, his tail swaying lazily, while Fenrin perched on the windowsill, her gaze fixed outward as snow drifted past in silent currents.

"It's strange not hearing the choir anymore," LuLu said quietly, her voice carrying the aftertaste of a long festival.

"Or Trip Danderly narrating his own survival story," Holden added dryly.

Calderis frowned faintly. "He leapt into frozen water of his own volition."

"Yes," I said. "And he will recount it for the next twenty years."

A faint smile tugged at LuLu's mouth, but the humor didn't linger long. "The wish," she said softly.

The room stilled.

This season's wish hadn't been romantic or whimsical. No whispered desires for new business ventures or love or lucky promotions. It had been quieter than that. More desperate.

Elliot had made it opening night, his shoulders hunched as if even the act of hoping felt indulgent. He hadn't wished for money. He hadn't wished to escape his mounting debt. He had wished for a bone marrow match for his mother. Just that.

A match. A chance. A way to keep her alive.

"The Wellies," Holden said, shaking his head faintly, "took that whisper and turned it into a full civic operation."

"They declared marrow a moral obligation," I said, unable to stop the faint warmth spreading through my chest.

Dot had arrived at the library with spreadsheets already drafted. Belle brought cinnamon rolls "for bone morale." Tilly claimed her spleen journal had predicted "marrow convergence." Within forty-eight hours, the library had transformed into something between a medical clinic and a bake sale, tables lined with swab kits and sign-in sheets, townspeople filing through with nervous laughter and powdered sugar on their sleeves.

Finch had stood in the doorway, with his arms crossed and expression unimpressed. He hadn't believed in the well. Hadn't ever tossed a coin into it or lingered at its rim during WishFest. But he liked Elliot, so he had stayed.

"Finch told me later," Holden said quietly, his eyes fixed on the fire, "that he didn't mean to sign up."

LuLu leaned forward slightly. "What changed his mind?"

"He said he'd walked halfway back to his truck," I answered softly, remembering Finch's exact words. "Said something wouldn't let him leave."

The fire cracked, sending a small spray of sparks upward.

"He described it like a splinter under the skin," Holden continued. "Persistent, irritating, and impossible to ignore."

Finch had never been sentimental. He hadn't been swayed by the Wellies' pastries or Dot's statistics or Tilly's aura commentary. But something had pressed him, a steady, insistent pull that refused to release him until he turned around and walked back inside. He signed the form, let the nurse swab his cheek, and left grumbling. And by the end of WishFest, the call came…

Finch was the match.

Calderis's gaze lowered slightly toward the floorboards as if he could see through them into Elarion itself. "The well did not alter blood," he said slowly. "It altered choice."

"Yes." That was exactly it.

The well hadn't rewritten biology. It hadn't conjured compatibility from thin air.

It had nudged a stubborn maintenance man into listening to something deeper than pride.

Elliot would still serve his sentence. Consequences mattered. He had helped steal from his neighbors. He had allowed desperation to cloud his judgment.

But his mother would live.

The transplant team was optimistic. Finch's health was strong. The surgery would take place within the month.

"And Dana?" LuLu asked gently.

The warmth in the room shifted, deeper now.

"She won't hurt anyone else," Holden said quietly.

Dana would spend the rest of her life confronting what she'd done. Percy would answer for trafficking the compound, but not for murder. Ozzy had confessed his part in the theft ring, his gambling debts now replaced with a far harsher but cleaner reckoning. Edward would repay every manipulated vendor count. Alistair Hawthorne's carefully curated façade had collapsed, and the women he preyed upon were no longer silent.

Justice had come. Not cleanly or easily, but fully.

Snow brushed against the window in soft waves.

"So, what happens now?" Holden asked. It wasn't a small question.

Calderis shifted his weight, and I could feel the weight of Elarion in the silence that followed. "We figure out who we are and where we stand."

"We stop reacting," I said.

LuLu nodded. "We start *acting*."

Calderis inclined his head. "We build what *should* have existed."

"And we do it without waiting for ancient men to bury it under stone," Holden added.

The firelight danced across the ceiling. "By the way...we signed the lease," LuLu said suddenly, brightening.

Calderis's expression shifted almost imperceptibly toward something softer as his gaze settled on her.

"For the townhouse overlooking the birch ridge?" I asked, genuinely happy for them.

"It has excellent visibility," Calderis said.

"It has charm," LuLu countered.

They would build something steady there, something chosen rather than inherited.

"And you?" LuLu asked Holden, her eyes gleaming. "Haven't you been here nearly a year?"

He nodded. "In a couple months, come spring."

It suddenly dawned on me what LuLu was getting at. "Then that means your lease will be up."

"That's right," he said simply, his gaze locking with mine and holding me captive.

The warmth in my chest settled into something sure and solid. "Move in with me," I said, with no hesitation or dramatic pause, just certainty.

His shoulders eased in a way that felt almost private. "Okay," he replied softly.

Vex sat upright suddenly. *But what about me? I thought I was the only male you needed in your life.*

Fenrin snuggled in beside him, making it clear there was a new female waiting to take my place.

He settled down beside her without another thought.

"Since The Covenant Three is no more," LuLu said, "We need a new name."

Calderis raised a brow. "We?"

"Yes, because it's quite clear you all need me." She crossed her arms, daring anyone to say otherwise.

Holden exhaled slowly. "Adding LuLu sounds dangerous."

"Four sounds good to me," I said.

LuLu grinned. "Because we're fearless."

Holden nodded once. "And there are four of us."

We all looked at each other.

"The Fearless Four it is," Calderis said.

I felt the well pulse, warm and steady and unmistakably present. It had allowed justice to surface. It had exposed lies buried beneath generations of stone. And now it had four protectors who no longer waited for permission from either realm. We sat together in the warm light of my house while snow fell softly beyond the glass.

Two worlds.

Four hearts.

One mission: no more lies.

Powers

Dweller Powers Linked to Water, Lava, and the Core

Because Dwellers live beneath the well and near the Earth's hidden layers, their powers tie into subterranean elements—water tables, magma flows, and the planet's inner energy.

Water Affinity

1. **Aquifer Calling** – ability to summon fresh water from underground springs.
2. **Mists and Veils** – conjuring fog or vapor to obscure vision.
3. **Current Shaping** – manipulating underground rivers and directing them to flood or recede.
4. **Memory Pools** – reflections in water that reveal truths, memories, or wishes.

Lava and Magma Affinity

1. **Ember Pulse** – channeling molten heat into bursts of energy or fiery weaponry.

2. **Obsidian Crafting** – forming weapons, keys, or charms instantly from cooled lava.
3. **Seismic Heat** – creating pockets of intense heat to deter intruders or destroy evidence.
4. **Infernal Glow** – eyes or markings flare with inner magma-light when power is used.

Core/Earth Affinity

1. **Seismic Whisper** – sensing tremors or distant footsteps through the ground.
2. **Stone Weaving** – reshaping rock, tunnels, or caverns for defense or concealment.
3. **Core Binding** – drawing strength from geothermal energy, boosting speed or stamina.
4. **Gravity Veil** – slightly altering pull of gravity around them (leaping, pulling objects down).

Hybrid Powers (Water + Fire/Core)

1. **Steam Veil** – merging water and magma to create blinding, scalding mist.
2. **Healing Springs** – heated water with mineral-rich, magical properties for mending wounds.
3. **Crystalline Growth** – forming luminous crystal clusters where water meets lava under pressure.
4. **Pressure Command** – controlling deep-earth pressure, causing geysers or controlled quakes.

Lyra's Hybrid Powers

As the only half-human, half-Dweller, Lyra bridges above-ground elements (air, light, celestial forces) with subterranean ones (water, magma, core). Her uniqueness gives her some Dweller powers and other ones that no full Dweller can access.

Celestial Affinity

1. **Sunfire Touch** – channeling warmth and light to heal or inspire courage.
2. **Moonveil** – manipulating moonlight for illusions, cloaking, or calming emotions.
3. **Star Echo** – heightened intuition or visions tied to constellations and night sky patterns.
4. **Skycall** – Influence over breezes, gusts, or even guiding birds.

Core Affinity

1. **Seismic Sense** – feeling vibrations through earth, sensing danger or hidden chambers.
2. **Lumen Wells** – pulling luminous energy from underground crystals.
3. **Magma Ward** – summoning protective heat barriers or obsidian shards.
4. **Aqua Vein** – drawing water from beneath the ground in times of need.

Hybrid/Balance Powers

1. **Eclipse State** – when sun and moon energies align, she can blend surface light with core fire for immense bursts of power.
2. **Breath of Worlds** – exhaling mist that merges steam, air, and memory-infused water.
3. **Harmony Pulse** – ability to temporarily stabilize cracks between worlds.
4. **Dual Sight** – seeing both surface illusions and subterranean truths simultaneously.
5. **Illusory Manipulation** – The ability to shift their surroundings, making structures disappear or entire

landscapes transform.

Vex (half-cat, half-Whispen)

**Whisper Magic
Abilities:**

1. **Shadow Phase** – slip between shadows in both realms.
2. **Mist Purr** – calming veil of vapor.
3. **Mind Whisper** – can communicate with others through their mind.

Fenrin (Full Whispen)

Abilities:

4. **Shapeshifter** – take on the form of other animals.

Books By Kari Lee Townsend

A WISHVILLE MYSTERY

The Well-Kept Secret

The Well-Laid Trap

The Well-Hidden Clue

The Well-Placed Lie

KALLI BALLAS MYSTERY

Mind Over Murder

Two Cents of Doom

A Touch of Malice

An Inkling of Evil

Mayhem on the Mind

Trouble for Your Thoughts

CECE MONROE MYSTERY

Harmful Habits

SUNNY MEADOWS MYSTERY

Tempest in the Tea Leaves

Corpse in the Crystal Ball

Trouble in the Tarot

Shenanigans in the Shadows

Perish in the Palm

Hazard in the Horoscope

Chaos and Cold Feet

Murder in the Meditation

SUNNY MEADOWS & KALLI BALLAS CROSSOVER

Cruising into Danger

Road Trip to Ruin

Bachelors, Badeges & Bad Luck

My Big Fat Fatal Wedding

DIGITAL DIVA

Talk to the Hand

Rise of the Phenoteens

Books By Kari Lee Harmon

COLDWATER COVE

Dark Seas

Frozen Waters

Dangerous Thaw

Deadly Frost

STANDALONE NOVELS

Valley of Secrets

Until Tomorrow

Project Produce

Love Lessons

LAKEHOUSE TREASURES NOVELLAS

James

Amber

Meghan

Brook

MERRY SCROOG-MAS NOVELLAS

Naughty or Nice

Sleigh Bells Ring

Jingle all the Way

TRIPLE R RANCH

Destiny Wears Spurs

Spurred by Fate

PORTRAIT OF A WOMAN

Resilient

Resourceful

Rebellious

Reclusive

National Bestselling Author, Agatha, RT Reviewer's Choice & Golden Duck Award Nominee. Kari lives in Central New York with her husband & Samoyeds. She's a lover of wine & travel (especially cruising), obsessed with reality TV, and loves a good book with at least some mystery, romance & humor. She writes cozy mysteries & upper middle grade as Kari Lee Townsend, as well as suspense, romance, romantic comedy & women's fiction as Kari Lee Harmon. To keep up with all of Kari Lee's books, check out her website, join her newsletter, and follow her on Amazon, Goodreads, and Bookbub! All links are on her website.

https://www.karileetownsend.com